T

Copyright © 2025 by Ann Goethals
All world rights reserved.

This is a work of fiction. Names, places, and incidents are the products of the author's imagination or are used fictitiously. Any resemblance to actual events or locales or persons, living or dead, is entirely coincidental.

No part of this book may be reproduced, stored in a retrieval system, or transmitted in any form or by any means electronic, mechanical, photocopy, recording or otherwise, without the prior consent of the publisher.

Published by Mission Point Press
MissionPointPress.com
PO Box 700028
Plymouth, MI 48170

Cover image by Jeff Bane

ISBN: 978-1-965278-58-1 (softcover)
ISBN: 978-1-965278-56-7 (hardcover)

Library of Congress Control Number upon request

Printed in the United States of America

The Doublewide

ANN GOETHALS

MISSION POINT PRESS

For the Caregivers

First Sight

From the sinkhole of her Goodwill couch, Candy sipped her coffee and surveyed the apartment which she had nicknamed "the Dump" shortly after moving in two years ago. She needed a house. But first she needed a donut. The Dump was located above the Pizza Palace, conveniently located on Main Street, in Cutler, Michigan, which, eight months of the year, saw fewer than a dozen cars per day. There had been a mass exodus over the weekend, with the summer people's SUVs packed to the hilt, kids tucked into back seats, already plugged into their devices for the trek downstate where school and jobs and real life waited. The pizza smells hadn't started migrating up from downstairs yet and she was enjoying her coffee without the shot of pepperoni on top.

Ok, maybe not exactly enjoying, because the familiar scroll of insecurities and excuses and "no, maybe not todays" had already started unwinding in her head, so she forced herself up from the couch before the whining could take hold. She walked the four short steps to her window which faced the back parking lot of the Palace. Vern's busted-up old minivan was there, along with Jimmy the cook's Camry. The day was bright and blue and the trees bordering the lot were still. No wind yet. It would be, was already, a perfect Northern Michigan day, with a yellow sun and green trees and the blue dome overhead, the new quiet of the offseason settling in. Of course it would ramp up again in another six weeks or so when the leaves started turning, but for now, Cutler was hers, and Vern's and all the rest of the village people who called the little town home.

By the time she had gotten out of the shower, she had mustered up enough courage to get into clothes that were decent enough to make her look like she was an adult with some money. Hopefully. She stood in front of the bathroom mirror, gathering her mop of strawberry blond curls behind a taupe headband while pumping herself up. For the thing to do. The thing that she would do. Today. Before she had more time to talk herself back onto the couch, she grabbed her phone and keys and headed down the back stairs to her '94 Tacoma.

Back when she was a kid and struggling in school, Candy's grandfather had frequently told her that while she was not the sharpest tool in the shed, she had talents. Among those were persistence. And patience. And powers of observation. Candy took this character analysis for what it was worth and, as she grew up, added a few other traits. She could do arithmetic in her head fast as lightning, not much good in high school geometry class but a real life skill at the grocery store with its fake claims of savings. And she knew all about color, had loved art class back in high school, although she only drew landscapes and her work was never chosen for the school art exhibits. She understood the color wheel and complementary versus analogous, value versus hue. As a little girl she had longed for the very expensive twenty-four pack of Sharpies, but had settled for colored pencils. With the puny allowance Granddah dropped on the hall table every Saturday morning, she bought coloring books, the grown-up kind that were designed to relieve stress and help people meditate, or whatever. She used them to create worlds of color, one or two shades off the normal palettes used in clothing and decor, and liked her finished pages so much she taped them to her bedroom walls.

These days she was guilty of hanging out in the paint section of Home Depot, picking up sample cards, particularly the ones shelved next to each other, and trying to guess what was different: which primary added or subtracted in the most miniscule way in order to create another shade worthy of a name. Or even more mysteriously, how white or black might have been used. Saturation. Her brother, Graham, had talked a lot about saturation when he took up photography in high school. On her way to work or the grocery store her glance would sometimes land on a color beyond her windshield and Candy would try to name it: November Woods; Autumn Blaze; Summer Sherbert. It made her less than a terrific driver. Good thing the roads were almost empty this morning as she pulled out onto Marra Road while pondering names for the impossible blue of the morning sky: Sapphire Glow, or maybe Cornflower Morning.

Her grandfather's pickup, which Candy now drove toward Edwards Homes, was a metallic greenish gray. Candy had once looked it up on the internet because for some reason she had to know what Toyota had named this color. Since her grandfather's Tacoma was ancient, its color faded by harsh seasons in the North, there was no way to know for sure but the color chart spit up by her laptop covering the years '76–'95 landed it as either Altair Green Met or Golden Topaz Met. The "met" being "metallic," which left the other two words for her to puzzle over. She never did bother to look up what "Altair" meant. Maybe it was a place, like Capri. Capri Blue was a color. And the paint companies loved to name colors after places: Miami Pink, Moroccan Orange, Antiguan Aqua, places far away which Candy imagined being saturated with colors found only in sunsets and sometimes the lake up here in Northern Michigan.

So. One of the things that Granddah had gotten right about Candy was her sharp eye, and not just for color. One day last week, driving past the Edwards manufactured home lot—"Let Us Bring You Home," the sign out front said—she had spied a doublewide sitting at the back of the lot that hadn't been there before. It was big and a kind of chalky sky blue with false white shutters framing its windows, and it sat up on concrete blocks surrounded by colored plastic flags which flapped insanely in any breeze. The flags surrounding it, and its location at the very back of the lot, had made Candy curious. That and the color. It was a kind of blue that was a few drops of gray different from the scrubs she sometimes wore to work, but there was something else about it that she couldn't name. A touch of lilac, maybe? Whatever it was, the color of that doublewide held her gaze like a magnet.

That first day she had not pulled into the lot. Instead, she had proceeded through post-beach-day traffic to work the night shift (a 5 percent pay differential; 10 percent more on weekends, and 25 percent more on holidays), and then gone home to check her savings account. Even though she already knew how much was in it: $21,376.95. Enough. Time to get serious. Time to go out and bring herself a home.

In the six days between her first sighting and this morning,

Candy had become desperate to see that doublewide again. She couldn't shake that blue and after a couple of days of slowing past the Edwards lot and letting her head turn way too long to keep her grandfather's pickup in the right lane, she gave in. She was going to have to find a way to buy that doublewide. Ok, maybe just look at it. Go inside. Inside she couldn't be bewitched by the blue: slate, or sky, or arctic, or whatever the hell it was called. Then something might not sit right, the rooms would be wrong, the halls too narrow, and then she could go on her way.

But on the other other hand—how many hands could a person have when they were arguing with themselves?—with the right down payment and the right deal, she knew she could afford a manufactured home. And what with Granddah's land now being as good as hers, even though his house, which is to say, the building that used to be their home, was now crumpled and threatening to fold in on itself like a milk carton at the bottom of a trash can, she knew she could do it. After she had moved Granddah into Glencrest Shores Retirement Home (not close to any lake and therefore no shore in sight), she had moved out of his house and let nature take its course. Turned off the lights and cut the power and locked the doors and windows and moved a couple of things that mattered to her into her one-bedroom shithole apartment above the Pizza Palace. She fixed up the place as best as she could on her budget, recycled taupe furnishings with burgundy accents picked out of the many resale stores in the area, but to Candy it had never really become a home. It had been more like a second job that she had to tolerate and get through until she could buy herself a real home. Which, she had decided, would contain no burgundy accents.

And now that new place might just be beginning to happen. She had checked prices on the internet. And she had saved. Boy, had she saved. Persistence and patience. Buying second-hand clothes and furniture. Eating the Shop 'n Save brand of ice cream instead of Edy's or Hudson's. Pizza out of a box from the frozen food aisle instead of downstairs from the Pizza Palace. Making sure she did her errands on the way to and from work to save gas, 'cause the truck, while it had been free, guzzled gas like nobody's business. Candy persisted, lived above the Palace, and paid her rent on time to the owner, whose name was Vern and who always called her Chrissie, bought cheap groceries, and went to the library to look at home design magazines instead of buying them, even though she craved taking them home and collapsing onto her Goodwill couch and eating Cheetos while she decorated her future home in her head. And every two weeks, part of her measly paycheck went into savings and that made the generic ice cream taste just a little bit creamier. Because Candy was going to do it. Sharp or not.

She pulled into the Quik Mart and noticed the gas gauge was inching close to E, so she pumped $20 into the pickup before going inside. Alyssa was working the counter and waved a hello. It was late in the morning so Candy's favorite donut, apple cinnamon, was gone and she had to settle for a glazed, which was what Alyssa looked like when Candy went to the counter to pay.

After hellos, Alyssa asked, "Day off?"

"Working third shift tonight, so yeah, sort of," Candy replied, and then tried to think of something else to say to warm up her vocal cords.

"How about you? Just starting?"

"Yeah. Stayed up too late last night, so it's gonna be a long one," she replied, dropping change into Candy's palm.

"Well, I hope it goes fast," she said, and smiled at the top of Alyssa's head. The clerk looked up.

"Hey, thanks. You have a good one."

And that was about all Candy could manage with the world of people. Not bad. She had witnessed plenty of people saying plenty less in the Quik Mart, or the grocery store.

Candy hopped back into the cab, fired up the truck, and steered it one-handed out onto the county road again. She had just turned twenty-eight, which made it four years that she had been saving. This get-your-own-house decision, made so long ago now it seemed, had given Candy's life a purpose, a goal that sustained her through her young adult life while she missed the many other goalposts which promised happiness and a full life. Once she had this goal, Candy's fantasy life, which had been her best friend, really, since her early realization that she would be a fat girl forgotten on the edges of the real world, had come alive. There were no more random meanderings about trying to fit herself into the kind of life that TV and magazines told her she should be in pursuit of. No, this dream of having her own home, of buying it by herself, for herself, had made her screenwriter, director, and producer of endless seasons of episodes about home and house decorating. This was her life now. This would make her complete, would shield her from the outer world's silly expectations, which seemed to Candy a one size fits all. And if it was one thing Candy had learned during her existence as a plus size, it was that one size definitely did not fit all.

The problem with this whole "make the dream home real"

scenario, or even the "yeah, not what I thought it was" possibility, was that the next step involved actually driving onto that lot and talking to a live salesman. And that was where Candy had gotten stuck. She worked at Granddah's retirement home as an LPN, but that meant that most of the time she worked in silence, or made small bits of conversation with people who had lost the ability to talk back. Or if they did, they never made much sense or cared about deep and meaningful conversation. So Candy spent much of her life not talking to anyone, or when she did it was quietly murmuring about lunch or washing up or the next Sit 'n Stretch session.

Her entire family consisted of Granddah, who was no longer in any shape to really share a life with, and her brother, who had disappeared long ago up into the UP, near enough to Pictured Rocks to land his pictures in galleries catering to those tourists he had talked about. She had no friends beyond Janelle and Marcos, who were really just work friends and so were probably only nice to her because she was around. Work friends were nice, but they weren't the kind you could ask along on a scary chore like this one. No, if she wanted to see that doublewide she was going to have to grit her teeth and do it. Now. Today. Solo.

Doing things on her own was not the problem. Candy spent her whole life on her own, especially after she had moved Granddah into Glencrest. She shopped, ate, slept, drove, and lived alone. This did not bother her particularly because the world made her nervous. It made her blush and sweat and become aware of her size and her clothes and her hair and her eczema. No, it wasn't the alone part. It was the NOT alone part.

This buying a house thing was going to involve people. Probably a lot of people. So many people.

Persistence. Blue. Doublewide. She cheerleaded herself as she drove north this morning, the sun lighting up the bug smears on the windshield. Over the past week, mostly on her commute, Candy had practiced in her head. Made up an episode or two about driving onto the lot and having a conversation and making eye contact and maybe cutting a deal. She rehearsed the episode until she decided she was ready. Or at least tired of the reruns playing in her head. Time to get to the next episode.

She finished her glazed, licked her fingers clean, and turned into the Edwards lot. She pulled into a spot marked "Future Happy Homeowner," and walked into the pale yellow trailer marked "SALES."

A man who was probably a salesman lumbered up from behind his crappy desk and extended a sweaty hand.

"Well hello there, Miss ... ?"

"Schein. Candace Schein."

"I'm Randy, Miss Schein, nice to meet you. And what can I do for you today, Miss Schein?"

Already it was like a commercial, or a bad movie. Somehow the familiarity of it made her less nervous.

"You can call me Candy."

"Of course," Randy cackled. And there it was. Of course her name was Candy. She had a round face and pink cheeks and a chubby cotton-candy body, and blond ringlets that she pulled away from her face with a hair band which was, thankfully today, not pink. Her size and her name seemed to be endlessly amusing to the world, which was one of the reasons she had stopped talking to it. She had every right to call herself Candy. It was the name her mother had given her before she left, her voice cooing that name the only real memory Candy had of her. Granddah, probably out of meanness toward her mom, his daughter, called her Candace instead. Always. But that name had made Candy feel like someone she wasn't. A lawyer, maybe, or a politician. Candy was the name of a large LPN from Northern Michigan. Which was what she was.

As far as that went, Randy kind of looked like a Randy too. Skinny, with a belly hanging over his cheap khakis, and a golf shirt in that crimson color that reminded her of a college football coach, only with "Edwards Homes" embroidered where the college logo might go. Randy's company shirt had stains on it and Randy had a long face and a moustache that was thin and fine, and hair that was no color: not blond or brown or anything in between. Faded Barn Door, Candy thought.

"I'm interested in maybe taking a look at that doublewide you got out there in the back?" she said.

"Ah, well, this is your lucky day, Miss Candy."

Don't I know it, Candy thought, and now you're going to tell me you can see me and my little ones in that place.

"It's just the perfect place for you and your little ones."

"Just me," she answered.

"Good for that too," Randy said, recovering quickly, "and it's priced to move because there is just a teeny problem with it. Happened in transit. Actually it happens all the time, but in this case the manufacturer decided to give it to me below cost and so I am ready to pass those savings on to you."

Candy thought there must be a school, or a YouTube video

that taught salesmen how to say all that crap without laughing at themselves. And of course, now that the sight of that blue doublewide with its false white shutters had drawn her onto the lot, there had to be something wrong with it.

"But never fear, let's walk on out there and have a look-see, and I can explain it all to you. Not a big deal at all. Really just cosmetic. No structural damage whatsoever."

Candy knew she should probably chuckle or sneer here, which was what Granddah would do, making his skepticism into a bargaining chip.

"Well, I wasn't in the market for a doublewide since it's just me." She paused for a beat. "But," she paused again, looking around the office, "if the price is right, maybe I'd be interested."

"Oh you're going to love it," Randy said, gathering up a wad of keys from the desk, and pointing her toward the door.

"What's that color called?" she asked.

"Ah, that blue? That's one of our most popular shades. We call it Mystic Blue."

Mystic Blue. Blue. Of a mystical kind. Sounded right. And she followed Mr. Randy out the door of the yellow sales trailer and walked across the dusty lot to the Mystic.

On the Lot

Candy had started sweating in the office so she was glad to get out into the mild September air. She was a sweater anyway, but now she was extra nervous. Right now the sweating was triggered by two discomforts. First, she had to keep talking and listening to this dweeb Randy who made all the clichés true, but was still a person and she was not comfortable with persons, and second, she was approaching this vinyl-clad house that she knew, like love at first sight, she wanted to make her own. It was a mobile home, for crying out loud, and she was falling in love. It was heating her up and she could actually see, in her mind, how pink her cheeks must be.

  The Mystic, as she had already started calling it, was big: it was a doublewide, after all, and all this time she had been looking at and imagining a single. She was single, after all, and would be forever; she knew that. Her world was small but roomy and she had come to appreciate the various empty places she had carved her life into. Besides, her world of choice was so big. The outdoors. Lake Michigan. The dunes. The hills. The woods. The storms. The snow piles in winter. The wildflowers in the spring, leaf storms in the fall. There was so much that was so spacious around her, that it had come to feel good and right to have a small life and she had imagined a small house. Randy was talking and Candy forced herself to listen.

"So, let's get the bad news over with first, shall we? And then we can go on to enjoy the many, many, wonderful characteristics of this home." Randy, and all the manufactured home websites for that matter, never used the word "mobile" or "manufactured" or "house." It was always "home." Randy was now rounding the corner to the back of the doublewide, which faced away from the lot. Candy followed. And there it was. A corner crunched in like it had taken a punch from a mailbox or something. It didn't look particularly violent, like it had gotten snagged or anything. It was more like a crease with an open cut in the middle. Candy looked at it. And then looked some more. She pasted a frown on her face, trying to look as skeptical as possible. She took note of the depth of the hole and where the creases began and ended, and how many layers of rip there were, and if it was wet or dry, and all the other things she thought a thoughtful person should be noticing about buying damaged goods. Randy's voice had now dissolved into a kind of background murmuring that contained words she sometimes caught: structural, water, took a corner, insurance, warranty.

"Can I go inside?" was all Candy thought to ask.

They climbed up the temporary, plywood stairs and Randy tried to make some sort of ceremony out of opening the front door. Candy didn't need it. She walked into a huge white space. There were walls, and a fridge and stove both still wrapped up in that blue plastic in-transit wrap. And there were windows, and light spilling in on the floor, which was finished in that kind of plastic-coated wood. It looked like oak, or maple. Something blond. Like her. And it made the whole place, along with the white walls and the sun shining in, luminous. Bright, open, but indoors. It was the largest, sunniest indoor living space she had ever been in. Like the lofts she had seen in magazines. She'd never been in a loft outside of a barn, but the pictures in the magazines of the renovated factories had been amazing. This light was like that. She turned around like a kid at a carnival, trying as hard as she could to keep the shit-eating grin off her face.

"So right here," Randy was saying, "we decided it would be good to take out the dividing wall between the second bedroom and the living room because it came just a little bit off square. Other than that she's sound. We have on-site engineers to guarantee its soundness and sign off on it. Also," and Randy paused for effect, "we are prepared to make a very attractive deal."

Randy was quiet but she could feel him looking closely at her face. She pulled the corners of her mouth down and avoided his eyes. Instead, she stood in a sunny patch and looked out a window, recalling once again how nearly impossible it had become for her to look at someone else's face. When she was caring for her Glencrest residents up close, she tried to look somewhere else: at their food trays or their feet or the brake on the wheelchair. Avoided their faces. She wondered if they noticed. If it made a difference. She guessed it did. She had read an article in her free *Elder Care* magazine about touch, too. That the sick and the old responded to touch. That they were healthier and talked more if you touched them. Like babies. Candy was working on that part. When she could, she put a hand on a shoulder or a forearm, working up to a hand or a head. Some residents leaned into her when she did that. She had noticed. But the faces. Looking into someone's face. That was a tough one.

Randy was still talking and Candy was half listening to hear if there was a question. There wasn't and so Candy said nothing. Instead, she forced herself to stop wandering around the house and headed back over to the dented corner. She could not see daylight, only some turquoise Styrofoam and some chalky drywall-looking stuff and some Mystic Blue vinyl. The layers of the wall all kind of folded in on each other. She didn't have the slightest idea whether any of this mattered and she had no one to ask.

"We're surely gonna make it right for you," Randy was saying. "As a matter of fact, we are prepared to offer this doublewide at a singlewide price."

Candy heard that. Loud and clear. She had budgeted for a singlewide. That's what she had in the bank, plus some for the washer-dryer and the new furniture and the microwave. She was still sweating, the cool feel of the damp gathering in her armpits and on the back of her shirt, and now she was also shaking inside. She needed a Tums in the worst way. And a Dr Pepper. Suddenly, she had to get out of this white, wide open, light filled space. Impossibly, it seemed to be suffocating her. Maybe it was just Randy.

"I'm gonna have to check it," she finally managed to say as she headed toward the door. Even with the windows open, there now didn't seem to be enough air in the room.

"Excuse me?" There was a laugh, or a sneer, in Randy's voice.

"I'm going to have to go home and get some tools and come

back and measure the damage and maybe get a second opinion and all before I make a decision."

Randy sounded like he was doing his best to be offended.

"Well, Miss Sheen—"

"It's Schein, like shine a light."

"Pardon me, Miss Schein." And then he caught himself, and the tone changed direction. Miss Candy had evidently left the building.

Randy corrected himself: "Well, sure, whatever you need to feel comfortable in making this your new home. But we also have some lovely singles which may be more your size." He smiled a gooey, liquid, sleazy smile.

Jesus. Unfat people just couldn't ever restrain themselves around big people. They had to sneak it into the conversation one way or another. Some thought they were being polite when they talked about how much they ate, how little they exercised. But no matter how much people thought they were deflecting the light off of her by babbling about themselves, really it was always about Candy and her plus size.

Candy, however, had already gotten lost in this plus-sized space. While Randy carried on, she had wandered around in circles, moving in and out of the cavernous living-dining area, the main bedroom which was almost the size of her entire Palace shithole, a utility room for her own washer-dryer. She tried to count the steps it took to walk from one end to the other, gave up, and asked.

"What is the square footage?"

"Well, Miss Candy ..." (They were back to that; there must be a playbook about names for salesmen.) "This is one of your smaller footprints—about 1,100 square feet."

That was a third more than what she had been looking at and dreaming of. Maybe she could get a dog or a cat or a stationary bike and lose some weight. Singlewides ran like an alley, one room following the next down a single hallway. In doublewides you could actually walk in two directions, down the hall and across it, like a real house. Suddenly this made a difference to Candy. She was sold. Randy must not know.

"I don't know. Like I said, I'm going to have to think about it."

"Well it's such a deal."

"I have a day off coming up, Wednesday. Could I come back and do some closer checking?"

Randy was not happy, and recited some other well-rehearsed lines about going fast, such a deal, have other people interested, may not be here long, as he led her back to the yellow trailer and filed brochures and documents and waivers and riders, and on top of all of that, a sales contract already filled out and into her hands. She pulled this last one out of the bunch, stuffed it in her bag, and clutched the rest to her chest. She'd need a bin for all the paperwork home-owning dreams generated.

And then she scrammed. Or she did the Candy version of scramming, which was more like a waddle and a clutching of paper and purse and a scrambling for keys and an awkward lunge up into the cab of her granddah's silver-blue Tacoma. Maybe it was green.

What, Exactly, Is Alone?

It wasn't exactly true that Candy felt alone in the world, although if one of those reality shows swooped down and followed her around with a drone they would think she had a miserable, lonely life. But it just wasn't true, or she didn't feel like it was true and that was what mattered, right? She didn't have a family of her own or really any close friends to spend days off with, and had always been, well if not exactly ignored, kind of invisible. And if she was being honest, Candy had come to feel comfortable that way. It made life, if not exciting and romantic and fun, at least easy. It felt like too much work to try to get people to notice her, to like her, to be in her life with her. It was so much easier to glide through the days taking care of herself and building the house dream.

Besides, there were humans all over the place. There were the checkers and baggers at the Shop 'n Save. She talked to them every week, sometimes more. She had had several sit-downs with the loan officer at her credit union, whose name was Evelyn. She made small talk with her landlord, Vern, whenever she saw him in the parking lot. She nodded and smiled at people at the laundromat. It was hard to explain to someone else, which she never did because nobody asked, but her life felt full. Enough. School and television and magazines had done their level best to convince Candy that she was supposed to be hankering for more: a husband, a career with happy hours at Applebee's at the end of the week, Saturday afternoon get-togethers at each other's houses for football games and such. And those TV images were tantalizing to Candy for sure, but more and more she would catch herself ignoring the happy people on the screen and zooming in instead on the interiors: the furniture and fixtures. She took to attending closely to commercials, scoping out the kitchens and the sofas and the side tables. It was hopeless. She was a home decorator hidden inside a caregiver's scrubs.

Candy didn't long for any more human contact than she already had; she no longer got depressed or wished for more or cruised dating sites for large people or extended herself beyond a "how's it goin'" to a former high school classmate when she ran into them at a store. Back in school, Candy had been the kid in the middle row halfway back. Average or slightly below. No trouble, no questions, no drama. As a student she sought so little attention that in fact, teachers often forgot to assign her a partner or a group. They would be busy smiling at all the chirping sassy kids doing their jolly dances, and then notice that Candy was still in her seat, trying to disappear. And there would be apologies and oh my goodnesses and occasionally an explanation having to do with how self-sufficient Candy was.

Whatever.

While a student at Northwoods High she had never gone to homecomings or dances, although she did really love a Friday night football game. The whole county loved their high school football. *Friday Night Lights* up here in freezing cold Lakeland County. For the home games she would buy popcorn and soda and choose a seat on the bleachers close enough to kids who knew her name so that she wouldn't look obviously alone. Or she would take Granddah if he was in the mood. Which wasn't often. Granddah was strictly a checkers/poker/VFW guy. Football belonged on TV. And bless him, he never asked even once why she didn't have a date or plans on a weekend. Most times she thought he was oblivious, but once in a while, a very great while—Candy remembered these times vividly—her grandfather would say something soothing about an upcoming weekend and how nice it was to hang around at home by the woodstove with a good movie or game on TV. Or, he would thank her for some chore she'd done that was part of her routine, nothing out of the ordinary. Or he would bring home a half gallon of ice cream and plunk a box of Duncan Hines brownie mix down on the kitchen counter and say, "Hope we got an egg. I could go for a brownie sundae tonight."

So Candy was by no means an orphan. Or an outcast, because outcast meant someone else had to cast you out, right? As she recited this familiar chorus in her mind, she would find herself visibly nodding, as if trying to shake loose the falseness of any claim. Was she lonely? Was she unhappy? The answers to these questions were always no. The only question she answered yes to, in her own mind at least: Was she nuts about not being unhappy? That one always tripped her up. Not and un- in one sentence sent her brain jiggling. In the end, Candy had settled comfortably inside her life. It fit her and she fit it. No tight seams or binding waistbands. Comfortable.

Granddah was starting to lose his memory but his self was still there, and she took her work breaks with him every chance she got and they talked about the weather or the game or whatever might be happening in the tiny town of Cutler. And her brother, Graham, well, he was up in the UP working in the iron-smelting factory and taking those weird photographs that were mostly black but had tree shadows in them, supposedly. He didn't come home, but she would occasionally get a text from him announcing an event worth mentioning: he had bagged a buck; he had sold a photo; the plant had to close down for safety maintenance. Candy and her brother were eight years apart and so hadn't really grown up together. Two different dads. Not that it mattered as neither of them ever saw or heard from the men whose last names they had carried until Granddah had switched them both back to Schein. And then their mom, Brenda, had left. Skedaddled. Booked. Made tracks. She and Graham used to think up all the words and phrases they could for their mother leaving. Graham remembered it, the leaving, but Candy didn't. She had been two, maybe three, and her mom, Brenda, had left Candy in her Pack 'n Play in the middle of the living room. Or so she had been told.

Granddah showed the note to her once when he had come home after a few or three beers at the VFW hall. She had been eleven, maybe, or twelve, just old enough to be left alone at home, according to him. He had turned on the TV, then started grumbling at it during an ad promoting foster care.

"Foster care, huh? Wonder what that pays."

"Am I a foster kid, Granddah?" she had asked.

"Hell no, Candace. You're family," he had replied. "But we

might could use some help now and then to pay for your school fees and such."

"Didn't Mama, my mother, say she would send money?"

"I'll tell you exactly what she said," he had muttered, and went to the sideboard, pulled out a folded piece of notebook paper, and handed it to Candy.

She had unfolded it and there in very round block letters was the following:

"Sorry, Pop, but I have to go. I'll send money and I'll be back just as soon as I can get it together."

"And THAT," Granddah had replied, grabbing the tattered note out of her hands and shoving it into the woodstove before she could stop him from ruining the only thing she had ever touched that her mother had also, "is all I heard from ... from your mother."

Their grandfather also made a kind of grunting sigh noise a lot when he thought the kids weren't close enough to hear, but in the end proved to be an able caretaker for his two grandkids. Enough to keep Child Protective Services away, at least. Then Graham had booked, skedaddled, made tracks, whatever, as soon as he got his diploma. Candy had finished her growing up in a leaning old farmhouse with her granddah, who dropped her at school in the morning and then went off to work for the road commission, which was the job he scrambled to find after the farm failed. Lucky for him and Candy, because the Social Security wasn't going to cover both of them and he had never been given legal custody of Candy for benefits, and so she was, well, invisible to the state of Michigan.

Because Candy loved color, especially loved to think about it on walls, and in clothes, and on couches and pillows, she liked to play a color-match game with people. Not which palette they should wear, but which colors came from them. Auras. Like the poster charts in the windows of psychics. Like Granddah was red and gray. Angry and quiet. He often wore a gray jacket and red shirts, and used to have red hair, which went gray, and his eyes were also gray now instead of blue. His cheeks went red and he had a red temper and red scars on his hands. His vibe, though, was gray most of the time, not the depressing kind, just quiet and smooth like a November sky or the lake on an overcast day.

Graham, of course, was black. Black in a good way. Rich, soft black like the night. Quiet. Black was a quiet color. Maybe that was why he took black photos, which he said were of the woods at night but often Candy couldn't tell. At first when he showed you a picture, you thought you were looking at a blank black print, something that the developer had messed up. Then slowly, if you looked long enough, and Candy certainly had because—as far apart as they were, she loved her brother and he loved his pictures—maybe some trees would emerge from the blackness or the line of the ground, or the sky above. Maybe a truck or a tractor or a fence. "Like you are out there and your eyes are adjusting. The picture makes your eyes adjust," Graham had once explained to her, and Candy had politely said, "Yah, cool," because he was her older brother and she wanted to be a sister to him. Graham also wore black. Well, not exactly; he wore jeans which were blue, but everything else was black: shirt, hoodie, jacket, boots. A black watch cap in the winter. And unlike Candy, he was dark: dark hair, dark eyes, dark skin in the summer, which went a kind of pasty yellow in the winter. Clearly two different dads.

Then there were her acquaintances. Evelyn, who she was on her way to see now before work, was definitely some kind of purple she could not quite land a name for. A dark shade for sure, but bright, and certainly nothing like a flower. Not an iris or a lilac. More like an ink color in one of those Sharpie sets she had so wanted as a kid.

Candy liked to make appointments with Evelyn before her shifts at Glencrest because she could show up in her scrubs. She never wore her purple ones. To Candy's way of thinking, this scheduling arrangement had two plusses: it reminded Evelyn, who would handle her mortgage, that Candy was employed, and secondly, it meant Candy didn't have to decide what she was going to wear. That had taken the better part of the early morning the day she decided to first visit the Mystic. Clothes of any kind suitable for non-work and non-couch slouching were always a problem.

Candy parked the Tacoma in the credit union parking lot and went inside, finding Evelyn trying to look busy at her desk. Small-town loan officer. Not an eight-hour-a-day job, Candy imagined. Evelyn was wearing navy and white today. Candy scanned her further: eyeshadow and nails: mauve and eggplant. She sat in the chair Evelyn indicated, and the banker smiled big. The smile looked real.

"Well, hello, Candace, so nice to see you. Do you have good news for me?"

And Candy pulled out the sheaf of papers Randy had dumped on her.

"Well, I found a place, although it wasn't the one I was looking for. It's such a deal, though. I dunno. I think I might have to take it on."

"Yes, it's quite large," Evelyn said, looking through the sales contract. "And what's this?" Her eyes had landed on the italicized description of the damage and the red-inked reduced price.

Candy explained. Evelyn scowled. Candy said she was heading back out to the Edwards lot with a friend for a second opinion. He was a contractor. He would give it to her straight. This was a total and complete lie. But Candy was not going to divulge to Evelyn that she just had a good feeling or that she sensed the Mystic was meant for her. After all, this was the bank officer who was going to lend her somewhere in the vicinity of 100K to buy the Mystic, move the Mystic, wire and hook up the Mystic, and move herself into the Mystic. So no vibe talk here. She had to have a man's voice saying it would be all right. So she invented one.

Dropping her voice, she reached across the desk, asked, "May I?" at the same time as she started turning more pages and pointing to another rider at the back. "Also, see here: Edwards guarantees and pays for the move, which they usually don't, and will cover all damage resulting from the dent for a year. On top of the five-year warranty. I figure that second one, the special rider, will take me through four seasons and I'll be safe from thereon."

Evelyn was frowning down at the language, running a nail under the words. Maybe not eggplant, Candy thought. Plum, or even a violet. There was some blue in that tint, but not enough to call it indigo. Color charts whirled behind her eyes, and Candy had to force herself to snap out of it. She always used color games when her nerves jangled and her stomach churned. God knows it was carnation pink moving up her neck right now. Evelyn finally lifted the fingernail off the contract, sank back in her chair, and looked up at a spot just past Candy's left ear. Bad news.

"Ok, well it seems you have thought about this, but I'll need to go back with these papers to the mortgage officer down in Grand Rapids and get it approved all over again."

Candy was mystified, especially as she had been so assertive; she lowered her voice and walked Evelyn through the important parts. After all, she was the one taking on the risk. She was the one buying an oversized, dented mobile home. She was going to be on the hook for the mortgage until she was on Social Security, for Pete's sakes. But she kept these thoughts to herself and put the smile back on her face that made her disappear. She looked down at her Casio and pretended she was late for work. Evelyn made copies of all of the papers and then handed Candy's back in a manilla folder. "For your records." As if.

Work-Life Balance

Candy pulled the Tacoma into the Glencrest senior living complex too fast, almost making the tires squeal. She was irritated, no, pissed. Review her application. Again. Banks. She had never played the lottery, having learned from her granddah's frequent tirades about never once in his life having bought a winning ticket, that that was a nonstarter. Too many times as a kid she had watched her grandfather tear his lotto tickets into tiny pieces while standing over the trash can, cursing that it was money down the toilet. But today she wished she had played and won and so she could pay cash for the Mystic, dammit.

Candy had the midday shift, twelve to eight, which normally she didn't mind, while most of the rest of the staff did. This was the shift when the residents were the most alert and therefore the most needy or the most ornery. There was trouble to be had of course, dealing with a place full of people without functioning brains or legs or hands. People would wander; some residents liked to undress and wander halls with their family stuff hanging out. There were a couple of ragers, and some criers, and the moaners. But Candy didn't blame them, and actually the hours went by more quickly when she had to deal with awake, if misbehaving, residents. The night shift was easy peasy but dull, and dull for Candy led to what-if thinking, and what-if thinking led to doubting herself and hating the world. Candy much preferred her oh-well thinking, which happened while she was busy attending to her people. So normally the midday shift was fine even though there wasn't bonus pay tacked on. Today, however, Evelyn had put her in a funk and a funk was a bad way to approach other people in a funk who you were supposed to cheer up, calm down, and clothe and feed.

She was louder than usual in the staff room, shoving her bag into her locker and slamming the door, grabbing her lanyard and her name tag, and sitting down to change into her work shoes. Janelle walked in, hung up her purse and coat, and pulled her shoes out of a Target bag.

"Oooo, I am running late. I gotta stop in the front office about my paycheck. Got it wrong again. How's my blue girl today?" Janelle always took note of Candy's color scheme. Candy could not for one minute compete with Janelle, but she made an effort to coordinate.

"I've had better days," Candy answered, slamming the locker door shut and twirling the useless combination lock.

"Ain't that the truth; my boys just about put me in my grave this morning, getting them ready for school and all. Scholars they are not, and besides, I OBJECT to giving first graders homework. Puhleeze."

Janelle was a mostly single mother to three: twin boys and a teen girl: Carter, Curry, and Christine. Candy thought Janelle was superhuman; she worked at Glencrest full time, and did two nights a week serving at a bar over in Traverse, all while raising three kids and trying to keep her useless but still lovelorn ex out of her hair, which, from what Candy had picked up in the staff room on breaks, took some effort. Janelle's hero was her own mother, who filled in on day care, pickups, doctors' appointments, and all that. Janelle and her mother were best friends. Sometimes Candy wondered what that was like.

"Yeah, I'm trying to do some business with my credit union and they are getting pickier and pickier, I swear."

"You know how Jesus felt about the moneylenders," Janelle said.

"No," said Candy. "How?"

"Did you not have to drag your ass to Sunday school as a kid? He threw the moneylenders out of the temple. Seems they were doing business in God's house and Jesus didn't like that."

"More things change," Candy said. It took a beat or two but then Janelle caught the joke and laughed.

"Learn something new every day," Candy added.

"Yeah." Janelle finished lacing up her purple Pumas. "Guess some things stuck after all those years. Damn, but that basement was hot and smelly too. I was always nodding off and getting pinched by the teacher."

Janelle asked no follow-up questions about the credit union or Candy's funk. The thing about Janelle, which was why Candy felt safe enough with her to have the occasional after-work, rosé-in-a-can meetup at the beach, and why she called Janelle "friend," was because Janelle asked no nosy questions. It wasn't that she didn't care. It was that she didn't pry. She was warm and funny and cheerful, but didn't ask now, for instance, what the bank business was about. Instead, she just slammed her locker and said, "Let's go get it on, huh, Miss Sweet?"

Candy followed Janelle, who was rocking kelly green scrubs today, with aqua nails and eyeshadow, through the double doors. Janelle was definitely all about the cool sectors of the color wheel. She took extra care to match her makeup with her outfits, she said, because it livened up the place. "Give 'em something to talk about," she always said. Janelle was blue, turquoise actually, like the stone. Deep but light, bright but soft. Like Lake Michigan on August afternoons.

Candy had checked the assignment board on her way in, the Glencrest administration having decided that rotating staff around to different "neighborhoods" increased the efficiency of staff. This of course was insane. The truth was, giving staff the chance to develop true relationships with the old folks made their jobs easier, and the residents happier, not that that mattered to Corporate. For instance, if you knew that Miss Gladys had to have a newspaper with her at all times open to the horoscope page, and she knew it was Candy who was coming to give her her pills, it was easier to get them down. And forget getting Samuel R. into the shower. If you wanted him clean, you had to use a face cloth with warm, not hot, water, preferably while asking him about his dead wife. That man positively hated water. And if you were working Birch, or the other memory-care hall, you had to learn not to upset people. If you spoke up, but not too loud, as you walked into any of the dementia residents' rooms or areas, you were less likely to have an outburst or a tantrum on your hands, or worse. And even if they didn't know who you were, Candy had to believe they were at least a little calmer if they even vaguely recognized your voice. The musical chairs system of staffing was hard on everyone but especially on the lost ones. And finally, Candy had learned the quiet dying ones loved to be touched. Petted. On their arms or shoulders, or their hair patted down if they had any. They would practically start purring, sometimes moaning in pleasure, when you petted them. And although a lot of touching was not her vibe, she made herself do it anyway, because although Candy had little use for the humans out in the world, she loved her old people. She petted them when she could and they purred and murmured their appreciation. There were more than a few whose families had left them there, alone. Candy's hands were sometimes all they had, it seemed.

But Candy wasn't in the confined section today. She was in Sycamore with Marcos. Ok. Sycamore housed the youngest and most mobile, most of them still with their minds. Granddah had done some time in Sycamore, but then lost his mobility: first a cane, then a walker, and now a walker with supervision. He was compliant because he knew if he wasn't, it was the wheelchair next. Granddah's moderately good nature would be down the tubes with a wheelchair.

Marcos was good people and Candy liked working with him. He had flunked out of high school and the military and then gotten it together to get a GED and then an associate's, and it turned out that what schools and military had decided was too slow, or too kind, ended up just right for working with seniors. He might be methodical and refuse to hurry through his care routines, but Marcos was not stupid. He was patient and kind and at the end of the day, Candy thought those two things, along with a sense of humor and a strong back, were what the job requirements should be, not some stupid associate's degree that quizzed you on science and pharmacology that you never got a chance to use anyway. The RN on shift and the doctors did all that. Liability. Efficiency and liability. The two words admins spat out of their mouths more than any others.

Candy hung her lanyard around her neck, hip checked the fire door open, and almost walked into Marcos.

"Buenos días, Senorita," he said. Marcos was also bilingual, which earned him extra treats from the kitchen.

"Hey, Mister."

They smiled at each other.

"How's it?"

"Passing. You?"

"Good enough, you know? Coming up on a payday, it's never bad."

The twelve-to-eight shift included shower duty and that could be tough, but there was a roving he-man staff member named Claude, who worked in the kitchen but was often called out to help lift. This was a total rip-off, but Claude was in school part-time too, trying to get degreed and out of the kitchen, so there was that. The afternoon was beautiful and warm and filled with autumn color and that cool slant of light, and so Marcos and Candy cajoled who they could out onto the deck. Some threw their heads back and drank in the sun. Others squinted and asked for shade but enjoyed the flurry of leaves when the wind blew. Any time outside made the day better. Winter would be here soon enough and they all would be confined to long, dark days indoors, breathing forced air under fluorescent lights. Better to grab any afternoon outside you could, and autumn here was a kind of beautiful that took you by surprise and gave you a lump in your throat.

This was another reason Candy was so excited about the doublewide. The Mystic. Her Pizza Palace shithole apartment in the center of town had no outdoor space unless you counted the treacherous back stairs she climbed up and down to get to her truck parked in the back lot. She could have used the inside stairs but that would mean she had to cruise through the Pizza Palace and say hello to people and that felt like too much to go through to get home.

If she could manage it, buy the doublewide and move it out onto Granddah's land, there would be ACRES out the back door, filled with pine and sandy soil and wildflowers all summer in the sunny spots and weird mushrooms in the shady places, and then at night, the sky and the stars. Candy was not sporty, but she loved being outside. She loved the color and the air and wind and the trees and almost more than anything in the world, she loved the lake. Lake Michigan, second largest of the Great Lakes, but to Candy it was as good as an ocean. And the beaches—some looked like they were straight out of an ad for the Caribbean. No wonder people flocked here all summer. Candy so loved the beaches, walking them, and watching the water change color and the waves change size and shape. That was how the lake told you how it was feeling. Waves.

As a teenager, after she had spent a long day being invisible or had been the butt of a joke which hurt her more than it should have, Candy would grab the school bus but get out at the stop closest to the beach and walk the lake, and then call Granddah to pick her up on his way home. It was at the lake in the wind that the voices of the day, or the lack of likes on Facebook, would get blown out of her head. It took a while, but Candy had learned if you just kept watching the water and you just kept leaning into the wind, you got some kind of clean, and then the human world went away and there were only colors to name and wind direction to track and maybe a stone or two to pick up and stow in her pocket.

If she couldn't get to the lake, then at home she would walk the woods. They were alive with noise and none of it was human. There was always a skittering, or a chirping, or a rustling that signaled a world apart, where a girl could be alone and not judged, not ignored, and not taunted. Candy had to admit, high school had been better than junior high. As they grew up, other kids, or some of them anyway, got manners, and the taunts had eased off. But the invisibility, well that went off the charts. Candy lost count of how many times she had been run into in the halls or coming through a door, with only a "my bad," or a "sorry," directed above her head or somewhere beyond her. The dream of the doublewide, set down on her own piece of land out on Lasso Road, would banish all those slights. And the thought made Candy lift her own face into the October light out on the patio at Glencrest.

After their afternoon sun and wind baths, the residents' cleanup and dinner passed quickly, and after clocking out, Candy walked the now quiet halls of the home. She found Granddah in the TV room watching a detective show. Not really. He was with his buddy Gus, playing gin rummy with the TV providing background.

"Up past your bedtime, huh, Granddah?" Candy said as she entered the room.

"Well hello there, Miss Candace," he said, and smiled without looking up from his cards.

Granddah had called her Candace since she could remember and then added the "Miss" just for fun when she graduated from grade school. As an adult, Candy no longer had an opinion one way or the other. Few enough people called her by her name anyway and "Candace" was what had landed on her name tag.

"Gus here keeps winning and I'm not going to bed until I get one round under my belt."

"Who's your staff tonight?" she asked.

"Black girl, what's her name, blue fingernails."

"Janelle."

"Janelle, yes. She's all right."

Candy was relieved. Besides being kind and not nosy, Janelle was one of the braver staff members who cared more about residents than rules. She would indulge those who could care for themselves and let them stay up past the Glencrest bedtime directives. Janelle rarely swore but she was heard to say on more than one occasion, "You know where they can put their directives. A mandated bedtime. For adults. Insulting."

Janelle, as if hearing her name, popped her head through the door. "What about it, Mr. Men? You even the score yet, Mr. Schein? Hey, Candy, what's doin'?"

"Just off, heading out to the store and then home. Feet up/ couch slouch/microwave/bed."

"Singing my song." Janelle laughed.

Candy sat with her grandfather for the few minutes it took to ease her guilt without interrupting his concentration on the cards he was holding. Over his shoulder she could see his hand was crap. Candy patted his shoulder, told him when her next shift was, and wished him good night.

"Who's got the kids?" she asked Janelle as she headed out of the TV room.

"Their father, praise be. He called and said he wanted more time with them. What he meant was he wants to enroll them in Pop Warner, but what I said was, start with covering a night or two and give their grandma a rest. He grumbled, but then showed up on time—what do you know?"

Candy laughed. "Progress."

"Don't know I'd go that far."

"'Night."

"'Night."

One of the bonuses of working the twelve-to-eight was that Candy could food shop at her favorite time of day. Or night, rather. Shop 'n Save hours were eight to closing, which was nine for the Benneville grocery store in the offseason. At night, aisles were often empty, the clerks and stockers cheerful, their moods lifting as closing time neared. But most of all, Candy could shop freely.

It wasn't easy food shopping while fat, or large as they now called it, in this America. People looked you over in your sweats and your Crocs and your tunic-sized sweatshirts and then they scrutinized the contents of your cart. Especially the thin summer people. Candy was by no means the only large one around here, but she was young, single, female, and fat. That put her in a whole other category of damnation. So rolling into the almost empty Shop 'n Save at around 8:20 was just fine. Candy grabbed a mini cart and began her now familiar interior lecture series, which was a schizo dance between "eat more produce, start diet now" and "wow, look at that new frozen spinach and cheese ravioli, wouldn't that be some serious comfort food after a hard day's work." Candy always managed to please both voices, conscientiously starting in the produce section, picking out bags of premixed salad and some bite-sized carrots, then grabbing that delicious blue cheese dressing that was so rich and fresh it had to be refrigerated. Yum. Then she rounded the corner to the meat aisle, which was where the third voice chimed in: budget, you can only spend $50, and that's gotta take you to Monday, so chill on the steaks.

What was on sale was not edible: pieces of animal bodies Candy didn't fancy. So she grabbed some frozen chicken thighs and some burgers and indulged in a package of pork chops. She just loved pork chops with apples and onions. And mashed potatoes.

And then the last lap, her favorite of course, was the frozen food section, which, since her childhood days, had expanded from one aisle to three. A person could now survive without ever having to make anything by themselves again, it seemed. Meals, side dishes, pizza, garlic bread, desserts galore, outrageously expensive meatless meals. This was where Candy had to really restrain herself from letting loose. It was always a bad idea to shop before dinner.

Her total came to $57.34. It was the frozen food that sent her over the edge. She routinely lost all control in the dessert section. But that was her passion and her comfort, and why else did she work so hard if she couldn't have a little comfort?

The ritual was to make herself wait until later in the week for the frozen-dinner indulgences. The first meal after shopping always included turning on the oven, cooking something, making a salad, and eating it. There was dessert of course, ice cream mostly, but for the first night, you had to make a dent in that produce that schizo number one had made you buy. Otherwise it was money down the drain. Or into the dumpster.

Her apartment, as usual, smelled of grease and cheese and pepperoni and, well, grease. This was fine except that it made Candy hungry all the time. The upside was that she rarely ate pizza anymore. Lasagna, and spaghetti with meatballs, yes. Pizza, not so much.

She grabbed some BBQ sauce out of the fridge, slathered it on her chicken thighs, put some water on to boil, and went to change. She showered, dressed in night clothes, and listened to the Palace's closing sounds as she paged through an old *Better Homes* magazine she had lifted from Glencrest with the TV in the background tuned to HGTV and muted. Tonight's episode looked like a massive ranch with a huge backyard and a kitchen that needed to be put out of its misery. A happy couple followed a buff remodeler in a tight T-shirt through rooms that had been staged to look worse than they were. Candy's fingers found the dog-eared pages with design ideas for her future home. Mostly couches and kitchens, the two centers of her universe. She loved blue and brown, navy and beige, teal and chestnut, aqua and cocoa, almost any combo of blue and brown. She knew from her research that this was a clichéd pairing but she didn't mind. Let the rich eat their black and white and bamboo and chrome. She wasn't going to order up driftwood or anchor prints or lighthouses. No bears or moose or deer. Just the colors. Stripes maybe, or splashes and splotches. Or woven heathers of blue and brown. Earth and sky. Lake and sand. That was going to be the whole nine yards in her new home. The Mystic.

The Doublewide. She was going to have to decide on a name and stick with it. But she was still split because Candace lived at the Mystic, Candy, in a doublewide.

She heard the water start to boil on the stove and got up to peel potatoes and preheat the oven. Happy? No. Lonely? Not a chance. Just hungry, was all. Just hungry.

Busted on the Peninsula

Candy woke late to no alarm and, rolling over in bed to look up at the deep blue morning sky, was reminded once again of why fall was her favorite time of year. It was true that daylight was leaking away like crazy, three or four minutes a day as Granddah liked to remind her, but the light and the leaves and the emptied-out roads gave Candy a reason to get out of bed even on her day off. Or so it seemed. More than that. Get out of the apartment, walk the beach, watch the trees, drive the roads and eat apple cinnamon donuts. All was good on a morning like this one.

She had an agenda today, though, and first on the list was figuring out ways to not sit around and wait for the phone call from the credit union. The sun was shining and the wind was not too bad, a perfect day to walk the semi-empty beaches. But this morning she was too antsy for beach walking. She wanted to go back to the house lot and check out the doublewide's crunched-in corner. Over the weekend, Candy had made her way back to her old, almost falling-down house and its not-quite-falling-down-as-bad-yet garage, where Granddah kept his tools and had scrounged up a square and the least ancient-looking level. She didn't know what else could help her, but at least with these she could go back out to Edwards and check the walls and floors and ceilings around the crumpled part. She didn't really know what she was doing but her grandfather had taught her what these tools were for when she hung around during fix-it time at the farm. And she figured at the very least she might look like maybe she had a clue and Randy might not be as tempted to rip her off.

She grabbed coffee and a muffin at the gas station, made small talk with a clerk she didn't recognize, and then began to head out to Edwards's. Then, at the T intersection, abruptly, and without thinking, Candy turned the Tacoma right instead of left and found herself driving out toward the peninsula. This was a small stretch of land that fingered its way out into Grand Traverse Bay, and perched on its shores was some of the most serious money in the county, hell, maybe even the state. The houses were monsters, many of them new. In the last five years or so, dozens of old cedar-shingled one-story cottages had come down, replaced by mongo five-bedroom mansions with three-car garages. As she drove east into the late, slanting fall sunshine, Candy schemed about how to steal onto a lot and take a peek at a kitchen, maybe, or a family room. Why a family room when she was going to live alone made little sense except that it conjured up visions of deep sofas and meals in front of a big TV, which was right up her alley. It was a Tuesday in October, so Candy was guessing owners might not be much around. Maybe she could find a place to sneak up to and see how the rich did their kitchens and decks, live and in color. Or actually, black and white mostly, she was guessing. Still.

The traffic up the shoreline drive was almost totally trade: landscapers, electricians, plumbers, contractors, random busted-up pickups driven by day workers who were hired for grunt work and clean up. There were no Lexuses, or Navigators, or Land Rovers, or Tahoes, summer people cars. In the offseason, the roads got repopulated with all kinds of trucks, mostly pickups, many beat up. This was one of the reasons Candy had loved inheriting Granddah's Tacoma. Driving a pickup well, she melted right into the morning traffic moving up Peninsula Drive. She kept an eye out for anything unfinished. A jobsite that she could slide into and look like she was a decorator or a realtor or somebody who might have business there. That morning she had put semi-professional looking clothes on because she had originally been headed out to the Edwards lot. Now, she figured the outfit could be cover: real estate agent, somebody who wasn't a snoop.

There was still a lot of building going on. Huge places in various stages of doneness. Some already had their asphalt drives and hardscaping, others were just getting their walls finished and clad. As fancy as these shore places were, there were precious few with wood siding. It was all cement board or aluminum, plastic decks and railings, false shutters, manufactured stone. It made Candy miss the old places she had driven past as a kid with her grandfather on their way up the peninsula for apples. The old places had been made of real wood, real shingles, paint that peeled, and porches that grayed. She now drove past a couple of new places that had that Mystic Blue palette thing going. Candy chuckled at that.

She drove slowly enough to scope out houses but not so slow as to piss off the trades trailing her. Luckily the road was narrow and winding, lake on one side, driveways, lawns, stone walls, on the other. The lake was lapping at the edges of the road, levels up six inches this year and four the year before. It didn't take too much to imagine these lovely new houses wading in water in a few years if you believed the disaster science. That was what people called it around here: disaster science. Like a type of reality TV show: Disaster Science: The New Millennium Invasion. Was there a sit-com science, or a bachelorette science? Candy usually tried to tune out the outside world, ignoring the news and the politicians and the crazy talk, but it seemed like climate change had become part of her inside universe: the lake levels, the polar freezes, the odd thaws; even the deer were eating differently, pushed off their normal diets by new weather patterns. She couldn't push the weather away like she did the crazy president, or the insane gun toters, or the wars in far-off places she couldn't find on a map.

Then, around a bend, she saw it up ahead: a mostly finished house, white with black shutters and a wide front porch, no finished driveway, no trucks parked on the lot. No landscaping beyond a few baby trees held up by staying wires which didn't look like they would survive a northern winter, especially if the lake splashed up and froze around their poor baby roots. She nudged the Tacoma over the rough gravel into what would probably be a backyard with a pool at some point in the future. She tucked the truck in right next to the back of the house and parked. She sneaked a peek around while pretending to look at her phone as if she might be meeting someone. Or pretending to look like she thought someone might look who actually belonged there.

Satisfied that she was alone, she looked around, spied an

overturned milk crate, got out of the truck, grabbed it, and set it below a back-facing window which looked to be about four feet off the ground. Took one more glance around. No one. Her heart was pounding and she felt like she should be doing this at night, but then what would be the point? Then there wouldn't be anything to peek at or anything that she could see in the dark. At any rate, she was out of sight from the road. She went for it, giddy with her new boldness.

    She stepped up carefully onto the crate, steadied herself, and looked through the windows, which still had the Pella stickers on them. Ah. A kitchen. A kitchen as big as the doublewide, it seemed. Two sinks, two stoves, built-in beverage fridge under a granite-topped island which itself was as big as her Palace kitchenette. The biggest fridge she'd ever seen. It had what looked like a TV screen on the front, except it was still coated in the blue plastic wrap that delicate surfaces were always wrapped protectively in. The scheme was all granite and wood, of course. Some creamy-taupe tinted granite, walnut-colored cabinets, stainless steel everything else. The kitchen island had a double sink and a breakfast bar to tuck into on a stool. Candy found herself a bit disappointed because it looked exactly like a magazine, except it was still empty, void of the blender and espresso makers and spoon holders and the like. It was as if the whole thing, every decision, had been lifted from Dream *Kitchens and Baths* magazine. It was true that Candy pored over these magazines when she could get her hands on them, and she coveted the furniture and the color schemes. But it had always seemed to her that the whole point of getting and filling a home was to create a place that would belong to you. That would be yours. That if you died or disappeared mysteriously, anyone who knew you could walk in and say, "Ah, this is definitely Candy's place," although with Granddah no longer mobile she couldn't think of who that person might be.

Candy had never liked the look of granite in magazines and liked it even less in real life. It was too hard, too shiny, sunlight gleaming off it like a mirror. Must be hard to cook there, she thought. Her distaste for the expensive counter material came as a relief, because of course Candy's doublewide, if it ever became Candy's, would come with a sandy, speckled kind of laminate and white appliances: stove, fridge, cabinets. White was always the default. Her possibly future bathroom would come with a shower, sink, vanity, and mirror already installed, the vanity a kind of honey brown lacquered wood. Menards. Lowe's. Whatever. The thousands of decisions like these homeowners could make were out of her reach, or the reach of most mobile homeowners. Candy would be able to choose rugs and couches and tables and beds and things to hang on walls. When she could afford them. First, she would paint the walls. They would not be white. These here were only primed white but she would bet good money that the owner would choose cream. Candy would not choose cream for her home. Cream was for coffee. Period.

Candy felt her face smiling at her own joke at the exact moment that a voice from behind her said, "Can I help you with something?" It was a man.

Candy had heard nothing. Had he just driven up? Had he been here the whole time? Was he security? And who was she going to pretend to be? Her mind raced through possible outs: Cousin? Designer? Designer lackey? Friend. Friend of contractor? Friend of owner? Cousin of owner? What if he was the owner? She became aware of the fact that she had stopped breathing. She tried to start again, breathing that is, then turned around, and stepped carefully off the crate, thinking it was no small miracle she got off the thing without tripping.

It was a big man who had snuck up behind her. When she looked up she saw he was round: round face, round body, round fingers curled into a tool belt. He was dressed in raggedy Carhartts, including a baseball cap that had seen better days and which shielded his face. He wore wraparounds over his eyes and his mouth was smiling. He had evidently walked up right behind her but when she turned around, had backed off to what he probably thought was a respectful distance. But he looked like he had her number. She just knew it.

"Uh, sorry. Just so curious. I drive by every day and always wanted to check out what was inside. Kept watching the trucks deliver stuff and you know ..." She was lying pretty well, she thought, and since he was probably not the owner, her fear of him eased off.

"Decorator?" he asked, perching his sunglasses on his hat. His eyes, circled by pale skin, looked directly into hers. This felt like a kind of scorching and she looked away again, vaguely waving her hands in the direction of the house behind her.

"Um, sort of. I'm getting my own place and am looking for ideas. Sorry. Hard sometimes to tell what something looks like in a magazine. Although this ..."

"Looks just like a magazine," he chimed in, and then laughed at his own joke. He seemed to be missing a tooth on one side of his smile and had reddish stubble growing out of his round cheeks and round chin. He continued to smile in a way that was not creepy, and so Candy was reasonably assured he was not going to hurt her. And he wasn't dressed as a security guy who would call the police. She had checked before getting out of the truck. Those obnoxious security stakes had not yet been punched into every corner of the property.

Candy heard the lake behind them and felt the red spread from her cheeks to her neck. It was one of the many reasons she found herself avoiding unexpected encounters with people. She reddened. It wasn't anything as cute as a blush. It was a full-on flush. All the time. And she was pale, and so she went from white to red without any intermediate stopover at pink. She often went from looking like she needed recess to needing a dermatologist. Annoyed didn't come close to how it made her feel. Now she forced herself to listen to the calm lapping sound of the lake.

"Don't you think?" the man asked, and Candy realized she had gone mute.

"Um, yeah, I was just thinking the same thing. The magazines come up with these color schemes, only they call them surface palettes or something."

"And these owners, or I should say the designers hired by these owners, don't have to make any decisions. Just repackage 'em as their own ideas and pick up their fee. At least it makes buying stock easier for us. The suppliers always know what people are going to want before they want it."

He was talkative, this guy, and hadn't returned to his first question, so maybe Candy was off the hook. She turned toward the truck. "Well, sorry to bother you. I'd better be ..."

"That's three," he said. The guy had this chuckle-in-his-eyes thing going on, like an elf or something.

"Sorry?"

"Four." And this time he held up his thick fingers, counting off. She could see his palms. They were covered in white calluses.

"Excuse me?"

"Sorrys. Four sorrys. Do you usually have a lot to apologize for?"

Candy felt herself move from bake to broil. Her back and neck were moist, heading to full-on wet. But this strange, smiling round man seemed to sense her unease and backed up another couple of steps.

"Want to take a peek inside?" he asked, and then by the reaction clearly visible on Candy's face, he seemed to realize how dangerous and crazy this would sound to a strange woman on a deserted building site.

"I mean," and now it was he who seemed to stumble, "you could." And then he stopped and seemed to be at a loss. "What I meant was ..."

This was fantastic. Someone was stumbling, stuttering, besides her. She tried not to enjoy it. Then his face changed, smile firing up again. "I know. I got a key to the back, and I'll give it to you and I can sit in my truck and you can see me from any window and I'll wait until you get out again and then I'll lock up." He was running at the mouth. And for the first time, Candy allowed herself a smile.

"No worries," she replied. "I wasn't that interested. Just curious." And then she added, "I actually have my own plans pretty well set." And once again she turned toward her door to open it.

"What kind of place?"

"What? Mine?"

"Yeah, you said you were getting ideas for your place. Are you buying? Condo? House?"

"Actually, manufactured home. They used to call them mobile homes but nobody moves them anymore, at least not the kind I'm buying."

He chuckled again. "Manufactured. I always thought that was a kind of funny word for them. All homes are manufactured, right?" The guy was a kidder, all right. And for reasons as mysterious to Candy's conscious mind as the ones that had pointed her east instead of west this morning, she remained outside her truck, engaging in a conversation with a perfect stranger who didn't work at the Shop 'n Save, or Quik Mart.

"Yeah, it's still on the lot. At Edwards. I was planning on a single but the salesman offered me a doublewide at a great price. It is damaged in one corner from moving. I'm on my way to check it out."

"Uh oh. Bad?"

"What do I know? I'm heading over there to check the dinged-up corner and then try to get them to extend their warranties and such. Besides that, I really like it. It's ..." and here she paused at the ridiculousness of what was coming next, "wide."

"Yep. Double."

And she rushed on, because of the word "wide" hanging out there in the breeze waiting to be snapped up into a joke. Jesus, Candy thought, what the hell was wrong with her? It was just possible that some people didn't notice her size or her color or her sweat. High school was in the rearview. Leave it already, she thought, and forced herself to focus on the man in front of her who was making conversation. She began.

"It seems like there's more light that way. At least that's the way it looked when I was shopping before. The doublewides have an open floor plan in the front, so there's windows on both sides that seem ..." And then she lost her words.

"Wider?" the man filled in, his face open and, well, nice looking.

Candy smiled and stared at her shoes.

"That would be it. Wider. Wider light. Whatever that means, I know it when I see it."

"Sightlines."

"Excuse me?"

"Sightlines," he repeated. "Places can appear to be lighter than they actually are when you can see outdoors in a 180. Like you swivel right, and then swivel left, and there's light and outside views in both directions. Or even if you can see more than one view from a single standing place. I learned that in CAD class in high school."

"That's it," Candy said. She felt the red fading, could feel her face cooling. And he was, or seemed to be, enjoying this conversation.

"Clint," he said, extending his hand, which was clean, she noted. "Name's Clint."

A Level and a Square

"I'm Candy. Candace. Candy."

"That two names or one?" Clint asked. He seemed about to chuckle again and she didn't know if that was his sense of humor or hers.

"Well, people call me Candy. Except for my grandfather. He calls me Candace. Says Candy's a kid's name. He may be right."

"Well, I know some grown-up Timmys, and my aunt's a Joanie."

A stuttering silence enveloped Candy along with the familiar fleeing response.

"I better be getting along. I want to get to the lot before Randy, that's the salesman, has a chance to pretend he has no time for me. I've got to get my 'I know my way around a dented corner' face on," she added, and resisted the impulse to turn away. Here she was, Candy Schein, admitting to a stranger that she was clueless. Candy's game face had always read "invisible." And independent. Or so she thought.

"What you got in the way of tools?"

"Me? Oh, a square and a level. My grandfather's. Enough to make me look like I know what I'm doing, I guess."

"Sounds like a start." And as she now turned toward her truck he fell into step beside her. There was no one around except the pickups passing by on the still busy shore road. The feeling that she should be scared or at least suspicious rattled around in her head. Should she have her car keys knuckled in between her fingers for a knockout punch? But he was this round, pleasant guy. Big, but somehow soft with his chuckles. Then again, those scary movies sometimes had round, chuckling guys. She shook her own head at herself.

"What?" He had seen her clench. Maybe. Maybe not. She forced herself to think of something to say.

"Just thinking about the sales rep at the lot. Name's Randy. He's so greasy and slick he's like a cliché."

"I had an English teacher once who told me that clichés were clichés for good reasons."

As he kept talking, Candy wondered if he was from around here, if he had gone to school here, if they were the same age, if he had played football and she had watched him. Taylor Swift suddenly came to mind. Speaking of clichés.

"They're true," Clint was saying. "Clichés. They're true. So true they become clichés. I always remember that."

"Huh," replied Candy, but in what she hoped was a friendly grunting kind of way.

Clint took off his hat to reveal a matted mess of dirty blond curls. "Mind if I ask you a kind of awkward question?"

Candy secured herself by putting a hand on the truck door handle. She felt a flash of heat, prickling of skin, cool of moist-hitting air.

"Ok ..."

"I mean, this is gonna sound sexist and all and it's not. At least I don't mean it that way."

Candy couldn't believe the word "sexist" had come out of this construction worker's stubbly face. And then she caught herself. Mean, she scolded herself.

"I mean, I don't mean it that way at all. I'm just kind of curious. About manufactured homes. I see them on the highway and I always think to myself, wow, that is never gonna make it to its final resting place in one piece. But they do. They make it. And then you told me your story and I started wondering, well, are they all dinged on some corner or telephone pole and then fixed up and sold as is? Has to be, cuz they sure are everywhere now. Working people's home of choice these days, it seems. So the price has got to be right and yet how do they get down those winding state roads?" He paused after his long speech, and then said again, "I'm just curious."

"How is that sexist?"

"Well. I was going to ask if you might let me tag along. I am dressed like I know my way around a construction site, or a mishap, or what have you. But actually, I probably don't know much more than you."

"Doubt that," Candy said, and then considered this seriously. She wasn't going home and so he couldn't follow her anywhere but the Edwards Homes site. He was a man and he was dressed for work on a jobsite, and he might have tools that said more about the crunched-up corner and she could use help. Any help. And. He was a man and that was how things rolled, she knew.

"And I am on tap to install bathroom cabinets here today

but I need to go to Traverse for hinges which they forgot to include, and that could take, well," and here he shrugged his shoulders and grinned in a way that made him look like a kid, "all morning, maybe."

And so she said yes, gave him the address, and climbed into the cab which still smelled of gas station coffee. The muffin was there waiting for her on the seat. Somehow it was reassuring, though she had no appetite for it right now.

Clint started back to his own truck, which was white. Like the park-service trucks, only without the logo. And then he turned back and practically jogged to the driver-side window, which she rolled down again.

"What am I?" he asked.

She was puzzled. "What are you?"

"To you."

Ahh, and she found herself smiling. At Clint.

"A cousin."

"Cousin Clint it is," he said, pleased with his new identity, it seemed, and went back to his truck, climbed in, made a quick three-point turn on the sandy dirt of the jobsite, and waited for her to pull out onto the shore road and head toward the lot.

It wasn't a long ride, but parts were tedious, the edges of Traverse City filled with strip malls and big-box stores and so many traffic lights. There were no lights and exactly one stop sign in Cutler. These big places needed big parking lots, Walmart and whatnot, and seemed to need their own traffic light to protect the left-turners. And because people bought so much they always needed big cars to haul it all home to places that didn't have a whole lot of room for sixteen-packs of paper towels and sixty-four ounces of peanut butter. Candy had shopped at these places a couple of times and first of all, because she liked math and could do it in her head, she had figured out the prices weren't any better than the Shop 'n Save. And they were just too big, the amounts too big. She was one person. A single person. She liked a store where you could shop for one person. And not for the apocalypse either.

The Edwards "Let Us Bring You Home" lot was still blazing with those irritating ropes of plastic flags flapping in the autumn wind. All around the edges of the lot, the maples and locusts and beeches and birches were changing, showcasing much better shades than the plastic triangles already tattered from the stiff breeze. Today, the fall foliage show was just warming up; next week would bring the hordes back in, clamoring for the maples especially: campers and cars and trailers. Roadside stands would hawk cider and pies and jams and honey advertised on homemade signs, and the breweries would offer a stronger cider and the cinnamon apple donuts would be everywhere.

There were not a lot of cars at the visitors' parking lot, Candy noticed as she climbed down from her cab. Clint was right behind her and stirred up dust as he pulled his pickup in next to hers. Randy came down the steps from the sales trailer with his hand outstretched to Candy. "I had a hunch you might be back so I went ahead with the repairs. She's all ready for you." He had forgotten her name. "Ready to fall in love forever?"

"We'll see," she replied, and then grabbed Granddah's tools out of the truck bed. They looked old and hopelessly out of date here on a sales lot where all attempts were made to keep everything looking shiny and new. They felt heavy in her hands and she felt awkward with them at her sides.

"And who's this?" Randy asked.

"Cousin," Clint answered. "Clint. Clint Houdek," he said, extending his hand. Houdek, Candy thought. Up here that name was like Smith or Jones. Houdeks and Hodeks and Hudecks were a dime a dozen: farmers, realtors, septic tank pumpers, schoolteachers. She had had a Ms. Hudeck in elementary school. Old. Mean.

"Well, welcome, cousin Clint," Randy said, extending his hand and not smiling at all. "Here to help this little lady out? Show her all is well, which it is of course." And he turned toward Clint with an outstretched arm toward the Mystic. He had turned away from Candy and was chatting up Clint. Men were so predictable.

But Clint was not smiling or chuckling or laughing. Or following. He had not taken off his wraparounds or removed his cap. This was not predictable. Cousin Clint was not the guy from the house lot up on the peninsula. Was this a performance? He was in a kind of stance, legs apart, his hands hooked over his tool belt. Like a cowboy. He swiveled his shoulders toward Candy, who held her grandfather's level and square, one in each hand.

"Here, Cuz, let me take those off your hands. We'll just have a quick look and then I got work to get back to."

"Certainly, certainly, right this way," Randy replied, holding out the other arm to include Candy.

But Clint had reached out and nudged Candy on the elbow and beckoned her to slow her steps. With Randy striding ahead of them, Clint leaned into her and said softly, "Do not commit. Say nothing. Grunt if you have to but try not to smile."

"I got that much from your opening, whatever that was."

"Game. It's a game."

When they approached the doublewide, the shimmying in her stomach started again. Candy couldn't help it. She was in love. It was a doublewide, yes, but it was the shorter model, so it was kind of a fat rectangle. The front door was white and had one of those arched windows, and the house windows had those dividers in them that made them look like they were multi-paned. Candy could already see the home on the lot on Lasso Road with herself inside, looking out on the back pines, covered in snow, maybe. She had begun to dream this, over and over again, until it was starting to seem as real as the life she existed in now. She had walked Granddah's lot leisurely, considering all the sites where a new home might sit. After all, she lived a lot inside her head, and inside her head the tales spun. A home. A warm home that belonged to her, that had her colors and her smells and maybe a cat but not a smelly one, and a full fridge and maybe Janelle might come over one afternoon after work, and they would drink rosé from a can and face each other on the couch and laugh.

And so here it was. Right here. Candy was absolutely certain because the vibration in her whole body was telling her so. Four years, no, five. One crumpled corner and a reapproved mortgage away, fingers crossed. And then she could plop down on a new couch with new pillows and look out a window onto a scene of pines and sky and say to herself, "Looky here, I did this. This is mine. And I belong here. So there."

She felt metal touch her skin and looked down at her hands. Clint was handing her back the square.

"Let's start with this," he said, and climbed the stairs to hold the door open for Candy as she walked over the threshold.

Inspection

"Don't you want to check out the outside first?" Randy asked Clint.

"Nah, we can start in here. This is where she'll be living, right? Like in January when the wind's blowing something fierce and such."

Candy was catching on to the script Clint was reading from and added, "Yeah, that wind, it can find any crack or crevice, right?"

"Right," Clint replied, furrowing his brow. Actually, Candy only imagined this, because Clint had kept his hat pulled down over his forehead, although he now perched his sunglasses on top of it as they moved inside, trooping up past Randy, who was holding the door. She turned to the questionable corner but Clint still didn't take the square from her, and so she walked to the corner which had been patched and primed and snuggled her square into it. Checked for gaps between the square and wall. Looked good, at least to her. Then she moved it up a foot. Still good. Then up another foot, still good. Then she handed the tool off to Clint.

"Could you?" She gestured toward the ceiling.

And he repeated her procedure, and then they went to the walls and worked the level and then, finally then, Clint squatted and squinted at the floor, laid the level down, and then laid down next to it so his eyes were even with the green bubble in the level's tube. Grunted. Candy had noticed the guy grunted really well. He seemed to have a whole language consisting of grunts. What was the word? A repertoire. Randy hovered and continued to repeat reassuring phrases which Candy paid no attention to. Instead, she glanced around, trying not to look completely gobsmacked. The view from the windows made even the Edwards lot look good. The lites, or fake lites, installed in the windows, gave the views an old-fashioned look. They sectioned off the landscape into snapshots. The narrow pieces of white plastic framed a tree or a section of sky or a piece of ground, and instead of there being one view, there were many.

Randy had given up on getting Clint's attention and now turned his comments directly to her. Candy had to turn away from the windows to pay attention: warranty, extended, free transport, permitting, bank papers. She felt like she did back at school when the teacher at the front of the room was saying things that were surely important, things that she would need to remember and do something about. But it had been hopeless then and it was hopeless now. There were home movies spinning out of her imagination that Randy's important facts couldn't compete with. She hoped he would repeat it all at least once or twice before they were rid of him.

She did pick up on Clint saying something about "outside." And they went out the door and Candy tried not to look back, and then they were leveling and squaring the hell out of the exterior corner. Clint was on his knees inspecting the underside, which made her blush for some reason. At least he had no butt crack visible, which was a mean thing to think. She forced herself to pay attention.

"That siding repair job?" Clint pointed to the barely visible patching. "Looks like a pretty amateur cut and paste. She might want the whole panel replaced."

"Well, it is sealed and secure, no doubt about it, but we could probably scrounge up a couple, two or three extra lengths and throw them in for free. You look like a pretty handy guy. Probably just a morning's work with the right tools."

"Not my work. Got my own job, ain't that right, Candy?"

Somehow, when Clint talked she could tune right in.

"Right. Right. It's got to be right when it leaves here," she replied in her biggest voice, trying to sound authoritative. And then she went for it and added, "And also. When it gets seated on the lot or whatever, I want it checked again, the corner especially. It could go off level in transport." She was making up conditions as she went along. "I'm not signing off until it's inspected again after it's in place. I'm buying damaged goods and I'm worried about that," she said, adding in a softer feminine tone, "being new to this and all. I'm a nurse, not a contractor, so I am trusting you to make it right for me." And she forced herself to look Randy in the eye.

She caught Clint stifling a smile. It felt like a star on her forehead.

"Sure thing. All part of the deal. All part of the deal," Randy replied.

Clint's stifled smile disappeared. He had put his sunglasses back on. Was this an act? Or was this who he was, and the nice chuckle guy back at the house was the act? She recalled with something like astonishment that she had only met the guy an hour ago. Cousins indeed.

"By the way, still haven't heard from your bank, Miss Schein."

"They are reprocessing the mortgage due to these new ... um, circumstances."

"And we still have a couple, three things to talk about, right, Cuz?" Clint interjected.

"Yeah. Randy, thanks for your time. I'll get back to you as soon as I hear from my credit union but there shouldn't be a problem."

"Unless there is," Clint piped in again. Well, not exactly piped, more like drummed. "Candy, I got to make tracks. Walk me to my truck."

And Randy followed them as far as he could, saying more words: "deal," "bargain," "time's short," "deal," "look forward."

Clint opened her truck door for her. Who was this guy?

"Try not to look so starry eyed, Cuz. It's not yours yet."

She blushed, climbed up into the driver's seat, closed her own door, and rolled down the window.

"If he's selling it at a singlewide price, sounds like you got yourself a deal," Clint said. "There's nothing beyond cosmetic wrong with it. At least nothing that I can see. Since these things aren't made of real materials, they bend like toys. Which means you can bend them back. And they have. Done pretty good too."

"It looked like that to me too, but what I know about this is close to zero." Candy shrugged and looked out her windshield onto the dingy yellow wall of the sales trailer.

"Thank you for doing all this," she said, waving a hand

toward the doublewide, "taking you away from your work and all."

"No problem. Spiced up my day, really. Otherwise it was just the Menards hardware aisle."

Was that a joke? She tried out a chuckle but directed it at her windshield.

"But really, keep up that anxious act. Works good. You might be able to get the slab poured gratis if you can just play anxious and unsure but with money in hand."

"Slab?"

"Yeah. We live on sand, Candace. You're gonna have to seat that baby on a slab and I'm guessing you don't have one yet."

"Geez. The videos I watched didn't mention a slab."

"Those things never show the drudge work beforehand."

"Ok. I guess I'll figure it out." And then Candy poked her chin in the direction of the sales trailer. "Have you done this before?"

"No, but I'm around all kinds of real estate and home buying shenanigans and I listen up."

"Ok. I'm all ears."

Clint looked off to check traffic and said, "Tell him you've secured the loan. Tell him you're still concerned. No offense, but play the innocent. Nervous first timer."

He paused, and although she wasn't looking at him, she could feel him looking at her. He went on, "Like, 'oh dear, what if it leaks, what if a storm blows it down, what if it gets damaged again?' Just throw everything at him. But keep up that other bossy, demanding thing you gave him a taste of too. 'I want this, I want that, let me see it in writing.' See if he tosses anything else into the deal and then grab it."

"I don't want to make him mad," Candy said, already imagining Randy barking and sneering at her.

"Biggest mistake in business. Worrying about who gets mad. Half the time it's an act. Slow down and think about it. Think about where old Mr. Randy's sitting right about now. It's the end of the season. He's got lean months coming up and probably some corporate guy breathing down his neck about sliding some last sales in. He needs you more than you need him."

Not sure about that, she thought.

Clint went on. "And it's damaged. And most people scare easy. Don't know how much or how little damage there actually is. And there's not a lot. That much I can see."

"Scare easy. That's me."

"Ah, no, doesn't look like it. At least from the outside." And he was still looking at her, and she was still looking at the pukey yellow wall of the trailer her truck was facing.

"Thanks," Candy said, again, looking down into her lap. She felt gratitude come over her in waves and the red running down from her cheeks into her neck. "I had no idea I was going to find this kind of help when I snuck onto that site this morning."

Clint didn't seem to hear. He was pulling out his phone. "Give me your number. If you do go through with it, and I think you should, by the way, I know people in the trades: plumbing, electrical, concrete, even. I can get trade prices. Especially for a family member."

And Candy made herself look up at him. He was turning his phone on. He was being helpful. To someone he didn't know, wasn't really, actually, related to. She didn't think people like this lived anymore in a world where families dumped their older folks in facilities and forgot about them, and struggling people were invisible and hourly wages got stuck somewhere between total poverty and the day-old racks at the grocery store. She was used to trusting only herself. Only. Or mostly. There was Granddah, still alive but locked up at Glencrest, and Graham, who sent the occasional text from up north. But here was this guy. Clint. Clint Houdek from God knows where. And this morning she had just learned that having someone else around in your corner might make you able to trust yourself more. It was like popcorn popping. She felt bigger, louder, in a good way for once.

That "Dream Home" notebook she carried around had every step mapped out, every purchase planned for. But there was a page with a list of to-do items with question marks after them. She had avoided turning to that page, but if this deal went through, that page and those items: permits, plumbing, moving, driveway, septic, electrical, moving guys, all that, would have to be handled before she had her Mystic. Doublewide. Home.

Not one single thing on that page, in that list, was anything she knew anything about, which was why she had tried not to look at it too often. But if the mortgage cleared and she signed the papers, the place would be hers, and she wanted that. Bad. And right here in front of her, or rather beside her, waiting outside the window, was someone who could help her take care of a few of those question marks so she could get going on checking the boxes. Clint had handed the phone to her through the window.

"Thanks," Candy said, and took the phone he had offered, construction-grade phone case, no cracks in the screen. She entered her phone number, pressed call, let it ring once, and then handed it back to him. She watched him as he added her to his contacts. She couldn't see what name he had used.

"Yeah, so text me if you decide to go through with it and I'll forward you some names."

"That would be great. My budget's a little tight right now, you know. I mean, I made one and all, but some of those bids are pretty scary. And I got most of the names from Randy."

"Well, there's your mistake. There's always more than one economy. He's in one. I'm in the other."

"Just don't try to sell me any meth," Candy laughed.

Clint didn't. Laugh, that is. Whoa. "It was just a joke," she wanted to say. The look on his face said it was a terrible one. A horrible one.

"Look, it was a joke. Sorry. I didn't mean it."

He wasn't smiling yet.

"Besides, what junkie in their right mind would buy from you?" A twinge.

"Too clean cut." She tried again, feeling the hole close in around her.

"Too clean something," he said, turning away. He waved goodbye as he headed off to his truck.

But the earlier cheer was gone. She had ruined it. She had been trying to say, what? That he was nice, that she had trusted him. But. What if he DID deal drugs? Or traffic in something else illegal? Clint? Her cousin Clint? No way.

She hollered one more thanks to his departing back, and he waved again without turning around. She let him pull out first.

The Beach

Candy was riled. She had been stupid. Mean. Where did that horrible joke come from? She'd just met him. She didn't know anything about him. You don't joke like that when you don't know someone, don't know what they've been through, what they're going through. What an idiot. She didn't know thing one about this Clint Houdek person except that he had been nice. To her. Totally unscary and kind of generous. Was that why she didn't trust him? Because nice people don't pop into your life and do nice things for no reason? This was too complicated. It was making her brain fry. Time for a walk.

Candy had the whole rest of the day off and while it was no longer a sparkling autumn afternoon, the clouds had moved in and the wind had kicked up; still, she couldn't go back to the Dump. There was no air in there and she needed air. She might have hurt somebody. This was new. Candy had always felt herself the target of the offhand snarky comment that was probably meant to be funny, she now realized, but landed on her thin skin after the speaker had walked past her, leaving her alone to lick her wounds, feeling good and sorry for herself. Feeling sorry for herself was one of Candy's go-tos, which often made her hungry, of course. But this made her hungry too, this new possibility of being the hurter.

She pulled the Tacoma into the lot at the beach and ate her muffin while checking out the waves through her windshield. Northeast. Cool. She changed out of her street shoes. The sand was probably still warm enough for bare toes but she put her slides on anyway. The clouds were moving northeast at a good pace but were high enough to not feel claustrophobic. Just before she got out of the cab, her phone dinged. It was Evelyn.

> you're RE-approved. 😄. just a few changes in the language. call me with a time to come by and re-sign! congrats.
> 👋

> thanks, Evelyn. i'll be in touch.

No emojis. She opened the glove box and put her phone in. No phones at the beach. It was a rule. Not because it dinged or rang. Because it didn't.

The waves were kicking the lake up, changing it from Bahama blue to a kind of murky sand. She didn't hate this churned-up color. There were all kinds of whites and beiges mashed up into a kind of mocha cream in motion. She headed south, wind at her back, and raised her hoodie to keep her curls from turning into a matted mess.

After the wind had cooled her down, she considered the crowd of thoughts circling her like gulls. Maybe he was a dealer. No. Clint? Cousin Clint? Not possible. Well, anything was possible but probably not that. Maybe his brother was a dealer.

His brother was a meth addict.

His brother was in prison.

His sister.

His girlfriend left him for a meth dealer.

His girlfriend was a meth addict.

His girlfriend counseled meth addicts; was the Florence Nightingale of meth addicts.

Whatever. She picked up a rock and tossed it underhand into the waves. He wasn't even a friend. He was exactly a one-day-long acquaintance. "Not important," she said into the wind, which was a lie and she knew it. This morning had been important. The doublewide and then this Clint person materializing out of nowhere. A stranger who had helped her and hadn't asked for anything in return, had even put on a pretty impressive act for Randy the salesman, and then she had gone and said something stupid and offended him. At least he had still said goodbye. Hadn't actually stomped away or anything like that. Well, he had turned away, that was for sure. And that smile he seemed to turn on her had vanished, just like that. Candy's stupid joke had wiped it right off his face. She was an idiot. She kicked sand.

This was why she didn't like a world populated with, well, populated. She preferred this: lake and trees and sand. Empty places that didn't cause thoughts to crowd up in her brain. Of course there were also movies and TV shows. But those people lived inside a screen and she could turn them off when they started to bother her. As in, make her feel something toward them. For them. About them was fine. But for them. That was when she reached for the power button. Off.

Reruns were a known quantity and as Candy walked down the beach following just above the edge where the wet began, she let herself slide into one of her favorites. The "building the driveway border out of beach stones" daydream. She had created this after-school special after driving by one of the summer places down on Crystal Lake. Not a new home but one of the older cottages, single story, green-painted wood with white shutters and lots of beach and water stuff piled up around the yard. The drive was long and went past the house to the lake edge, no doubt for boat trailers. But the driveway, Candy had noticed one day driving by, was bordered on both sides with round, good-sized beach rocks. Rocks, not stones, like the size of a turkey breast or a roll of toilet paper or something. Big ones that you could only lug home one or two at a time in a beach bag. Large enough to cause a wicked bump if a vehicle meandered over the border. From a distance, they looked like granite, most a kind of light smoky gray, but not uniform, except they were clearly lined up with care along each side of the sandy drive.

And so a home movie of sorts, which had become one of her favorites, unspooled inside Candy's head. It was a family: three generations. This was the grandparents' place and they had, over the years, gathered up the stones to make their own driveway border. No, not they, the grandma, and the grandkids when they could be cajoled with a reward. The family would go to the big lake and at the end of a summer's day, fill the empty coolers and beach bags with just the right sizes and colors of rocks and bring them back to the cottage. But first they had to pass the grandma test. She would decide if they were the right size, the right shape, the right color. Candy ordered up a close-up of this scene: some grandkid, wet and sandy and blond in a baggy bathing suit lugging a stone up to her grandma's beach chair, and the grandma taking it and turning it over in her arthritic hands and smiling and saying something like "yes, this is a good one." (Grandma, if that's what she was called; sometimes she was Oma, sometimes Gran, sometimes Nonny or Babcia.) Each time Candy wove the story the grandma changed. Sometimes she was cranky, sometimes a cookie baker, sometimes a widow. A widow was convenient. Fewer people to cast and be concerned about. That was the thing about living inside your own head. You could live inside a story and change it any time you wanted and let go when it was done. Or even when it was not done. It was entirely her own world and she got to live inside it, but not as one of the characters. It could, at times, feel like family, these people who lived in her dreams. And they were better than TV because she got to write and rewrite them and cast them and direct them and redirect them.

She had developed this magical movie-making part of her brain while still in school, friendships and gatherings and jokes and hilarity swirling around just beyond her. And when she discovered that she could populate her own world with people who never asked her in because they didn't know she existed in her director's chair up there in the dark, writing their lives, well then it was the best of all possible worlds. Safe, and hers alone. No wonder she didn't need anyone. She had enough people inside her own mind with enough warm and fuzzy storylines to keep her company. It was "Grandma's Driveway" today, and in it, today's grandma, who was a crank, turned the stone around and then tossed it away from the family circle and told her granddaughter to try again. Then she took a sip from a drink, a lemonade or a Sprite or something, and turned to laugh at one or another thing one or another one of her grown children said to her. It was a big family. They all got along. Not a meth addict in sight. Clean, cheery, surrounded by all the bright colors of the day and the towels and the chairs and the umbrella which Grandma sat under.

The story spun out to the return home and the tossing of the stones out of the truck bed to a corner of the drive, and then the story sped up like the end of a movie when you've got five minutes of film and the credits have to roll and there are candids of the future of the plot which somebody had decided would end up in the trash bin. These last bits in Candy's story involved family members piling into the house for showers and changes, and some man in the family lights the grill and there are brats and burgers and a cold salad or two that nice Grandma had made in advance, and then of course some fantastic sweet things for dessert. Obviously, Candy would linger over the dessert scene. She didn't like s'mores so it would be brownies or cookies, or better yet, cookies and ice cream. Moose Tracks. Yep. Some little one would lug out the ice cream container and some adult would holler for some other family member to bring out the scoop. And the next morning, the children and their families would pile into minivans and go back to wherever they came from, which was a story Candy never pursued.

She always chose to be left with the grandma and the stones. The quiet would descend on another early morning that had emptied out and instead of loneliness (there was not a lot of loneliness in any of Candy's productions) Grandma would wander down to the new pile of rocks and pick one up and wander up and down the drive, placing it, sometimes on a yet to be bordered spot and sometimes switching an old stone out for the new one and then admiring her work.

These driveway borders never got finished because the whole center of the movie was this task. This piece of landscaping that cost nothing but someone's thought and sharp eye, and a filled cooler at the end of the day for some minor character to lug back to the car.

As for Candy, she had recently taken to bringing a backpack with her on her walks, often picking up one or two rocks she found. If she got the doublewide, bought it and actually moved into it, there would not be a long driveway. She had already figured out that it had to be close to the road because she couldn't afford plowing, and it snowed heaps up here and she would have to make her own way out of a snowed-in drive to get to work. Maybe there would be a rounded drive; they called it a pull-through, like an egg on its side, so you could pull in and out again without having to turn around, but whatever it was going to be, she needed a path to turn in and park and then leave again and that path would need borders, and those borders would be beach rocks.

This afternoon was a good haul. Too good. Four stones made the backpack heavy. The lake and the wind had done their part, clearing out the debris of other people, real people, that is, from Candy's mind. She turned around and faced the wind, with the backpack weighing against her lower back as she made her way to the Tacoma and dumped the rocks into the truck bed in a big plastic bin. She fired up the truck and headed out to the credit union. Clint was history. Nobody. But he had contacts who could save her money. So not nobody. Damn.

The Pour

Candy had a notebook for the new house project. She had dog-eared pages that served as dividers which marked off sections. The scariest one looked like this so far and she was worried that she was missing something, something even scarier:

Contract/Mortgage/Paperwork

Lawyer?
Permits ?
Utilities?
Move ?
PO Box?
Insurance?

Candy had been told more than once that she was no brainiac and so she had a lot of expertise in knowing what she didn't know. She had Googled the hell out of every single step in the process. She had learned to skip the first three entries on a search and only go down the rabbit holes of URLs that had actual names that sounded like they might contain the bits and pieces of whatever she needed to know. And then she took notes. She was turning out to be a better student in this one notebook than she had ever been in school.

She had learned, for example, that permits were "pulled," not gotten or issued. And she learned who pulled what permit. And she also discovered, happily, that the seller of a manufactured home had all kinds of responsibilities to the buyer from the point of sale to the point of a habitable domicile. "Habitable" was another word she had learned from Google.

However, she also learned, unhappily, that she had to pour a concrete slab. Clint had been right. They couldn't seat a home on sand and that was what it was up here, sand, sometimes with a six-inch topping of soil, but really, sand. Sand shifted. So, slab. She added it to the scary list. After scoring a considerable number of freebies from Randy, he had held the line at pouring her slab. She was also responsible for septic and electric and water. She wasn't going to get a propane tank, so no gas here. She had banned those ugly, huge tubs of rusty steel long ago from all of her home dreams and she wasn't going to have them clutter up the real thing. No propane tank on her lot.

That page in her notebook, the one with the lists peppered with question marks, had to now be faced. You couldn't just Google forever. You had to pick up the phone and make some plans. With people. Contractors and installers who knew all kinds of things Candy didn't and who could do what she HAD to get done in order to have her house. And the first couple of calls, made to Randy's contacts, had taken her breath away. The costs. The initial visit and then the hourly and the materials and the permit fees and the inspection fees. She paced the small floors of the Dump night after night, fearing she wasn't going to make it.

But she had to make it. She couldn't move in, she couldn't own, possess, move into, this doublewide place without plumbing and electric and septic and a slab.

She needed Clint. Clint could save her hundreds, maybe thousands. Clint had connections. He also had hurt feelings. The meth epidemic up here was no joke, and it was the rare native whose life hadn't been scarred by a loss. That much Candy knew, but she had done such a bang-up job of hiding from the world that this hadn't registered. On her tenth circuit around the apartment, she paused and kicked a doorway. "Idiot," she said, the word floating out into the grease-scented air.

Her fear of making contact and having to apologize battled against her need for advice and connections. After a couple more turns around the Dump, the connections won.

She dialed and he answered.

"Yep?" was apparently how Clint answered the phone.

"Uh. Hi," she managed.

Clint didn't seem to recognize her voice. Why would he? They didn't know each other. Not really.

"It's Candy. The blue doublewide?"

"I know," he answered.

This wasn't going to be easy, and Candy usually did what was easiest. Blame the other guy. He was going to make her work for it. He probably knew what she was calling about and he had offered, after all, and so what was his problem? She cursed being human. And dumb.

"I'm calling because—"

"You want some names, I'm guessing."

"Uh, yeah."

"Where do you want to start?"

"I don't actually know. I mean, I know what I need but I'm not sure in what order."

"You need a contractor. They run the show and set the sequence and all."

"Well, I'm in the DIY world. My debt ceiling is gonna be blown and so ..." And here she was at a loss. She felt her stomach turn.

"You're asking me?"

"Not to be my contractor or anything. I mean, I would. Hire you and all, but I just can't."

"I know."

"You know a lot," she said, aggravation slipping into her voice.

"I know some."

She struggled to apologize. Do it now, she said to herself. Do it NOW. Simple. "I'm sorry."

But his voice came back on the line before she could manage it.

He put her on speaker and asked her if she had paper and pen; she fumbled open her notebook and he started naming names and giving numbers. She wrote and then read back names and numbers. He said, "Yep, that's it."

At the end of the call, Candy said thank you about a dozen times and Clint had said no problem, this is my wheelhouse, and the rest is up to you.

"Let me know if you hit a snag," he said.

"I will, and Clint?"

There was a beep.

"I gotta call. Happy hunting." And he was gone.

Along with all of the names and numbers Clint provided her with, he added a few lines about how he knew the guy and why he could be trusted. He also reminded Candy to refer to herself as Clint Houdek's cousin. Since Houdek was like Smith up here, that would not be hard to believe. The call to the electrician was her first, and proved to be kind of a model for all of the ones that followed. Candy would call a number, which was never an office with a secretary but the guy's cellphone, and he himself would answer or call back. She would introduce herself and relay her connection with her cousin.

"Houdek? Clint? He's your cousin? Well, I'll be damned. What can I do you for?"

And Candy would tell her story and the guy on the other end of the line, whose name was Elliot in the case of the electrician, would insist on some small talk. This was a steep learning curve for Candy.

"Well, how is the old goat?"

"His mom move yet?"

"Tell him he owes me a game down at Dooley's."

"Yeah, me and Clint go way back. All the way to the Neidersons' place up on Catherine Road. That was a hell of a job. Five baths. Clint, he had him some extra overtime on that one."

Candy would murmur in agreement when she could, lie when she had to (he had a mom? where was she moving? what kind of game? where is Dooley's?) and try to move the contractor toward a date.

"Well, things is slowing down but not enough yet. What did you say you needed? And when?"

And then there might be the: "I'm sorry, I know it's a small job but I don't think I can squeeze it in," followed by, "oh hell, Clint's good people / a nice guy / did me one last year. Call me tomorrow and I'll see what I can do."

And Candy would pace a bit in her apartment before each call and then slowly, guy by guy, line by line, the calendar filled. The calendar was one Candy had drawn herself on the very last page of her notebook: October/November/December: M/T/W/R/F. This page with days and dates was a sign to her that it was going to happen. Time was going to pass and days would contain steps to the finish line. There was a sequence. Slab had to be poured AFTER lines pulled for water and electric. She, or rather Granddah, HAD lines, which had gone back to the farmhouse now copping a lean just out of sight of the cleared lot. So the guys, the electricians led by Elliot, had brought some fancy tools with lights that they beamed down on the ground and then spray-painted all kinds of different colored symbols, or hammered in stakes, which obviously meant something to them, and then told her all kind of good news about placement and cutting in and no problem and on schedule. The water turned out to be easy too. There was so much good news that the sections of the notebook started getting checkmarks added to the question-marked items. Candy never crossed off an item. She had, instead, always drawn little square boxes in the margin next to each item. A tiny home for a check when it had been earned. And the checks, almost unbelievably to Candy, started populating those little squares, even on the scariest page. And in her quiet moments when she wasn't at work or checking her bank balance or running errands, she forced herself to acknowledge that this was possible because Clint had helped. He had brought her calendar to life and now it was in motion. Clint.

It was all becoming both too good to be true, and too frightening to wish for. Her mind carried on a split existence. Half of her dreamed endlessly of finally owning a home and her other half entertained all kinds of scenarios of the ways that it was all going to blow up. Construction plans never went this way, even though HGTV tried to convince their viewers otherwise. There would surely be monster surcharges and impossible add-ons and hidden boulders or buried toxic waste or SOMETHING that was going to destroy it all, and Candy would be left at the Palace with its pepperoni smell and Lean Cuisine dinners which she would continue to supplement with ice cream and cookie desserts for the rest of her dull, stupid, aimless life.

Both of these thought streams, the good and the bad, when they really caught hold of her, made her sweat so much she often had to change shirts before heading out to the site to meet a guy who was going to do a thing or show her a thing that she would have to sign off on and write a check for.

Clint never texted to ask how it was going, or did the guys work out, or what the move date was. Surprisingly, Candy was disappointed in this. So used to working inside her invisibility cloak when it came to the real world, she now seemed to have lost it somewhere in his vicinity. Not only had he helped her, she had felt he had really looked at her, seen her, and it was a feeling she found herself wanting to feel again. Not that there were movies about him swirling in her head. Her imagination didn't do romance as a genre, or even buddy movies, and besides she had made an ass of herself and that was that. No, it wasn't romance that came to mind when she thought about Clint. It was like having a business partner. Or, more honestly, it was just company along a road with all kinds of hidden potholes.

Candy pushed Clint once again to the side of her mind and forced herself to focus on the realities before her every day. This morning the slab was going to be poured. There were lots of stages to this pour she had learned on the internet, and the first stages had been completed: the long boards placed into the ground marking the perimeter, then the leveling of the dirt, then some sort of gravelly, sandy stuff poured down. More leveling. And now today was the pour. Seth, the concrete guy, had told her the mixer was due early; Candy was the first job of the day and so she was up early.

What did you wear to a slab pouring? She owned not one piece of Carhartt anything and it had been a while since she had tried on her one pair of jeans but this morning she attempted them. They were too tight. No surprise. They were like five years old. She was not going to show up at a pouring, or whatever it was called, wearing jeans that made her look like a blown-up latex glove. It was going to have to be pull-ons. At least they were corduroy. Lands' End. Starfish collection. Thank God for Starfish.

She pulled out of the Palace parking lot at eight thirty. It was a fifteen-minute drive down 673. Pretty straight shot. She stopped for coffee and a muffin. She lingered at the coffee station, poured slowly, stirred in her creamer, disposed of her garbage carefully. She even wiped the counter with a napkin. Then stared at the muffin case. The coffee cake ones were sold out, but it was now pumpkin spice season and she grabbed one of those, took it all to the register. It was Nate this morning, and she said hello and remarked on the colors and practiced her eye contact. They exchanged a joke about the leaf peepers and she told him to have a good one as she left.

October was flying by and leaves swirled on the road and fluttered out of the sky. You waited for months, it seemed, for the colors to reach their peak. But really there was no peak. No one day. Instead, there were early maples and then the aspens and birch, and then the ash and beech, the oak having browned early and fallen late. And then, all of a sudden there was a windy stretch of weather and then a blizzard of beautiful leaves would swirl down from branches and pile up in mounds made by the wind into hills of color which then browned and were soaked by the early winter mush that fell from the sky, and then autumn was gone.

Today was a falling day. Winter would close in on them soon and the peepers would retreat back south to their other lives. Candy would be tucked into the doublewide by December. Edwards couldn't move the Mystic until the week after Thanksgiving and so Candy would move the second week of December. It was on the calendar. In ink. Almost real. On the other side of real of course, there were "Christmas at the Mystic/ Doublewide" stories swirling around in her head almost every night. They were so fabulous and cozy and filled with delicious details, she found she had to drag herself out of them in the morning. Groggy from the joy of a fairy tale world of warmed apple cider and Christmas cookies and her grandfather in the new armchair she would buy just for him. Except she wanted it to be a recliner and those were pricey, and so she would have to move his old one from the farmhouse into her place and buy a new one in installments, maybe next year.

She pulled onto the lot. Her lot. It was empty save for the boards in the ground and the stakes, some with little flutters of fluorescent ribbon waving from their tops. She took it in. Today was the day the world, or rather her world, was going to change. This piece of her granddah's land was never going to be the same. She had lived for weeks in fear that the pulling of the permits would require her granddah's signature. And then she would have to explain. And he could get confused easily and that could lead to the grumpy questions borne out of his frustration, because he was no longer large and in charge as he had been all his life. He was an old, stooped man with a walker and an early bedtime and not much more to do than keep up with the box scores and beat Gus at gin rummy when he could.

But miraculously, and for reasons Candy could not figure out but was grateful for, there had been no phone calls about land titles or property rights or anything. She had Granddah's last name and the plot was simply labeled "Schein" on the county records. The permit pulling went on without Granddah knowing. They needed a signature and Candy had power of attorney and so that was that. It felt like betrayal as she added (POA) after the signature line that read "Albert Schein," but her life, this new life, had to move forward. The thing was in drive and there was nowhere left to pull over until the thing was done.

And why didn't she want him to know? Why hadn't she told her grandfather yet? Because for once she was going to make one of her fairy tales come true and the story went something like this: Snow would be falling and she would bundle her grandfather up in his winter clothes and put him in the truck, and he would badger her about why they were going out on such a cold and crappy night, and she would lead him toward his old home and she would pull into the clamshell driveway, and the doublewide would be lit from inside with those lites segmenting the window, making it look like a home for the holidays commercial. And the wreath on the door and the fire in the ...

Whoops. No fireplace.

But there was also her new reality, right here, rolling out in front of her and she couldn't risk having Granddah stomp on this, her dream that was on the brink of becoming true. She just couldn't tolerate the thought of him saying no, or what a stupid idea, or those homes are built like crap, or worst of all, you're doing it all wrong, Candace. Nice idea, but you don't know what you're doing.

And that had been true, of course. She hadn't known what she was doing. At first. But bit by bit and search by search and step by step and with the notebook as her bible and Clint as her unexpected and unasked for wingman, it had taken shape. It was going to be. A Dream. Come. True.

And until it did, Granddah was not going to have the opportunity to tear it down. She realized this was another reason she actually didn't shy away from Clint's texts. Not one of them said, "Do you know what you're doing?" Or worse: "Hate to say it but you can't do this." Or: "Not this way." Or: "Not on this budget." No, Clint had just dutifully, from far away up on the peninsula or wherever he was at those moments, forwarded contact info, reminded her of their cousin status, and then went back to radio silence.

So Candy was not a little surprised when she heard a vehicle on the highway behind her that wasn't loud enough to be the massive red and white striped mixer she was expecting and turned around to see a white pickup slow and then pass and then do a U-turn and pull in behind hers. And Clint climbed out of the truck.

"Hey, Cuz," she heard herself saying through a smile. She was happy to see him. Happy and nervous as hell, her belly suddenly full of acid.

"Hey yourself," he said, slamming his truck door and zipping up his jacket. "Sorry to show up like this without texting first, but my curiosity got the better of me and I took a detour off my route. Seth said they were headed out and did I want to take a peek. And I did. Do you mind?" he asked, dipping his head in a strange way, kind of like a horse when they are adjusting their bridle or whatever.

"'Course not." How did this go? What to say next? She was dying to apologize again, but thought, no, don't rip off the Band-Aid, you fool. Instead she attempted easy chat. "Thanks for all the referrals. Saving me buckets."

"No problem. These guys get paid the same. It's just the skim off the top taken by the middle guy. Or Randy. Or Mr. Edwards or whoever."

They walked together over to the marked-off slab site. There were pipes and tubes sticking up out of the ground. The septic had been dug the week before, an act Candy had skipped, but she took note of the green "approved" sticker inside a Ziploc attached to a pole. She had been told to put it inside her bathroom cabinet for the final inspection.

The mixer's arrival saved her from making more talk. Four

guys tumbled out of the truck's cab and got busy doing the things concrete guys do, Candy guessed, slipping on gloves, swinging the chute out, pulling levers, yanking shovels from slots in the side of the truck. One man waved over in the direction where she and Clint had retreated, close to the pines and out of the way.

The pour was over in minutes, it seemed. The rakers leveled and the measurers pulled out more laser-like thingies that took pictures and shouted things like "she's good" and "ready to set" to each other after learning whatever they needed to know from a tiny screen smaller than a phone which was attached to the laser doodad.

"How's it, Houdek?" said a guy who seemed to be doing little if anything. Candy figured he must be Seth. The boss.

"Good enough, Seth. Thanks for fitting this in for my cousin here. This is Candace. Candace, Seth."

Candy waved a mute hello.

"Yeah, we crazy busy but like I told you over the phone, Houdek family's all right. Still pulls some weight around here. Small job. We'll be up and out in about five." Then he started talking about set times and where was the gas line and once again, this Seth guy was directing all of his questions to Clint.

And Clint turned to Candy. And Candy said, "Hmm?"

"The gas line. Do you have gas coming into the place?"

"No. It's all electric."

"Going clean energy, huh? A green prefab. Will wonders never cease. Solar panels go in next week?"

Candy had to check Seth's face for ridicule. He was making fun of her? No? Yes? Wow. She had failed the construction site banter class or any kind of banter class, for that matter, long ago. The mute buttons were going off like crazy inside her head, but she forced herself to unmute.

"Village gas lines don't come out here, and honestly, I kinda hate the look of propane tanks," was all she could muster before she realized that probably both of these guys had propane tanks in their yards.

Clint added, "Well, it is cleaner too. You see those windmills out on 72 by Traverse? And all those solar panels out there too? They're not converting into propane, that's for sure."

"I don't see my bills going down," Seth muttered, kicking gravel.

"The planet. Gotta think of the planet." There was sarcasm in Clint's voice.

"Yeah, and Ima bet you love those Green New Deal chicks in Washington too, huh."

"Wait 'n see," said Clint, smiling. He had not failed any banter class, that was for sure.

Seth tipped an imaginary hat in Candy's direction. "Nice to meet you, Candace. Be sure not to recommend us to any of your friends. We're full up till snow season. Clint, I'll catch you around. Topper's this weekend?"

"Nah, gotta stick around home. The place is a mess and I can't keep up. She's slowing down and the house is falling down around her."

"I hear you. But you can't be working the place on a Friday night. Swing by if you can. There's a Halloween MGD special and I want to take your money."

And then Seth scrambled back up into the truck cab where the other guys were already waiting and turned some lever which sped up the mixer behind them and they were off in a cloud of dust and noise.

Candy turned back to the slab.

"This'll have plenty of time to set up and cure. Seth told me the move isn't for a month or so."

"Long time to wait, but it is what it is," said Candy, and then faltered.

"So your mom? Slowing down a bit?"

"Yeah, you know how it is. All my brothers and sisters have moved downstate and so I'm left holding the bag. It's a pain but she's been good to me. She's alone up there with just me to help her, and I'm always at work, sometimes commuting over an hour to worksites and back. That leaves her alone an awful lot in a house which leaks and leans." He was shaking his head, and looked down at his boots, which were kicking gravel.

"I'm working on her to move, but she's not liking that. Not one bit."

"How's her cognitive functioning?"

"Come again?"

"Sorry. Her brain. Her mind. Can she still take care of herself?"

"Oh, the problem's not her mind. It's her hands. And her back. She can barely get out of bed in the morning so I got to get her up super early every day so I can help her get started before I go to work. And then her hands. She can't manage bottle tops or her phone even though I bought her one of those senior citizen ones with the big buttons. She fumbles a lot."

Candy watched silently as he scraped his fingers through the mess and suddenly saw a man, a son, standing in front of her who was stumped by the caring that was now required of him. Up until that last chunk of words, he had been some kind of superman, giving her just what she needed to make her house a real thing. And now, in just one minute, he had limped, wounded, it looked like, into Candy's orbit. Her wheelhouse, as he would say.

"I'm so sorry," she said, and meant those words in all kinds of ways and thought about the next sentence and immediately felt the sweat beading at her hairline. Helping would mean talking a lot, sharing who she was and what she did and what she knew. A drop of sweat threatened to drip down her forehead and she swiped it away, then pulled out her phone to check the time and made her excuses.

She had to get to work, thanked him again. Wished him good luck with his mom and turned to go.

When she was almost at the truck, she heard his voice again.

"My niece."

"Excuse me?"

"My niece. Nineteen. Gone. OD. Speedball."

"Oh. Clint."

"So."

"I am so sorry. I'm such a ..."

"Never mind. I just wanted you to know."

And he pointed at the slab, and said, "Ready for landing."

And Candy couldn't find a single thing to say.

Caregiving

At work that night, Candy took notice of the residents' hands and saw, as if for the first time although she knew it wasn't, how many of them were swollen at the joints, especially the thumbs. She and her coworkers often handled the residents' small motor tasks without thinking, but tonight she thought about it. About how much they could no longer do and how that had landed them here at Glencrest, worlds away from the homes they had built and loved with those same hands. And Clint's mom. Could she unroll toilet paper? Could she push the buttons on her microwave? Could she open Ziplocs? Not likely.

As Candy worked her way through the nightly duties: showers and baths and dinners and cleanup and bedtime rituals, she was momentarily distracted by the soap opera drama that was sometimes nighttime at a retirement home. Marvin refused his pajamas, again, and trotted up and down the hallway trying to find female residents to terrorize in his birthday suit, which would have been funny if he also didn't sometimes backhand caregivers out of the way on his quest. Marvin needed a chill pill in the worst way, but his family refused, claiming it hurt his memory. They of course did not witness Marvin's rampages, which called for restraint, which meant making more work for the male caregivers and sometimes the kitchen staff. After they got him calm and in bed and temporarily locked his door, Candy finished with her quieter, albeit shook-up people. Wanda wanted to call 911. Millicent wanted a lawyer. Bedtime took forever.

But when it was finally over, Candy still couldn't shake herself loose from worrying about Clint, or Clint's mom. It sounded like it was time for her to go, to be moved somewhere that was not another falling-down house that she could no longer keep up. Candy felt almost physically ill as she flashed back on her own weeks of returning to the same conversation over and over again with Granddah, slowly wearing him down, convincing him it was time to move. She had to keep tossing rusty daggers at him, or at least that's what it had felt like. He could no longer drive or climb stairs. She had had to rush home from work on more than one occasion to bail him out of a spot he'd gotten stuck in. She had shifted his sleeping to the recliner in the living room because she couldn't move his bed downstairs and she hadn't had anyone to ask. He hadn't seemed to mind, what with the pillows and comforter she arranged around him every night, but then she started having to wake up when he called for her for his many night trips to the can after he had fallen a couple of times and it had taken them forever to set him right again.

She had finally worn him down by using the dirtiest trick.

"I, I mean we just can't do it on our own anymore, Granddah. I've got to work and you are not safe here. If you fall, it could be curtains and then instead of a home you are sent to it might be a bed in a hospital for God knows how long."

Pause. Sigh.

"Or, we could hire someone to come in and help you ..."

And as she could have predicted, Candy hadn't had to finish the sentence before he had erupted with something along the lines of, over my dead body and no one's coming in here and I can manage, I can, I can, knowing full well that he couldn't. Not anymore. And then a Medicaid-funded bed had opened up at Glencrest and while the move wasn't smooth, they had done it together, and now he had Gus and also Charlie Cook, when they could stand each other. Charlie had been the supervisor at Granddah's last job, and Granddah had been the union steward and out in the real world they had clashed too many times to count. They were now on equal ground at Glencrest with nothing anymore to grouse at each other about except who needed to be traded from the Tigers or whether to back the Wolverines or the Spartans. And Candy was sad, but relieved. She had been sprung from that cage to live her own life.

And now Clint, nice, round, quiet Clint, was in the same awful, impossible spot. And alone in it, it seemed, just like she had been. He would have to cajole and plead and convince and rinse and repeat and not lose his temper when his mom did and not succumb to her requests for a little more time, and maybe the new meds would help, and a million other weak pleas.

Candy had heard this script unroll many times at Glencrest as well. She had listened to it from outside a room while standing in a hallway, or at an opposite corner of the TV or dining spaces. The residents would complain and plead to go home, either because they had taken that last step into complete disorientation brought on by the move, or because they were mad as hell and wanted the whole thing undone. And the sons or daughters would shrink into a chair or a corner and murmur the same lame responses and finally everyone would leave, miserable. She knew she could help Clint through it, coach him a bit.

Or maybe she would just bring him a brochure?

No. Bad idea. Brochures galore would be tossed at him, all promising golden moments and loving care, and not a single one with a rate schedule printed on them. No, she could, she should, help him. Explain the process. Tell him things to say to move the ball down the field and help his mom to see that her son loved her and that was what this was about. She assumed Clint loved his mother. He seemed like the kind of guy who would love his mom and not even be ashamed to admit it. Candy was making all of this part up but still, she should reach out to him, ask if he needed anything. She had a break in a couple of hours. She resolved to do it.

As the rest of the residents settled in for the night, she went to go find Granddah. He was nodding off in a chair in the TV room with the *Traverse Times* sliding off his lap.

"Hey there, old man. Isn't it time you headed off for bed?"

Granddah got special treatment, on the sly of course, from the staff who knew he belonged to Candy. So they didn't corral him back to his room before he asked and they let him be when he wanted to be let be. He didn't look up, hadn't even recognized her voice, it seemed.

"No. Haven't finished reading the ... the ...," and she watched him scan the paper in his lap to get his bearings again, "this story about the new county road commission. I swear those guys don't have a clue. Cutting budgets when the snow drops have been bigger and longer every winter."

And then he looked up and seemed to recognize his granddaughter. "How's it going there, Miss Candace? Any news from the outside world?"

"Nothing much. Good leafing this year, as you can see yourself. Warm weather's holding. Went to Meyer Beach the other day and had a good long walk. Had the place all to myself."

"No friends to walk with?" Granddah wouldn't have asked this a year ago, even a few months ago.

"Happy to keep my own company, you know, Granddah." He was losing track of her, and who they had learned to be with each other.

"Huh," he replied, and then "huh" again. And then again.

"Say, how's the house doing? Are you staying warm? Did you ever get that back screen door fixed?"

She had not, of course. She looked at him and saw his milky eyes and his loosened lower jaw, noticed how the cuffs of his shirt were frayed and his belt hitched in another notch.

"No, Granddah, you know I moved out of there when you left. I got a place in town, real close to here. I told you. Remember?" And then caught herself. You never asked residents who were slipping into dementia if they remembered. Especially those prone to outbursts. But he didn't flip, although his eyes did slide away from hers and went back to the paper, snapping it back into its folds and tossing it onto the table next to his now cold cup of tea.

Marcos came in and saved her from more blunders with the only family member she had ever truly loved. The gentle giant of a man jollied Granddah off to his bedtime ritual, but as he was shuffling away on his walker and Candy was tidying up after him, he stopped and turned. Marcos had his fingers tucked into the back of her granddah's belt to steady him.

"Say, maybe we should think about getting that back door repaired, huh? Whyn't you look into that? Call up whatshisname, the handyman."

"Sure, Granddah. I'll do it soon." And then she said her goodnights, feeling like a heel. A lying, cheating granddaughter.

She wasn't off duty until midnight but during her break, she settled onto a stool in the kitchen area and took out her phone. She found Clint's name in her contacts. Somehow she now had a grand total of twelve contacts: Graham, Janelle, Marcos, Work, the Credit Union, the Pizza Palace, the Town Bar and Grill takeout, AAA, the electrician Elliot, the plumber Neville, the septic dude whose name she had forgotten and so typed in "septic" instead of a name, and now Clint. Her favorites list was empty. Her finger hovered over the message icon, then she checked the time again. Nine more minutes on her break. She checked the forecast on her weather app. Rain due by Sunday. Temps dropping. Eight minutes. She played a game of sudoku. Five minutes. She clicked back to her contacts list. Selected Clint. Every minute she did not reach out to him about his mom after all he had done for her made her more of a shit. A little selfish shit. A big selfish shit.

Two minutes. She put her empty Dr Pepper bottle in the recycling. She popped the rest of her Reese's into her mouth. The peanut butter and chocolate dissolved together lusciously on her tongue.

She couldn't do it. All the years of snubs, and snorts and jostling in halls and corridors and aisles of stores as the rest of the human race blew by her, all those little slices of hurt now piled up against each other like a traffic accident in her brain. Back when she was a kid, she had made herself rise above it all, imagined herself in one of those hang gliders people jumped off the dune with, viewing the mess of her life below from way above, numbed into a neutral zone, a place where reaching out, making contact, talking human to human was no longer possible.

But had it been that bad? Or was she just a crybaby? Maybe it hadn't been that many snubs and snorts. Maybe it had been only a couple and she had blown them up in her head, just like she did her dreams, until they were so huge she couldn't see past them. This was not the first time Candy had doubted herself, doubted her own version of history. But wasn't history just a story of how people felt about the way things happened? Who knew what was fact and what was not once your crazy brain got hold of it.

Anyway. This text she would have to write to Clint about family and feelings and pain were way different than a plumber referral. This text would lead to another, and they would have to exchange experiences and then maybe the texts would have to become phone calls because it was all too hard to type out in tiny boxes on a little screen. Then maybe he would come here, and she would help him and his mom as best she could and then, sooner or later.

The old script started up again. She would do or say something stupid, again, or maybe even not, but people would see it that way. She would be rolling along, right next to Clint, occupying a shared space in his world and talking about important feeling-type things and then another person would enter and command his attention and whoosh, just like that, she would disappear. She would be invisible again and she would beat her familiar retreat back into the world of "poor me." Or she would step in it again, say something meant to be funny but that came out mean without her realizing it because she was slow at this type of thing. She kicked herself for the millionth time for the meth joke gone south. She could not navigate this world. So, nope. Better to just let it be.

Clint was a smart guy. He'd figure it out. She slid her phone back into her pocket and left to finish her shift in the quiet halls of the home for mostly lonely and sometimes forgotten people who had once been family members: fathers and sons and sisters and aunties who were now watching their own slow-ticking time clocks, no doubt waiting to finish up their shifts on this earth and clock the hell out.

Josie and Janelle

Halloween came and went. The kids had good weather and the pumpkins, or jack o' lanterns was what they were called when they were carved and lit up, glowed in the night. Candy saw them perched on front porches and edges of drives as she drove to and from work. More and more of them came from Michael's, the plastic ones with battery lighting inside. Less pumpkin smashing later on, that was for sure, but Candy did remember as a kid carving pumpkins with Graham and Granddah, making a big mess on the dining room table which was covered in old newspapers. Graham had a thing for pumpkin seeds and would roast a cookie sheet or two of them and then, half the time, wander away from the kitchen and let them burn.

Candy tracked the dark as it fell earlier and earlier each evening. Every day, two or three more minutes of light slipped away, the earth folding itself into the dark corner of winter. At least one leg of Candy's commute was in the dark now regardless of shift, but she didn't really mind. So much of this kind of darkness wasn't ominous or scary or middle-of-the-night pitch black. It was more like a hover cloud of darkened gray. Not exactly charcoal or smoke; there were definitely not enough good words for gray. Plus, the growing darkness meant moving day was nearer and the biggest deal in all of Candy's life was approaching. She was coveting it like a treasure found and stowed away in a pocket, mentally turning it over in her fingers, a beautiful lucky stone from the beach, waiting for the day when she could bring it up into the light, confident that the ring around it had done its work. Sure, there wouldn't be crowds to ooh and aah, but there were her and Granddah if it struck him in the right mood, and she would write Graham a text and include a picture. When it was done. Right now there were days to grind through and wait. Candy had become a champion waiter.

She filled up her free time taking all her crappy stuff to the Goodwill and cruising the aisles of Bed Bath & Beyond. New bath rugs, new dish drainer, new this, new that. But she had to be careful. She saved up her coupons and bought the big stuff with those. The Dump was littered with blue and white bags with new treasures as yet unpacked.

One day, leaving the Goodwill drop-off, she had noticed a flier: "Warm Meals Needed." And then a description of how food supplies were low and what the shelters really needed were pans of warm food. "Are you a good cook looking to share some holiday joy?" the flier asked. Candy took a picture of the phone number and the website. This would be good. Cooking was always good. She could buy some of those aluminum pans and make up a mess of mostaccioli, and maybe a pan of brownies. Nothing fancy. She had never been a volunteer before. With her salary she felt like her job was volunteering enough. But cooking. Now that was something Candy could get behind. She promised herself she wouldn't spend too much, and when she got to the checkout line with her pans and her ingredients, the cashier—it was Josie today—asked, "Heading out for the holidays?"

"No, I ... I just saw a flier for St. Timothy's food drive and it said they could use warm dishes. It's not much, but I do love to cook and thought I might lend a hand," Candy replied, feeling warm and chatty and trying out some eye contact.

"That's nice of you," the cashier named Josie said, keeping her eyes on the groceries and her head down. But Candy could sense a sneer on her face. The cashier was itching to say something, Candy could tell. She was bagging her own groceries when Josie said, "Hard to tell the really hard up from the lazy ones these days, huh?"

The meanness in that voice felt like a slap across Candy's face. Who would think that people showing up to a crummy meal in a church basement with a bunch of burnt-out, ragged poor people and plastic chairs would see it as a chance to take advantage. She had no reply for mean. Josie was still talking.

"I mean, I'm sure there are the needy and all, but the druggies and the meth heads and the bums, they spend all their checks on dope and then show up wanting to be fed, wanting to get their medical care for free when the rest of us are out here earning a living."

What could you say to a world drawn like that? Who was this woman and what had made her so mad? And then, she thought, really, how different was she from Josie? She didn't trust people either; she didn't believe, really, all that much in kindness. What was she thinking, spending her money for other people's dinners? The sparkle in the pans and the goods she was packing vanished.

Josie was watching the grocery tape print out and then folded it and handed it to Candy, who noticed that Josie had a bright red T-shirt on under her Shop 'n Save apron, and Candy could make out the big white M and the A on either side of the bib. Candy didn't pay attention to politics, or tried not to, and had never voted, but the hate that spewed out of people these days she wanted to blame on somebody. The president was as good as anyone.

Candy thanked Josie anyway and told her to have a good night. She shouldered her bags and left the store, feeling stupid and angry. Josie had rained on her parade of generosity the very first time she had ventured into it.

Back at the Dump, she dumped the groceries on the counter, and looked around. There were full bags and empty boxes all over the place. She wasn't going to clean again until she had moved out. Vern was letting her use her security deposit as last month's rent and had chuckled, "I don't even have to look. I'm betting you are gonna leave the place better than when you found it."

"Well, I don't know about that but I'm going to try," she replied.

"Say, where you moving?" Vern asked one morning as he watched her load up the Tacoma with junk for the Goodwill, without offering to help. It had taken her landlord several months to figure out that moving out of the Pizza Palace probably meant moving in somewhere else. Candy had lied to him; Vern was a gossip and was not getting a piece of her life to spread all over town when he cozied up to people at the bar who were willing to stand him to a PBR on the house.

"Um, over by Cort and 656," she responded, and then wondered, why was she lying? What did it matter if Vern knew she was going back to her family's land, that she had done this buying a doublewide thing all by herself and was going to move a house and then herself onto her granddah's lot and make a life there for herself? And why did it matter if the whole township knew? If the whole county found out? They would anyway, especially as it was happening in the offseason, where every sneeze was heard, and every screwup published in the weekly police blotter in the news.

"Hmm. Don't recall any apartments over there. Housing's tight, you know, and I usually know where things open up," Vern said.

He certainly did. This was a tourist economy and rents were so high that anyone with a place to lease kept a sharp eye on rents and openings, which were high and not many, in that order. Vern had let Candy know on more than one occasion about how much more he could be getting for the Dump (he didn't call it that) if he could just get an air conditioner up there and rent it by the week.

"Course it would be a pain and I'd have to get a cleaner and all, but the money, Jesus, you can get seven, eight hundred a week."

Here Candy was supposed to thank Vern for his generosity in renting the piece of shit to her for half that. And she had thanked him over and over again, every time he brought it up, which was practically every time he saw her. It was another reason she was in a hurry. She couldn't stand the place anymore and she wanted out. Instead, she mumbled that now that the place was going to be empty, he could spend the winter fixing it up real nice for the big money next summer, and pulled out of the Palace parking lot as fast as she could and still look like she had some manners.

Even though Candy tried to fill those November days of waiting with Goodwill drop-offs and kitchen and bath store cruises and extra shifts at work, there wasn't a whole lot to do except wait for the days to pass. Except now she had the cooking and drop-off at St. Timothy's, which took up a whole day off. The cooking distracted her. And she had to admit, despite Josie's criticism, she loved it, loved the feeling that she was cooking and feeding other people, felt some sort of balloon around her, expanding. She even sprinkled powdered sugar on top of the brownies, and extra parm on the mostaccioli. She relished every minute of the cooking and the sealing up and the labeling of what the ingredients were, and while she was being thanked again and again by the volunteer who accepted her donations, she silently sneered back at Josie inside her head. She was doing her part to make America great again. So what if she were feeding drug addicts? Poor things.

The next Tuesday, when the weather was fine and Janelle and she were working the same shift, Candy brought the four-pack of rosé wine in cans she had at home and asked Janelle out for a beach happy hour, spur of the moment. Janelle called her mom and wrangled an extra hour of child care and they squealed happiness as they headed out to Candy's truck after their shifts ended.

For their happy hours, they always used Candy's truck,

which did not smell as bad as Janelle's. Candy's smelled like muffin wrappers, Janelle's like dairy products long ago spilled under seats. Kids. They parked in the lot at the beach and watched the stars appear in the deep navy sky over the lake. It was chilly and too windy to sit on the wall, so Candy left the truck idling and they popped open their cans of wine and chatted easily about work being over and the holidays coming and the kids and the ex-husband. Janelle was so easy to talk to, and had a bulging life that spilled out all kinds of stories Candy gobbled up and laughed into.

"What about you?" Janelle asked. "Now that your granddad's at Glencrest, what are your turkey plans?" Candy froze for a second. Janelle was always careful with questions but maybe she had noticed an opening in Candy's laugh or even her face. Janelle always turned to Candy when she spoke to her and looked her right in the face. Candy rarely looked back but felt the eyes on her right cheek.

"I think I'll just chill with him at the home. No big deal. No cooking, no cleanup. Free meal."

"Girl, that is beyond depressing. You are coming to my house. I got my mom and aunties and the kids coming."

"Not a big crowd," she added. "I know how you get." Janelle's face was lit up by the dashboard. "Shy," she added. She was still facing Candy, who realized she was holding her breath. This might have been the first personal comment about Candy that Janelle had ever made. The grumbling started in her head: she just feels sorry for me, she's only asking to be polite.

Jesus, she was nuts.

Because really, the question felt real. And ok. Fine. Really. And Candy suddenly knew why she had come to love being with Janelle. She trusted her. The feeling was a warm one, an orange glow.

"Thanks," she said, half turning to Janelle. "Seriously. I appreciate it." And she did. "But I have a lot to do. I am moving the week after and I'm short on cash for the move and all, and so I grabbed up a heap of holiday shifts. Wednesday second, Thursday third, and then Black Friday too. Good bonus bucks."

"You know, if you tell me when you're moving, I can help," Janelle started, and Candy knew what was coming. Even Janelle couldn't resist just one or two more questions. And in that moment, when Janelle's kindness had filled the cab of the truck like some kind of bakery smell, Candy made a decision. She unclasped the armor from around her heart and decided Janelle was going to be the one who she would tell, who she would share the doublewide with. Well, besides Clint, and he didn't really count, did he? He appeared and then disappeared like a ghost in her phone, and besides, he was a guy and Candy had hated guys all her life for sneering and snickering. Calling her names when they thought she couldn't hear. Or making her disappear. Walking right through her in a hallway or a shop aisle or a bank line. No. Thanks for the contacts, Clint old boy, but you're off the list. It was Janelle.

Haltingly at first and then in a burst of detail and dates and pent-up anxiety, Candy spilled the details of the doublewide all at once. The cab of the truck filled up with her own voice, saying more words in a row outside of her head and to another person than she could ever remember. She had the strange sensation of hearing herself talk and for the first time she seemed to truly hear the sound of her own voice. It didn't come out squeaky or girlie. Her sentences didn't end by going up at the end, like girls in movies. It was her voice. It sounded just like her. Candy. Candace. Candy Schein. Person. This seemed to be just about as amazing to Candy as the story of the doublewide was to Janelle.

"Wait, slow down, slow down. JUST A MINUTE," Janelle was saying. "You did what? And when? And how?"

And so they popped open a second rosé, and Candy hit rewind, back to four years ago, and explained about it being a dream at first and needing a new place to live and the old farmhouse a shambles and then Granddah's mind and legs doing nosedives, and how the rents were ridiculous and getting worse since *Good Morning America* had decided this area was the most beautiful place in the country. (Whoever decided that had clearly not seen Glencrest or the Palace, but the park and dunes and the lake were nice, Candy had to agree, and she felt lucky to live there most of the time.) So, as she now told Janelle, she had decided four years ago, when she was beyond broke, still paying college loans and living with her failing grandfather, that she would try to save up and buy a place because the old place that was supposed to be her inheritance was leaking and falling down and never felt like hers in the first place. She had opened up a savings account and bought a notebook and started to save. And to plan. And here she was.

Janelle still had some questions, which she posed gently.

"By yourself? Don't you have a brother? What about your granddad?"

No, Granddah had not helped. No, her brother didn't know. No, it wasn't there yet but would be, all the permits were pulled and the slab laid and the move scheduled and the, and the, and the, and then finally Candy ran out of words. She had made it back to the present and she was exhausted.

And Janelle said, "Well I'll be damned," and then said, "Really?" a couple times. Then they fell out laughing and Janelle kept up a constant stream of praise, and the cab was now filled with "damn, you are one determined woman," and "I cannot BELIEVE you saved for FOUR years," and "I wouldn't know the first thing about permits and slabs and houses," and "you did this—you," and "amazing."

Janelle circled back again, just to be sure it seemed, that the curly headed, pink skinned, round woman in green scrubs and white Crocs was the same person who had pulled off this feat.

"You saved for four years."

"Yep. Almost five, actually."

"And got the down payment."

"Uh huh."

"And the mortgage."

"Looks like it."

"And did all that utility stuff and called the builder guys and signed contracts with them and got them to do it and then paid them."

"Yep, that's how it works, as it turns out."

"When it turns out."

"I guess so. Maybe I got lucky in a few places?" Candy acknowledged and then tipped the rest of the rosé into her mouth and let the sour sweetness of the cheap wine slip down her throat.

"Well, I'll be good and goddamned."

There in the green-white light of the darkened truck cab, Candy also decided that Janelle, if she could and if she wanted, would be her first guest, even before Granddah. Because the truth was she had been nicer to Candy than Granddah ever had. He had been a good guardian, no doubt about it. He had taken care of her and fed her and kept a roof, even a leaky one, over her head. But it felt like Janelle actually liked her. Their friendship, and now Candy believed that they had one, had seemed to grow slowly over this past autumn, almost without her noticing, and it felt full of what felt like forgiveness. There was no other word for it, at least none that Candy could think of. Janelle seemed to immediately understand how big this was for Candy and how hard it had been. By her exclamations while Candy told her the details she could sense that Janelle understood how Candy had had to break everything into pieces she could lift, and then she lifted them, and then she had to go back and find the next piece to lift. Or to manage. Or to Google and figure out. And always to pay for.

And Janelle had never, ever, in the whole time Candy had known her, asked the wrong question. Do you have a date? Why don't you join a gym? Don't you want a boyfriend? Why do you always eat pasta for lunch? Where's your brother? What did you do last weekend?

Nope, Janelle had always taken Candy as she found her. Seemed to sense that Candy was not shy, but private. That was the word. Private. And Candy liked it that way. And Janelle wouldn't even ever ask why she liked it that way. At least that's what she hoped.

Now, she pulled out her phone and said, "My mother will hit the roof if I am late getting home. She has her shows tonight and she already stayed an extra hour so I could chill with you."

"No problem," Candy replied, and clanked the transmission into reverse, and had Janelle back at her car in ten minutes. As she was getting out, Candy had to tell her, "You're the only person I've told. The only person who knows. Besides this guy I met."

"This GUY you met?" Janelle leaned back into the cab.

"Another long story and not the one that plays on the radio," Candy laughed, "but seriously, you are the first and only person I told about this. And I'm glad. Really. That I told you."

"This GUY you met?"

"Another night, another can of rosé," Candy said. "But you are also gonna be my first house guest. You may have to sit on the floor of an empty trailer, but it will be mine and we are going to toast my homeownership together."

"You real people, Candace Schein."

And Candy felt in every pore of her now cooled skin what Janelle meant.

The New World

This shiny new piece of pretty in Candy's life, the fact that she had a real friend, someone who liked her, someone who acted like she had done a big, big thing and should be proud, had the effect of puffing up and pinkening Candy so that she did a swirl in the middle of her living room when she got home. Or tried to. It was pretty much a total disaster in there.

And it was why she decided that she was NOT going to move her grandmother's dishes into the new place. Even if she had to eat off paper for the next six months, she was going to get new dishes.

And she was going to get a full-sized couch, not a love seat or a small one. A good, deep long one with extra pillows. The one that was five hundred dollars too expensive and that she was coveting because as she was finishing her swirl and moving onto dinner, she realized that if you bought the thing you hated, you had to live with it. And if you bought the thing you loved, even if you couldn't afford it, you could keep loving it all the while that you were paying it off.

And this came as such an epiphany to Candy, such a world-changing, mind-blowing new fact, that she plopped down on her old, smelly, hard, sunken couch and without letting herself think it through or delete it, she sent a text.

hey, how's your mom doing?

And as she pushed send and her phone gave the little swoop sound as it sent her words off to wherever to land in his phone wherever, she realized she had just taken a second dive. Into the world. Of people.

Maybe he wouldn't reply. Maybe he wouldn't even remember who she was. Wait, that was an old Candy thought. Of course he would remember. They knew each other now. Her name was in his phone. They had walked the lot side by side and stood together at her slab pouring.

She put the phone down on the couch and headed to the fridge to uncover leftovers. No leftovers. Cheese. Crackers. An apple for show. She had just finished cutting the apple when her phone dinged. She felt the air leave her lungs and her head.

No big deal, she counseled herself. She was just going to offer advice to Clint. She was a nurse in a retirement home, for God's sake. It was going to be hard enough to explain why she hadn't offered to help before.

ok, thanks.
    glad to hear it. i'm an lpn up at glencrest. heard of it?
huh. yeah. visited there last sunday
    really? when?
morning.
    i had third shift sunday. who did you talk to?
margaret somebody
    hmm
hmm is right. did not like her.

And then immediately a second ding: **ONE BIT**

Oooh. Clint in capitals. Only Margaret could ruffle feathers like that. And from what little she knew of Clint, he didn't seem like the feathers ruffled kind of guy.

seen other places?
    yeah. all the same.
anything I can do to help?

That last one had taken Candy about ten minutes to compose. Well, that wasn't true. It took ten seconds to type and ten minutes for her thumb to hover over the send button. But she made herself. She was not going to spend the rest of her life being a jerk just because she didn't trust anyone. She was going to give being generous a try. Try not to become a Josie.

There was text silence for another ten minutes.

too many questions for texting.

Candy made herself keep going.

we can talk.
    i'm bringing mom to glencrest for a visit on tuesday noon.
i'm working then. can meet you there. i can take my break and answer questions if you want. without margaret
    smile. thanks.

It wasn't an emoji. Clint had written out the word: smile. Huh.

Miss Maeve

While the permit guys had not made a big deal out of which Schein they were dealing with, they did forward a letter to Edwards to be forwarded to the owner of parcel 168 saying that the existing structure would have to be secured prior to final approval for new domicile usage within one hundred yards, etc., etc. Candy had received the notice in the mail the day before but had let it sit on her counter, unopened, as it had Edwards's return address on it.

Domicile usage. They meant living, Candy knew. What she didn't know was what the secure part meant. So she called and asked Randy.

"Well, Miss Schein, that means that there can be no points of ingress or egress for humans or animals. Nor can there be any outbuildings, excluding structurally sound barns or garages, left standing within one hundred yards of the original farmhouse. And all electrical and gas lines must be permanently sealed or cut off." He sounded as if he was reading from some kind of rule book. Candy started composing a list, wishing she had her notebook in hand. She had to ask Randy to repeat it, then thanked him and faced the list.

She had turned off the utilities. Check. She had locked up the place. It was as secure as she could make it. Check. She had even called the propane guys and paid seventy-five bucks to have the tank removed. Even if it was out of eyesight from her new place, Candy would know it was there and those tanks, sitting and rusting and rotting in the backyards of most homes up here reminded her of Armageddon. The apocalypse—everything else would be gone, toasted or flooded or rotted or otherwise destroyed. And the goddamn propane tanks would be left standing.

It turned out that you had to buy some sort of extra cap to seal off the gas access to the house.

"In case someone else comes and wants to inhabit the place," Randy said.

"I'm not going to let anyone do that. It's not exactly a rental property."

"I mean they are thinking stealth-like. Like squatters or something."

And here Candy thought she detected a kind of sneer in Randy's voice, reminding her that a girl on her own out in the country, well, maybe not the best idea. Not without a family, or a man. For a single lady it might be better to score a place in town. A townhouse, a condo. But places in town had been flipped and turned into weekly rentals that made so much money during high season that even if the owners did want to rent to people in the offseason, which they didn't, Candy couldn't afford them. Besides, she wanted to live on HER LAND, in HER HOUSE. No neighbors or smells from downstairs or up, for that matter. No more landlords. Bank mortgage, ok, she had to live with that. No landlords. And why would he discourage her from buying this hulk of dented aluminum he wanted to move off his lot?

Candy made a new "Securing the Property" page in her notebook and then marched off to Menards and got a nice man to help her gather more locks and chains and locking gas caps, and he urged her to cover the windows in plywood as well, but that was way too big a job. It meant ladders and saws and big nails or screws, and wow, the thought of all that took Candy's breath away. Unless.

But then Clint had happened. Tuesday had come and he had arrived at Glencrest not wearing a cap or Carhartts. And without his mother. He wore regular clothes and no toolbelt and he looked strangely naked. He said hello and dipped his head in that horsey kind of way again, and she led him down to the TV room to talk and there they came upon Granddah. So there would have to be introductions, and Candy hoped for some kind of miracle sent straight from heaven, that Clint wouldn't mention the move or the doublewide. When she first caught sight of her grandfather in his favorite chair by the best reading light, she paused at the door and murmured, "Oh," and then "um," and then finally, "uh."

Clint looked over at her.

"My grandfather. Over there. His name is Albert. Albert Schein."

"All right then," Clint said, and then strode over to Granddah like he was some kind of car salesman and said in a big voice, "Hello, Mr. Schein, I'm Clint. Clint Houdek. Candace here is showing me around the place for my ma."

"No need to yell," Granddah said, but he was smiling. "My legs don't work so good but my hearing's fine."

"Sorry." Clint reddened. Another blusher.

"Houdek. Which Houdek?"

"Harris was my father. The place out by Burrville. Used to farm soy and corn. Now we're looking to sell. A couple mini-storage places have made offers, and my ma's back is bothering her something terrible. And arthritis. In her hands, mostly. She's not looking to move, but she needs to. So the time might be right, as sad as that might be."

Granddah grunted. He didn't go in for conversations about "sad" or "glad." "Mad" he could do. He added, "This place is passable. Better for my granddaughter being here. She makes it pleasant even, some days."

Nice. Granddah didn't often spread around much praise and she learned to accept his grunts as approval.

"Well, I imagine she would. She's been helpful to me. I want her to meet my ma; maybe she can talk some sense into her."

"Might be."

"Granddah, we're just going to take a seat over there and go over some details."

"Don't let me stop you," he said, and went back to snapping his paper back to the page he was interested in. Today he was wearing an old flannel shirt. Red, blue, and gray, a nice plaid, but the chest pocket was ripped. She started another list in her head: Christmas presents for Granddah.

Candy led Clint over to a nook with two chairs. She sat in the most stained one and tried to restrain herself from sweeping the cookie crumbs off the coffee table.

"The place is fine," Clint was saying, "and Margaret says they have a room for her. And we have enough to tide her over until the property sells. I was looking to take some of that cash to get some land of my own, but that's on hold for now. I'll just hole up at the old place for now. We got some space heaters and such." He paused, then looked across the room at Candy's grandfather. "I just don't know how I am gonna get her to the yes part."

"Why didn't you bring her?"

"She was in terrible pain this morning so I made her breakfast and brought her her pills and put her back to bed. I just knew if I brought her when she was feeling some kind of way, I wouldn't make any progress." And here Clint's head dropped and Candy could see that he was in pain too, along with his mom; a mother couldn't ask much more than that.

"Probably right. Good call."

And then Candy walked him through the steps, like one of those furniture assembly manuals. She detailed for Clint how to lead his mom into the conversation and then circle back in excruciating round after round of talks, worrying the parent like a dog with a bone. Wearing them down. It was cruel, really, but it had to be done, Candy added, because Clint seemed too nice a son to figure it out himself, the part about not always being so helpful and available at a moment's notice.

"I don't mean leave her to get hurt or anything. But little things. Like maybe forget to unscrew the cap on the sugar jar. Or don't bring in the mail. Or be late a couple times with breakfast."

"That's harsh." Clint looked up at her in surprise and then shook his head. "I mean, I'm her son and all and the only one she has here. She raised me. Food and church and manners and such. She came to my football games even though I never played, and put my high school diploma on the wall and all. Like that." He sighed, took a breath that contained a shudder, then went on.

"And after Pops died, she just carried on and kept up a good front and made do. She still bakes me cookies, for chrissakes. Last time she dropped a full pan on the floor. It was terrible. The look on her face when that happened. I wasn't there at the time and when I came home she was just sitting in the living room clutching her hands together cuz they hurt so much, you know? And the cookie pan or whatever was still on the kitchen floor, cookies and all."

They both shook their heads at the sadness, and Candy let the silence be for a beat, then went back at it.

"I know it's hard to believe because you probably think you're doing a crap job, but it's because of you that she is able to keep living there. I'm not saying starve her or anything. I'm saying help her to see what her situation really is, not how it is with you propping her whole life up every day. Look at it this way. Every time you rush home to help her keep living the life she is used to she never gets used to the life she now has to face."

Clint's head had been bowed, sunk down practically between his knees, but now he looked up again at her.

"Wow. That was deep."

"Look. I don't know you or your family that well or anything." And here Candy paused, thinking that might not be true. She was beginning to know him. His chin dips and his blushing and his efforts to dress to impress. His kindness and good manners that seemed out of place in the world she roamed around in. And now his hurting heart. "But I think you are heading for caregiver burnout and that won't be good for anyone. If you don't start the process now, you might end up neglecting her in a way that you don't mean to."

"I would never do that." He said it loud: he was offended, angry, frustrated. Something that Candy sensed she had to push through, instead of ducking. In for a penny, in for a pound, Granddah would say.

"People never intend to. They don't set out to say, 'I'm gonna make my mom or my dad suffer because they've become a pain.' But you'd be surprised how people act when they get to the end of their rope." Let that hang there, dark, awful.

"Clint," she used his name to get him to raise his head, "you're a really good son, seems like."

Then she checked herself. This conversation was heading down some lane that looked like friendship: warmth all around and between them; she could feel it. She resisted the impulse to back up, but this whole counseling thing was the job of the residential supervisor, Margaret, not some LPN. But the fact was that they were mostly terrible people, the cynical bosses buckling under pressure from Corporate on quotas and filled beds and mandates to avoid quoting monthly rates and extra charges. Candy had been down this road herself and she knew what was in store for Clint and his mom. She couldn't help it. She felt for him.

"And I'm guessing you want to keep being a good son. And this is what good sons have to do. Look, I'm not saying this place is the solution. If I could have cared for my grandfather

I would have. Believe me. But growing old is no picnic, and it's no picnic for the kids or the caregivers either."

Clint looked over at Granddah hunched over his paper and slurping his coffee, and Candy spent a quiet minute watching Clint watching. The whole thing was overwhelming, she knew, even suffocating at times, but they were humans and humans didn't leave their old ones out in the cold to freeze or be eaten or whatever. They had to take care of them, and wait, forever it seemed sometimes, for them to pass on. Sometimes Candy wondered if the wilderness laws of nature were actually more humane, instead of this endless caring for and cajoling old sick people into the next day and the string of endless days following. God knows she cared for enough residents around here whose painful and pathetic existences screamed for the curtain to fall. And she had worked at Glencrest long enough to know that the longer these people lingered in their illnesses, the healthier the parent company's profits were. It was a sick business. And not her business. Her business was to care for people once they got there and to make the endless days feel less like torture and a bit like a life.

"Would you meet her?" Clint's voice cut into the silence.

"Pardon?"

"Would you meet my mother? Over at our place? And talk to her? Help me talk to her? I mean, it's a lot to ask."

"No. I mean, yes. I could do that."

And Candy had taken down the address, and the next morning before her shift followed the Google directions though she didn't need them. It was a simple two-turn route. The house was still modest and neat, but Candy could see the signs of rot and ruin along with some half-finished repair jobs that Clint was no doubt attempting in between his job and his caregiving. Clint's mother, Maeve, was a sweet little white-haired lady whose face was scrunched up in pain along with the rest of her. There were bottles of generic Tylenol and ibuprofen scattered around the place on every tabletop. They were open, tops nestled beside them. When Candy asked about her dosages, she was hazy.

"Oh, I know. It's supposed to be every four hours, but I read an article in a magazine that said you could take both off and on, like so." Miss Maeve was doing her best to hold on to the situation but right off the bat Candy could see she could hardly focus for her pain. There was a cane hooked over the arm of the couch and a walker in the kitchen doorway. The house was chilly despite the radiators clanking and hissing under the windows.

"Did you ask your doctor about that? About the doses you can take?" Candy tried to smile. It felt like a cruel question somehow.

And the sweet old thing had lied; she could tell from Clint's face. If she told the truth, which was that she might be gobbling them like candy, the pain got so bad sometimes, well then her doctor might have prescribed Oxy and then another kind of hell would have broken loose. A quick glance at Clint's face told her he wasn't going to be able to carry the conversation. All of a sudden he looked about eight years old, slouched down in what probably had been his father's chair. Helpless. It made her like him more.

Candy took over. She sat down gently on the couch next to Maeve and faced her to begin the siege. She started by talking up Glencrest big time, coming at it sideways by talking about how happy she was to work there, and how Granddah was comfortable there, and that was because it was a happy, comfortable place. She described all the services Glencrest provided right there on-site so her son wouldn't have to take time off work to keep running errands, and that would give them more time to spend together and they could manage her pain better and help her communicate with her doctor more, and on and on and on until the lady started shaking her head, saying, "I don't know, I just don't know," which Candy knew was a signal for the beginning of the end. She had heard that refrain before. It didn't mean "I don't know about this moving idea," it meant "I now know that I don't know how I am going to move forward in my life as it is."

With all the cheeriness and sympathy she could muster, she delivered the final punch: how amazingly brave Maeve had been in managing up until now. Candy said she knew a lot of people who hadn't been able to hang on like Maeve had. And she let that sit in the silence. Candy calculated that there would be another week of percolating, maybe less, depending on whether Clint could face the music. Then he could move her closer to agreeing, even if it was just a maybe. Then he could swoop back in with all the details settled and all the questions answered, and then it was a done deal. She looked over at him. He looked up from his boots when he registered that silence had fallen, and gave her a pathetic smile. He may have just dodged a bullet, but there were more coming his way.

Candy knew there was no final asking for permission. No final "So Ma, is it ok if we move you?" There were just acres of doubt sown, and then waiting, and then more tiny conveniences left unprovided for, and then the done deal and the elaborate charade of moving forward as if the parent had actually agreed.

Candy made some more gentle conversation with Maeve about how lovely the family home was and how it was obvious she had a decorator's touch. She commented on the red trim in the kitchen and the coordinated pine greens and acorn browns of the living room upholstery. There were needlepointed pillows she oohed and aahed over until Maeve, her voice cracking, admitted she couldn't hold a needle anymore. Finally, when Candy sensed the silence that came with exhaustion, she rose to leave and thanked them for the coffee and said the cake was delicious even though she could see it was store bought.

Clint walked her to the truck.

Candy slammed her door shut, then rolled down the window.

"I have to ask you one more thing and it seems harsh, but I don't mean it that way, ok?" Candy had previously pegged Clint for a warm rust. Right now he looked puke green.

"Ok."

"Does your mother have a will?"

"Yeah, I saw it when my dad died. Everything went to her and then," he paused, "then it all goes to us three kids equally. After."

"Did she sign a power of attorney or any medical allowances, like a DNR or medical proxy?"

"I don't even know what those are."

He was standing outside in his shirtsleeves. It was cold. Candy gestured for him to get into the cab, where she walked him through those too. That had been a tough one with Granddah. He fumed about having all his senses and even, cruelly at one point, lashed out and said he had more sense than any of the rest of his family. Candy remembered she had had to leave the room at that point and let the lawyer calm him down, and out they came with the papers signed, and now Candy had control legally and medically over her grandfather's life. She tried not to think about it too much. She answered all of Clint's questions, and there were not many, and by the time she pulled out of the Houdek driveway, she was worried. In the rearview, the poor guy stood in the drive, looking sick to his stomach, and she felt like a butcher who had cut the legs right out from underneath him.

As she drove back to town, she was feeling so many feelings and thinking so many thoughts she thought she might have to pull over. This being out in the world of people and actually caring about them thing might not be such a good idea. Maybe time to pull back. Go back to Candy 1.0 or something. She could practically feel her nerves reddening. And then, in what felt like a bucket of Gatorade poured over her head, came the shame. What a coward she was. Here she had spent all this time, practically all her adult life, dodging the world in order to protect her own thin skin, never realizing that there were all kinds of pain out there being carried by all types of people besides her. How had she missed this little detail about the universe? Candy 1.0 might be safer, but she was selfish. Here she was talking big about how people had to move forward, and she had been idling in neutral for too long.

As she slowed the truck to drive down Cutler's main drag, she glanced at the few people out and about. And for what felt like the first time in her crazy selfish life, she saw them as people who were also likely toting around their own pain or joy or anger or fear. How could they not be? Maybe most of them couldn't afford the armor Candy had bought and paid for with her solitude. Or more likely, they were way smarter than her and recognized that that was the price you paid for being human, while Candy, in her pouting self-pity nourished way back whenever, had decided to forge her way through the world not needing anyone, refusing to pay that price, the price of being human.

She was a Dollar General kind of person. Cheap. Pay little. Get little. In trying to avoid getting hurt, Candy now realized with a kind of belly sickness, she had only succeeded in remaining a child. For all his hang-dog cowardice, Clint had grown up. More than she had, it seemed.

Thanksgiving

Candy was bracing for the three shifts in a row she had signed onto over the holiday. It was Tuesday night and she was planning an early dinner and then tucking into bed. She had stopped off at the hardware store to buy boxes but when she got to her back stairs at the Palace, they were already slick with ice. It had been overcast and wet for days and the nights had turned frigid so the darkness was now filled with slick and glittery things frozen in the night.

She looked up at her back door, sighed, and then swore out loud. Goddamn it. She could put the boxes back in the truck and wait till morning or she could go around and through the front. The lights were on and the lot was full, or full for November. Tonight was Vern's annual "Employees & Friends" Thanksgiving dinner when he closed the Palace and ordered in a turkey with all the fixings from down in Honor, and he also opened the taps and people seemed to have a good old time. Or so Candy had heard the last two holidays that she had lived upstairs. She was always invited but begged off, claiming work, which was no lie as she felt best when working the holidays.

The order-in complete dinner reminded her of the Thanksgivings she had shared along with Granddah when he, too, had ordered up the same and then some. And although they weren't close in any TV family kind of way, she was so grateful, so thankful for him during those holidays, more so than any other. Because these two, Thanksgiving and Christmas, they were killers for people with broken up or scattered or fighting families. Or people alone. And she learned from an early age, as soon as Graham had left, that she and Granddah were people alone.

On the Thanksgiving eves of her young life, Granddah would arrive home late from the Gobble Gobble Happy Hour at the Lodge over in Crystal. He would stumble through the front door, jolly, with foil trays and plastic containers and lay it all out on the kitchen table and let Candy put it away. There was turkey and two containers of gravy and dressing and sweet potatoes and mashed potatoes and green beans, which they always threw away because they never kept right. And there was a pumpkin pie, and Granddah almost always remembered to buy a can of whipped cream because he loved it so much, or maybe he knew that Candy did.

The next day, Candy, even at ages eleven and twelve, would rise early and put a tablecloth on the dining room table and set two places, and write down a list of when things went in the oven. Then she would make Granddah his coffee and his English muffin with butter and jam, and they would sit and talk about the weather. They never made themselves wait until late afternoon, which was when the meal was supposed to be, no doubt due to all those traveling relatives who were coming over the river and through the woods. No, the meal was on the table by one, with the TV blaring one football game after another in the living room, providing enough background noise so that the pauses in their sparse conversation were filled.

And afterward, Granddah would fall asleep in his recliner and Candy would slide the remote out from his lap and switch the channel to *A Charlie Brown Thanksgiving* or *Home for the Holidays,* or even some black and white movies on the Classic movie channel, although Candy found those were harder to watch because the families were huge and in them everyone did travel over the river and through the woods. This was when she still missed her mom, or the idea of a mom. So, Charlie Brown was more her speed.

Late in the day, Granddah would wake up and the two of them would eat more pumpkin pie and finish the whipped cream canister, and Candy would clean up, and it would have felt like a holiday. And she had been thankful for that, even as a kid. However distant Granddah was most of the time, he showed up when it counted. After they had given up on Graham coming home or her mother reappearing, it was just the two of them and Granddah made it count.

Now, standing at the bottom of her icy stairs, the memory made her hungry. Vern always invited Candy to stop by and this year was no exception. Or maybe it was. Her last days here. And there was also the possibility that maybe she was different this year. Was she? Who cared. Really, right this minute all she felt was hungry, and so she was now seriously considering going in there and sitting down and eating with other people. She couldn't remember the last time she had sat down and eaten with anyone besides her grandfather. Ok, why not? She was almost rid of this place and its stink, and so she hitched the flattened boxes under her arm, about-faced, and walked around to the front entrance of the building before she had a chance to change her mind. She was beginning to figure out maybe this was the way people engaged in the world with other people. They probably just didn't think about it too much. Otherwise, the ones with enough sense, that is, would retreat as she had. People in general, Candy was finding, while not as cruel as they used to be, like back in high school or when she went to community college, or worked in service, took no small amount of energy. She still couldn't shake this new idea that her life choices, made when she was eleven or twelve, maybe should've been revised once or twice in the following dozen or so years. Then again, it had become so comfortable and easy, like an oversized T-shirt. It was sure easier than this, she thought, as she braced herself to try to make it through the front door with the boxes under her too short arms, and the wind blowing, and then ...

"Hey, hey, let me help you there," said an older, stooped man who nevertheless spryly jumped up from the nearest table.

"Thanks," Candy said, handing over the boxes.

"Well, hey there, Chrissie, nice of you to drop by," Vern hollered from across the room. "Put those down there over in the corner and pull yourself up to the buffet. Guys, this is Chrissie, my tenant. Or as you can see from what she dragged in, my soon-to-be former tenant. Chrissie, this here's the guys." And Vern named some names and Candy smiled. It was dark enough to hide blushes which, oddly, she did not feel rising. For once. What was happening? Next thing you know she'd be asking Clint to board up her windows in exchange for all the nice things she had done for him.

Candy shrugged off her coat and hung it on a peg by

the door as her new door-opening friend took her boxes and propped them up on the far wall. As her eyes adjusted, Candy took a look around the place. The pizza makers and the drivers and the counter staff and a couple, three, or four of Vern's old codger friends were tucked into mountains of food piled on Styrofoam plates around four-top folding tables that Vern had crowded into the front room. People raised their heads and made hello gestures with their hands and went back to their plates. The Palace wasn't really that much of a sit-down place in its regular life. A couple two-tops and a window counter, that was all. Not a restaurant.

Tonight, Vern had taken a stab at making it festive. Those decorations which you could buy flat but unfanned to become 3D were perched on the back counter: turkeys, pumpkins, pilgrims. And he had strung lights across the ceiling and turned off the god-awful overhead fluorescents. This made it hard for people to see their food but from the way they were forking it in, there seemed to be nothing wrong with how it tasted. And it was free. Candy began to fill a plate, which soon started growing a mountain of meat and gravy and potatoes and yams. She skipped the beans. She turned around, spied an open seat at a four-top in the center of the room, and headed for it.

"Hello." And inside, she patted herself on the back. Well look at you, Candace Schein, walking up to a stranger and sitting down. Will wonders never cease.

"Make yourself at home. Happy holidays to you," said the man sitting at the table in front of a well-picked-over but by no means empty plate.

"Thank you. I'm Candy. Candy Schein."

"I thought Vern called you Chrissie."

"Yeah, I let it go. He's been making that mistake for two years now and I don't want to correct him now. You know how it is."

"Well, I'll be damned. Don't it bother you?"

"Oh yeah, but truth is, we would go months at a time without really seeing each other. I always use the back stairs. And he always wanted the rent in cash. So you know, no check with my name on it or anything."

The man, who looked to be in his seventies or eighties, smiled and scooped some stuffing onto his plastic fork. "That's right kind of you, Candy. Candy, right?"

And they both chuckled. Candy began to dig into her plate. The flavors were exactly those of her young years. It made her eyes fill and she was grateful for the dark. The man across from her, whose name she hadn't asked about and he hadn't offered, said, "What did you say your last name was?"

"Schein," Candy replied, and spelled it, because like Houdek, up here, there were three or four varieties of Schein.

"By any chance are you related to Graham Schein?"

"He's my brother."

"I'm Irving. Irving Habendecker. Graham worked for me one or two summers back when he was in high school."

"Is that right?" Candy managed to mumble in between bites. This was small-town life. Someone always knew someone you were related to, even counting Candy's tiny family. She tried to focus on her food. The stuffing was average but the sweet potatoes were outstanding. Gravy was B+. Made the stuffing better and the dry turkey edible. God bless gravy.

"Yeah, I was a supervisor over at Lawn and Garden Specialists."

"Right, right."

"How's he doing, your brother?"

"Up in the UP. He is working at Nuveen, up in Munising."

"Good job, sounds like. Get home much?"

"Not much."

Irving was warming up to a full-on interrogation. Candy knew she was up next, and then there would be Granddah and then her ma, maybe, and all that. Small-town talk got sticky. Fast. Never more than five minutes into what seemed like polite conversation and people started to get curious about things that you may or may not want to share. Now she automatically thought of beating a quick retreat. But her plate was still half full and it occurred to her that it might be rude, and she didn't want this nice Irving man to think she was rude. An image of her notebook came to mind, oddly. So how did you do this? Stay in the room but keep people out of your business? Ah-ha. The light bulb clicked on.

"And what about you? Do you have children of your own?" she asked.

"Me, I got two. Both grown. Both gone." And he was off on the familiar tale of they were so great or maybe they weren't, but now they were getting it together, or not, and then they left town and went down/upstate for a job, and now they hardly ever come home. Sometimes for Christmas but not really on this holiday. Blah, blah, blah. Candy excused herself to get seconds. This time she noticed the cups by the soda dispenser and grabbed some lemonade.

When she returned, Irving started his family history right up again without missing a beat. Vern came over and bragged what a great tenant Chrissie had been and how much he was going to miss her, but now he was going to redo upstairs up like a Verbo. That was how he pronounced it, and while he and Irving commiserated about the times they are a changin', Candy thanked them for the great meal and gathered her boxes and made it up the front stairs to her apartment.

Before turning off the light, she went to plug in her phone and noticed a text. Two texts.

From Janelle: invite's still on the table. i do make the best pumpkin spice cake in the world. dinner at 4

And from Clint: wanted to thank you. not usually that tongue tied. so thanks. sibs are in town and i'm gonna talk to them. thanks again and let me know if i can return the favor in some way.

Three thank yous and a dinner invite.

To Janelle: working 12-8. maybe stop by for dessert?

To Clint: no problem. it'll all work out. and actually i do need a favor. talk later.

And just like that, Candy felt like she had been born into the world. All day she had been chatting, texting, making conversation, and even had possible plans. It was exhausting, but it hadn't hurt. She was still entirely unsure if this brave new world of people was the right move for her. After all, there were many, many memories of sticking her toe in the waters of social life only to be bit by a casual jab or insult. Or worse, the invisible cloak would drop over her and she would be gone. Anyway. Enough pity-party talk. Today had been nice and that was enough. She had three shifts coming up and the turkey and gravy were working their sleepy magic on her, and so she tucked herself in and called it a night.

Working the Holidays

The Glencrest Shores Homes, LLC decorating team had obviously shopped the same aisles at the Hobby Lobby as Vern. The stand-up paper decorations and such were all over walls and halls, nooks and ledges, along with garlands of fall leaves framing the windows and those cornucopia arrangements on the sideboards. The dining room manager had pulled out the holiday tablecloths: kind of a pukey sienna brown for Thanksgiving, which would switch over to a nice hunter green for Christmas. Today was the second busiest day at Glencrest for visiting relatives and the home had to put on a good show. This made Candy a little sick, even if she did love the way a holiday broke up the routine.

She was working the twelve to eight, and visitors had not jammed up the place yet. Marcos passed her in the hall and murmured a busy hello. He was carrying residents' sweaters and a couple of ties draped over one monster forearm.

"Ties?"

"I do what I'm told."

"Cuckoo's Nest," Candy sneered.

Marcos laughed. Neither had seen the movie but it was standard nursing home humor.

Janelle wasn't working. Good on her, taking the day off to be with her kids and her mom. Candy signed up for holiday shifts every year because, well, because there was nowhere else to go and the money was good. One shift equaled two on Thanksgiving, Christmas, New Year's, and Easter. You didn't have to ask twice at those wages.

Candy checked the shift board and saw she was assigned to Birch. The locked-down crew. The ones who didn't get dressed or couldn't be trusted not to disrupt or God knows even sometimes attack other residents, and so they didn't make the guest list into the main dining room. These were the ones who had the fewest visitors, and even those who attempted a family rendezvous never stayed long. What was there to say? Candy thought staff should get triple pay for spending Thanksgiving with the Birchers. She generally hated the admin's decision to switch staffers all around every shift, except when she was assigned to this wing. This wing was tough for anyone with a heart. Or a pulse, for that matter. Once in a while, on her Birch shifts, Candy found herself thinking about helping these poor souls end it. What was the use of going on like this? You couldn't even call it living. Why did the human race cling to some belief in a god who wanted you to suffer just to satisfy some commandment that Moses had supposedly received from the Big Guy? The thought of pillows over faces or double dosing at night occurred to Candy more than she liked to admit, especially when she was caring for the ones who asked for it. Or asked for their loved ones, their husbands long gone, or their daughters since moved away. As she went into the staff room to switch her shoes, Candy promised herself that she would continue to visit Granddah right on through to the end. And you could bet he would be asking for the knockout punch, no doubt about that.

Candy murmured hellos to other staff members as she headed downstairs for her shift. Didn't need terrific views once you were classified Birch material, so these rooms occupied the lower level. No one called it the basement. Miss Gladys was nodding her head back and forth, back and forth, on her pillow as usual. The head nod was her language now that she had lost words. In the next room, Samuel had been dressed and put in his chair by the window, where he often raised a finger at something that had caught his eye, but the words sometimes didn't match what he was seeing, or what other people saw outside the window. Samuel's hair had been combed down and still shone with moisture from whichever miracle worker had been able to get close to his head. Nobody down here liked to bathe anymore. It was too cold or too hot or too scratchy or too hard. Candy agreed. After initialing Samuel's medication schedule: BP meds three times a day, second dose after lunch, she headed toward her toughest customers. These were the people who had not completely lost track of reality. They were still at that stage where they knew they were losing their senses and they were good and pissed about it. She remembered to start talking as she entered the room so the poor things wouldn't be immediately startled out of their reveries or stupors.

Miss Olive started in right away, asking about her car keys. Over and over. Not angry but persistent. "I thought I put them in my purse just like always, now where's my purse?"

Candy's role in the Miss Olive drama was to say she didn't know but that she would certainly look around when she got a chance, and that would satisfy the poor thing for a couple of minutes and then the exact same conversation would be repeated. And repeated. Candy stayed for two cycles and then headed off to Mr. Thomas's room. Mr. Thomas didn't like to be called by his first name. Mr. Thomas's first name was Eben, or Eb, as he had once been known. He had, as he lost his mind, lost his taste for his first name and was newly and wickedly delighted that he could order people to call him Mister. And so it was. Mr. Thomas had gone mean. All-the-time mean.

"Ah, I got the fat one today. Why are you so fat?" was his standard greeting to Candy.

"Guess I like to eat, Mr. Thomas."

"Well, that's a silly answer; don't you want a husband? You got a husband? Bet he'd throw you out on your big fat keister. Least I would."

"Thank you, Mr. Thomas, I sure do appreciate that."

Candy moved about the room and asked if he wanted tea or coffee and he said no, he wanted a beer, and so Candy cycled through that much repeated conversation, momentarily relieved as Mr. Thomas's target briefly shifted to Glencrest instead of her while on his "why can't a man get a beer if he wants one?" tirade.

Candy tried to say as little as possible about herself when he cycled back for more attacks. She had learned to never give these types any personal information, because even though they didn't know where they were or what day it was, they had the capacity, these lost ones, to grab on to a random detail and shake it for all it was worth. Nope. No details for Mr. Thomas.

"Why you so fat? What's your name?"

"Here's my name tag, Mr. Thomas. Name's Candace, or Candy, if you like."

"Candy, huh? You sure ain't sweet," the old man sneered as Candy moved behind him to straighten his sweater so it wasn't twisted around his neck. This was especially tricky, but she had learned to adjust clothing from behind while saying what it was she was doing. This seemed to take the threat out of it. Otherwise, she opened herself up to a random slap. Approach from behind, keep talking, tell them each step, and adjust gently, keeping an eye out for the backhand. Some residents would slap, then apologize, ashamed of their loss of control, but Mr. Thomas was not one of them. He seemed to really enjoy a slap back at a faceless pair of hands messing around in his clothes. Once in a while, Candy mustered up some hate for Mr. Thomas, no doubt, but she also felt bad for him. He was on Norco three times a day because his legs had become useless but he had terrible phantom pain. Watching someone in pain, like Candy did with Mr. Thomas, could, or should at least, soften anyone's heart.

Candy forced herself to spend the same amount of time with the mean ones as the docile ones. It just didn't seem fair. Mr. Thomas, or Eb, as she called him inside her own head, he might've been nice at one time. His wife might've loved him. He had kids. They had visited quite regularly up until about three months ago when the off-and-on meanness became his full-time job. But now he lived in a world of pain, eased only for a couple of hours at a time by the Norco. No way to live. Or die, for that matter.

"Today's Thanksgiving, Mr. Thomas; you're going to have

some turkey and fixings. You would like that, huh? I'll come back in a few, and we'll go down together to the little dining room and you can celebrate Thanksgiving with the others. George and Gladys and Ruby and them all."

"Looks like you ate already," he said, before he swallowed the tiny white capsules she shook into his hand.

"Well, helloooo there, Mr. Thomas," came a voice from the doorway.

Candy turned. It was Vicky. Vicky was a saint and a demon all rolled into one tiny bundle of skin and bone. She was another work-every-holiday-you-could LPN. Not because she didn't have family, but because she had too much. And a daughter in college. First kid to make it past high school. Every holiday shift she would tell Candy, "Money's better, company's about the same." And they would chuckle together. And here she was, Vicky, coming in to stop the carnage, and Candy dreaded her intervention. Wickedness was sure to follow.

"Who are you now? I already got one after me, don't need another. Get out." Mr. Thomas was yelling now, waving his hand in dismissal at Vicky.

"Well, Mr. Thomas, I'm just coming in here to wish you a happy holiday, see? Because all of us at Glencrest want you to enjoy yourself the best you can."

And here Vicky paused. "Under the circumstances."

Pause. Mr. Thomas was silent, his mouth gaping open. Vicky kept smiling. She was moving in for the kill. Like a bullfighter. Candy saw it coming. That smile on Vicky's face. Wicked.

"Seeing as how your family doesn't seem to be coming."

Pause.

"Maybe some friends will drop by later for a visit?"

Pause. Mr. Thomas's chin dropped to his chest.

"Or your grandchildren. Home from college, are they, for a break and coming to see their grandpa?"

It was all delivered with a smile pasted on her face that said nothing besides: "Hello, my name is Vicky, and I work here at Glencrest." But Candy knew that smile meant: "You're a mean sonuvabitch and I don't care how lost or scared or sick or forgotten you are; I'm going to make you pay." Candy was fearful that if caught, Vicky could be fired for elder abuse. But then again Mr. Thomas, or Eb, rather, might never remember and the admin, or at least the one admin on staff during this holiday, was hiding out in their offices no doubt watching a football game or a parade on their phones.

Candy smiled at Vicky in an attempt to call this all to a halt. She didn't particularly like being saved. This kind of meanness drove her nuts and belonged back in some beyond world that she was no longer a citizen of. The world she had made for herself did not have cruelty in it. There weren't a lot of rules in Candyland, but it was a cruelty free place, just like they said on the shampoo bottle. And Vicky regularly violated that rule. In the past, Candy had said nothing, told herself to be grateful, hoping Vicky acted like this out of love and a sense of decency and not because she enjoyed it.

But recently Candy had come to doubt it. Vicky was just mean. They both turned and headed out of Mr. Thomas's room, leaving him deflated and silent in his chair. In the corridor, Candy, who had never done so before, said to Vicky, "I appreciate what you're doing—"

"Bastard," Vicky hissed.

"But see, he doesn't know what he's doing and it doesn't bother me. Nothing new. Hear it all the time."

"He's got no right," Vicky sneered.

"He's got no mind," Candy shot back, and Vicky was silenced.

"And, as you also pointed out, no family to speak of either."

"What do you care?" Vicky asked.

"I don't know. But I do."

Vicky turned and went off in a huff, and Candy imagined a superwoman cape drooping around her ankles. Candy turned into Miss Ivy's room. Miss Ivy would die soon. She had the dying smell on her. Her chest barely rose or fell. There was nothing wrong with her but total exhaustion. This woman was tired of living. She wore a diaper she never filled, and she lived on a couple of sips of broth a day. She had good family, though, especially her daughter who came in a couple times a week and would be here soon, Candy was certain.

Candy reached over to pet the sleeping woman. Candy made petting part of her rounds in Birch. Lonely, cold, basement Birch. She patted and petted and stroked those who seemed to ask for it. She did so on their arms or shoulders or smoothed their hair down if they had any. They would practically start purring, no lie, some of them, when you petted them. And let them, was what Candy thought. Grant Tortenson had loved to be petted too, and he had finally passed last week, and Ivy would join him soon. Ivy especially liked being petted on her head, which was bald except for a few tendrils of white wisps here and there.

"Today is Thanksgiving, Miss Ivy."

Stroke.

"Your daughter Melanie will surely be in today to see you and wish you a happy holiday."

Stroke.

"Maybe some yummy stuffing later too, huh?"

Stroke.

"It's a lovely day, Miss Ivy, not too cold, and the sun came out."

Stroke. And though she couldn't hear it, Candy imagined Ivy purring.

Black Friday

Candy had worked an exhausting midday shift Thursday with many visiting family members needing their own kind of triage:

"How long has he been this way?"

"Her pain has increased; what can we do?"

"When does the doctor come in?"

"Isn't there any way to get that old codger into the bath?"

"I sent a card; do you know why it is not in his room to cheer him up?"

"She tells me you are not giving her enough to eat; is that true?"

"We called the doctor. Do you know if he came in to pay a visit?"

"We would like to see the manager."

And then there was the turkey dinner that was so overcooked even Granddah threw his napkin in disgust over his half-finished plate.

And the residents, as exhausted as they were after all of the festivities and the food and the visits, threw their own kind of tantrums later on in the day, just like over-excited toddlers, only without the mobility. Or the toys. Really, sometimes bonus pay didn't match how much work these holidays were. After Candy and the rest of the shift managed to maneuver most of the residents back to their rooms, if not their beds, Candy went to see Granddah. Knowing what a disaster Glencrest's holiday meals were, Candy had made an extra plate at Vern's the night before, and now she popped it in the microwave and gave him a plate where she found him in the TV room.

"Well, Miss Candace, if that isn't a nice surprise," Granddah grumbled through a smile. "Didn't have an appetite for that other meal. Looked pretty worked over, if you know what I mean."

"Yes, I do, Granddah. I've seen enough of them to know I gotta bring some backup."

And she settled a napkin on his lap, wishing she could tuck it under his chin but not daring to. That was what laundry was for, she figured, and she wasn't going to humiliate him like that. Not yet.

They passed a nice moment or two, Candy munching on her KitKat bar and Granddah making his way through the meal, grunting approval at practically every bite. After he finished, he pushed the paper plate across the table, looked over at his granddaughter, and asked, "What have you been up to these days, Miss Candace?"

"Oh, this 'n that." She was too tired to spill the doublewide beans. Not today. She expected the worst and Mr. Thomas had filled her quota for one day.

"Buttoning down the place for winter? Did you get the storms in?"

"Not yet, I've got to get someone to help me, 'cause you know how I feel about ladder work."

"You're gonna have to learn, young lady. It's your place now. It's your inheritance. Not much of one, but if you care for it right, it'll give you shelter for years to come. Got to keep after it, you know."

"Oh, I know, Granddah; I am going to get someone out soon as the holiday's over to get it all done before Christmas."

"Am I coming home for Christmas?" he asked, and the way his voice went soft, almost like a kid's, made Candy's heart jump. She felt the blush rise and the sweat pores open. Did he think this was a little stay at a hotel? Some broken-down resort he was vacationing at? This was a damning part of dementia. You'd be rolling along with your loved one, basking in their presentness and their ability to keep up a conversation without repeating, and then it was like they hit black ice and spun out into the dark, where they no longer knew which way was up. Candy was tired, and wanted only to retreat, as soon as she could, into her now well-scripted "home to the doublewide for the holidays" fantasy. So, she kept lying.

"Yeah, well, that would be real nice, wouldn't it, Granddah? Ima do my best to make it happen. I'll have the place fixed up all nice and cozy and then we'll see how the ice and snow are and whether we can manage the walk." At least this part wasn't a lie.

"I can manage the walk. I got this goddamn set of wheels here," he said, patting his walker, a deluxe one. It had four wheels and a fold-up seat for his newspaper and his glasses and tissues. They had had to give it some racing stripes with green painter's tape because it was identical to three other residents' walkers and squabbles had ensued.

Her grandfather was shaking his now bowed head.

"Holidays around here are a losing game." He was back in the real world of Glencrest: present and miserable.

"Well, I'm here, and I brought you a nice plate. Looks like you enjoyed that right enough, eh?" And she pointed to the empty plate and tried to get a laugh going.

"Yup. That was some good eating. I appreciate it, Candace. Everything you do, I appreciate. I am thankful, as they make us say around here on this day."

"And I'm thankful for you, Granddah, and all you have done for me all my life." Candy practically choked on this, but it had to be said; she needed to say it. He looked so pathetic and another thing dementia did or had done to her grandfather was make him sometimes sentimental and sometimes angry. Maybe it was Alzheimer's, after all. They kept changing the definition. It didn't matter what you called it. He was fading.

And then out of the blue he asked, "You heard from your mother? She around?" He was gone again.

"Um, no, Granddah, I've never heard from her. Neither have you. She's history, as you always liked to tell me." The air filled with black thoughts. Candy took a swipe at them.

"Remember when I was a little girl, I would daydream out the window and make up stories about how she was on an adventure and was coming home?"

"Christ. That was terrible. A terrible time." Granddah was shaking his head, now remembering.

"Not so much, Granddah; you'd play along, I remember

that clear as day. You'd say yes, she was on a trip and she was going to come back one day, you just didn't know when, and then you'd plop me in front of a favorite movie, *Parent Trap* or *Toy Story.* And make popcorn in the microwave."

"But it was wrong to lie like that," he said, remembering. "I knew she was no good as a mom and wasn't coming home as long as she had one monkey or another on her back."

"No, it was all right to lie then, Granddah. I was little. I couldn't handle anything about forever, or never. You did good by me, Granddah," she said, and wished they were the touching types. She wanted to touch him now.

Instead, she said, "Speaking of, I got to go clear out the stragglers from the other TV room and get people off to bed. Who's your person today?"

"Miss Vicky."

"Ok, you'll be fine."

"Witch."

"C'mon, Granddah. Be nice."

"Not likely." But he laughed a little and she helped him up and he got the walker going and she followed him to his room, where they said goodnight. It was an hour after her shift had ended and so there was no rounding up to be done. But that was another thing Granddah didn't need to know.

Candy was back the next day, a Black Friday indeed. Two scheduled caregivers had called in sick, no surprise there, and had been replaced by contract workers who moved silently through their tasks and quietly mumbled to each other in Spanish. The residents were in a funk. Too much stimulation, or too much disappointment. Candy had the early shift: eight to four.

She made her apologies to Janelle; she was just so tired. Janelle understood.

"Those holidays are killer," she said as a comfort to Candy, all bright-eyed and bushy-tailed in the morning. She reported on her good holiday: the kids had been nice to their grandma and her teenage daughter had actually helped with cleanup.

"They do grow up and come to their senses."

Candy murmured assent. Murmuring was all she was up to this morning. After a quick apology text to Janelle last night, she had collapsed as soon as she got home, too tired to face a box or a mess. But once in bed she had been unable to sleep, and tossed and turned in a funk of shame about lying to Granddah and correcting Vicky. The first made her doubly anxious about the doublewide, the second made her nervous. Once again she had said too much to a person and now there would be another conversation and then the person would think Candy was normal.

And now the sun was shining and many residents were still nursing their holiday hangovers. They didn't want to dress or go to Sit 'n Stretch. Instead, they glumly slumped in front of the TV which screamed at them about Black Friday sales and Christmas right around the corner. What a world.

Candy slogged through her shift with Janelle playing cleanup behind her, acting like a real friend. The best kind, though, in Candy's book, backup without question. Candy knew that Janelle knew that holidays were kind of a triple whammy for her: no mom, no home, no relatives to cook with or for. So however miserable those shifts were, work was the best alternative.

At their lockers, after Candy had said her goodbyes to Granddah, as she had the next two days off and wasn't sure he kept track of her like that, she spoke to Janelle without looking up from her shoe change.

"Thank you. I needed the help today."

"You're fine. Everybody needs a lift one time or another; am I right?"

"Always are."

And as Candy stood up and turned to say goodbye, Janelle held her arms open. Candy walked into them, and was wrapped up in a fragrant, soft, warm hug. It was a brand-new experience.

Flu Shot

Glencrest was offering four hours of PTO for proof of a flu shot. And another four hours paid for evidence of an annual checkup. Candy hadn't had a checkup since she had been hired six years ago. It wasn't mandatory and she was healthy. Or at least she figured she was, minus the extra thirty or forty pounds she was carrying around on her otherwise pretty small frame. But this was the first time Glencrest, which couldn't mandate anything like this legally—after all, this was Michigan, home of crazy survivalists who surrounded the capitol anytime a politician wanted to pass a law making people do anything—this was the first time the job had offered an incentive. A financial one. And Candy was going to have to take time off to move. This way, one of those days would be paid, so she went down to the Rite Aid and got her flu shot, making sure to stash the paperwork, worth half a day's pay. And since she was on a roll, she then drove to a Minute Clinic in Martinville's only strip mall and asked for a physical.

"Do you mean an annual checkup?" the receptionist asked.

"Yes, that's what it's called," Candy blushed.

"We don't do annuals here. This here is more of a triage,

on-the-spot place. You'll need to make an appointment with your primary care physician."

"What if I don't have one?"

"Then I would Google it," the helpful receptionist said. "Got to be a ton, especially in and around Traverse."

Candy went away aggravated. She had hoped she could get it all done in one day and instead she had to go back to the truck and Google up a doctor and make an appointment. Which she got. But it would be after the move, so she checked with HR at Glencrest Inc., or LLC, or whatever, which, after a fifteen-minute hold, told her that she would be paid the four hours of PTO even if she didn't take the time off during that pay period.

"Even if I work a full week?" Candy felt like an idiot, but she didn't get it. How do you get paid for time off when you don't take the time off? she wondered. And then it came to her before she heard the bored and exasperated voice on the other end of the phone. They could do whatever they wanted with her paycheck. Duh.

So now all she had to do was drop twenty pounds in the next ten days so she would be gently reprimanded instead of scolded. If there was one thing Candy hated to do, it was diet. After many failed attempts and interrupted exercise routines she had realized her heart just wasn't in it. Her size had become a kind of armor, a convenient defense against playing sports or shopping at the mall. An excuse for why she didn't get asked to parties or out on a date or to homecoming. When she had started to pack on the pounds, or rather, not take them off, in high school, she was just as unhappy as all fat kids were but she also found it could be a kind of shield. Even though if she was being completely honest with herself, which she tried to be from time to time, she did notice that some big girls got asked out and fat boys didn't seem to have this problem. Still, it was an easy out. And Candy didn't have a lot of other options to consider. She didn't want to dwell on the other possibilities of why she didn't have friends. Like she was a pain. Or unlikeable. That was the worst. She had done enough Googling to know that parental abandonment showed up in all kinds of messed-up ways in kids. But she hadn't been sent off to a foster home and Granddah, bless his heart, had never, ever, well hardly ever, implied that she was a pain or a burden.

Candy figured she couldn't be entirely unlikeable. Janelle liked her, she thought. And Clint might like her. She tried to smile out at the world from a distance. Made nice small talk. The Shop 'n Save. The Quik Mart. The laundromat. This was as far as she had been willing to venture out in a long time. Her past dips into social media demonstrated she certainly wasn't in demand; she wasn't friended or liked, and the internet universe had been another face slap of invisibility. It had hurt because back in the school hallways or classrooms, people had to still move around her, or hand out a test to her or wait behind her in the line at the cafeteria. Not on social media. Just WHOOSH, not there, unfriended, unliked, unseen. It had been brutal for her teenage self and so, after community college, Candy had closed all of her accounts. Now her new besties were YouTube and Google.

Jesus. And there she was stopped in her tracks by what she was coming to call Candy 2.0. Was she going to remain that scared and hurt little teenager for the rest of her life? Was it going to come down to the gas station and the grocery store with occasional field trips to the laundromat or the Rite Aid? Was that what the doublewide was going to be? The Mystic? Another hidey hole just like the one she had made out of her bedroom back at the farmhouse?

As a kid, Candy had never asked a lot of her granddah. But once she got her license, or even before when they went to town to do errands, Candy would ask to be dropped off at the Goodwill and would make a beeline to the back of the store to look at the furniture section. In a town with a rich tourist population, it wasn't all that hard finding things that were cheap and good. And by good, Candy of course meant good taste. Wood, rattan, good colors, pillows that didn't smell of someone else's life. Candy would bum five or ten bucks from Granddah to buy things for her room. A white wicker-framed mirror which she carefully hung at chest level. A quilted bed cover, in lovely patterns of violet and pink and orange, and then a throw rug to match, in orange and gray stripes, which she laid by the side of her bed. A side table that she painted some kind of yellow she had found in the garage. In that not-yet-falling-down farmhouse, Candy's childhood bedroom had become her refuge. Her home inside a home, a nest inside a tree hollow. Granddah splurged one Christmas and bought her a little TV and even paid the cable guy to run some wiring up to her room. So that was that. Her first place. Her magazines, her desk, her bed, her windows which looked out on the pine forest behind the house. The heat registers carried noise from downstairs so she could always tell when her grandfather was up and about and nearing the time when he would stand at the bottom of the stairs to holler to her for breakfast or dinner or a ride to school or town. Then she would hop up and head downstairs just before that moment, thinking if he had time to think about how much time she spent there, he might say something and she would be sent back into that hellish place where she had to think about why she wasn't out in the world.

She had gotten her driver's license at the earliest possible age. Sixteen. Took the early-bird driver's ed class and did her "on the road" hours in the school parking lot before school. Granddah had had to drive her because the school buses didn't run for before-school classes, but he hadn't seemed to mind. When she got her license, the old man took her on a few practice runs in his then new Tacoma, and one day when they arrived back at home without incident, he laid the keys on the side table right next to the front door and said, "You can use it whenever I'm not needing it. But no driving past eleven until you are eighteen. You know the law."

Past eleven. As if. Still, sometimes Candy drove into town to see a movie. Sometimes she even went to the mall, but spent most of her time in furniture or kitchen stores, dreaming up a place of her own where no one would ever come asking why she didn't have a boyfriend or a girlfriend for that matter, or where she was headed for Friday happy hour, or any other annoying prying questions which made her comfortable life feel like she didn't measure up.

The driver's license led to her first job at a Tim Hortons out on US 31. Minimum wage but the hours were good. Candy could grab the BATA bus from school and make it there to work the four-to-nine shift. And weekends. They had a hard time filling weekend slots and Candy was happy to take them when she could get the truck. The uniform was pretty ok: brown with red trim. The hat was annoying, but the hairnet was worse, and so she had tucked up her curls under the hat, tried to find lip gloss the color of the red trim, then gave up when she wore it one day and one of the donut makers said she looked like a clown.

"No offense," the baker had said. They all said that. Tossed words at her that felt like punches and then said "no offense" without ever even looking at her.

She pulled in behind the Palace. Her arm hurt at the injection site and she still had packing to do. She lugged what she figured might be the last load of groceries up the back stairs into the Dump and popped a meal into the microwave. The doublewide transport was tomorrow, the move next week. Then installation took a week. Was supposed to take a week. Randy had promised a week.

At first Candy had reserved a U-Haul, then, still uncertain whether she would need it, cancelled it. She thought about hiring movers: Two Guys and a Truck, but it would only be one trip and she was junking almost everything: the bed, the couch, the coffee table. Somehow, the thought of throwing things out felt like a day at an amusement park. Woo-hoo. Out you go, smelly, faded old things that had never really belonged to her. These were furnishings Candy had settled for, so many of them someone else's first choice. The payoff in these castoffs had been her savings account. Every time she had settled: a set of sheets here, a couple of juice glasses there, she imagined her savings account getting a snack. She fed it any way she could. But that was over.

Candy used a spoon to scoop up the last of the marinara sauce from her Stouffer's spaghetti and meatballs, then cleaned up her small dinner mess. As she wiped her hands on a dish towel, she cheered at the thought that there would be new things. Things that would be hers first. She was not taking much. Clothes, kitchen, TV, coffee pot, microwave, the blender she had bought back when she caught the smoothie craze. In the back of her notebook, she had written down the delivery dates of her new items. Bed, couch, but no recliner for Granddah. Yet. For now she would have to still use the laundromat. She couldn't afford anything other than what she had already bought. Her credit card balance scared her and for once she would not be able to pay it off. She'd have to eat all that interest for about six months. She had already figured it all out in the "Finances" section of her notebook. It was true that she had always liked numbers, except when they told you how much interest the credit card company was going to squeeze from you for overspending. You set numbers up and made them do things, and they did: product, sum, difference, quotient. That was the good part. But what the numbers had come to mean in her planning for a home, well, that was like moving to the high-stakes table at the casino.

Canceling the movers had helped pay about $500 worth of her new couch. That was at least a third of the cost. She would do the hauling herself. She had the Tacoma. She would sleep in the emptied-out Dump for two days, waiting for her new bed frame and mattress, and then she would raid the farmhouse for old furniture that she would use until she could fill in with new. And for a while, she would make minimum payments that never shrank the balance because that was the game.

Her arm felt better when she moved it around and it got a good workout as she packed up what she wanted from the kitchen, minus one of each thing to get her through the next couple of days. The plates she wrapped had belonged to her grandmother; she would drop them at the Goodwill. The glasses she had picked up at an estate sale along with the pots and pans: good old-fashioned Revere Ware with the copper bottoms. She had gotten them for a steal. A buck apiece.

Her phone pinged. It was Randy, telling her the movers had sussed out the site and all was in order and they would be on the move at eight. Due at the site at ten. Said the site looked good, and they would place it and secure it and anchor it down, and then the hookups could begin. They had their own electricians and plumbers to take care of all of that, and since it was November there shouldn't be a delay. Hers was the only installation on the docket that week.

Candy had looked up how all of this was supposed to happen. There were dozens of YouTube videos that showed a bunch of guys running around and crouching down and jacking things up and moving things around and nailing things down. The videos all played in double or triple time, no doubt to fool people into thinking this was an easy process. Apparently it involved all kinds of cranes and wheels and dollies and jacks and hookups before the final inspection. It made Candy so nervously nauseous she had decided not to take the time off to watch anything other than the first day.

What made her feel sick was that she had no idea how to tell if it was all done correctly. No idea if the guys who were doing the job actually knew what they were doing. And this was a lonely thought. Not alone, as in, ok, this is how I live, but lonely, as in scared. Beds, couches, color schemes, beach-rock-lined driveways. All that she could do. Alone. But this part. This was the part that she had cut out of her daydreams. Her storyline here was that she would buy the place. Then, on the appointed day, she would go to the site and watch efficient, trustworthy people prepare the site. Watch as the house, her house, was gently plopped down and secured in one day. Then she would move into a world of perfectly color-coordinated furniture and fixtures and continue life as Candy Schein with an upgraded cocoon.

She took out her phone, looked at her contacts. Clint. Clint would know. Clint could talk to those guys. Clint could tell if something was wrong. Clint would know a guy who knew a guy.

Guys. Guys who knew guys.

Hi. hope you had a nice holiday. Hope things with Mom are going ok. I actually have a favor to ask.

Candy used capitals and punctuation. This was important.

She ground her teeth. Candy ground her teeth whenever she had to do something she hated. It was why she had stopped going to the dentist, besides the fact that she didn't have dental insurance and one trip without a single thing wrong was 150 bucks. She ground, and thought, I won't have to ask for any more help from anyone once I'm settled. Once the doublewide was plopped down and secured and hooked up and the inspection was passed, and the address change filed with the post office. She would never again have to put herself in a position where she had to ask for help. She hated asking for help. People always turned away. Ok, she imagined they would. Maybe they had? Maybe she had never asked.

Jesus. She was a mess. She got up and went to the back window which looked out over the Palace parking lot. She stared into the night. It was dark. And cold. And windy. She could see the bare trees bending under the streetlights. Now on top of everything, she had to worry about the weather. The beautiful fall was gone and the shit season of drizzle and freezing rain and sleet and wind, so much wind, was here. Would the doublewide be blown off the truck bed before it even arrived?

She pushed send.

The Wizard of Oz

When Candy had texted Clint to ask him this huge favor, he had actually suggested that Candy call so they could talk. That was new. So she placed the call, relieved in a way, because there was so much to say, so many pieces of information she felt she had to lay down to justify her fear. It would have taken all afternoon to type. She had no time to ponder how new this was, this calling someone on the phone and talking to them. In her life, the phone was, or had been, a mute machine, used for the weather and for work and for Googling and texting. It was not for talking. But Clint picked up on the first ring, just as all these fleeting pieces of thoughts were flying out through her eyeballs. She tried to fix her attention on the horizon. And then she let all the fears tumble out into the phone, making sense as best she could. At last, she paused for breath, and Clint spoke.

"When is this happening again?" he asked.

"It's supposed to arrive on-site by ten. Then they lower it or roll it off or something, and it sits on jacks while they build the foundation. Honestly, I've watched YouTube videos about a half dozen times but I don't know what I'm looking at and those construction clips are always so sped up you can't really tell what is real time."

"True that. Double the cost and triple the time frame. Rule of thumb. But if he, Rusty or whoever, says a week and the internet says a week, I can take a look and see if it looks like a week's worth of work. You under some kind of time crunch?"

"No. Really, I didn't hire movers or anything. Not taking much with me. Starting new, or whatever." Then she forced herself back onto her track of fear. "But today I'm scared I'll just faint or something if it looks wrong but I won't know if it looks wrong but you might, and I wouldn't normally ask you but you've been nice and all and I promise I will always look after your mom as my own." She heard the string of "buts" as she tried to rein in the tumble of words spilling out of her.

There was a pause.

"You would do that anyway."

Silence. And Candy heard the ugliness of what she had said. What the hell? She wouldn't take care of his mom if he said no?

"I didn't mean that." And Candy fell silent and sensed herself turning into kind of a mashed-up, disintegrating blob of humanity. She hated herself.

"I don't know what I meant." Another pause creaking out through her phone screen.

"So tomorrow." Clint was picking up the thread once again.

"Yeah, tomorrow. Ten. If you can. Please."

"I might have to move things around but no one's on-site, so I'll just let them know I got another side job and then I should be good to go."

"Look, I understand it's kind of a stupid ask, and I don't know why I said that about your mom. You've got to know I will care for her always anyway, but I just ..."

It was quiet for so long, Candy pulled the phone away to look that they were still connected. She was waiting for Clint to say it was all right. But it wasn't. For once, she didn't want to stop talking. She had the impulse to babble on until some kind of magic-eraser words formed so she could send them out over the phone to this nice guy who kept doing nice things for her. Where was the delete button when you needed it? She threw herself again into the silence.

"I can't describe it. But I'm freaked out and it makes me say stupid things and ask stupid favors."

More pauses. The silence felt like a poisonous ooze coming at her through the phone. She pushed on, babbling. Like an idiot. And so she added, "I know. I'm an idiot. And a coward. After this one more thing, I'll never ask another favor of you. But this is ..." By this time, Candy was sick of the sound of her own voice and gave up. She breathed heavily and didn't even care anymore if he heard her on the other end of the phone sounding like a beast in a barnyard. She waited. Just as she was about to sign off, he spoke again.

"Too big. I get it. You sound like how I felt the day I had to tell my mom she was going to move. I spent the entire night before wishing someone else could be there to be breaking it to her. Anyone but me. But there was no one but me."

"I know. I'm sorry you had to do that alone. I did too. With my grandfather. It was horrible."

"But you helped. You did. You know that, right? You started

the ball rolling for us, for me and my mom, and then after that, I could use your name. I could say, 'Well, Miss Candace tells me,' and 'Candy says,' and it seemed to help."

And just like that, he had moved on. Had it been her apology? Her craziness? What was up with this niceness?

"Both names, huh?"

"Yeah." He chuckled. "I can't tell which one fits you better yet."

Yet? Candy thought. Better? His chuckle helped her to exhale, quietly this time.

"Anyway, I can stand in for you, although I really think you should be there to ... you know ... assert yourself." He said the word "assert" like he was trying it out for the first time. "And you'll be able to see as clear as me if they ding it again, or drop it, or screw it up."

"But if it looks like that, you can just call me, and I'll hop on over there. It's the waiting for it to happen that I can't stand. Once it happens, then I think I can handle it. Like watching a glass fall. After it's crashed and broken, I know exactly what to do."

"You're a funny girl."

"Aren't I just."

"Huh."

"So you'll do it if you can?"

"I'll be there. I know I can be there. Just got to move things around."

"Thank you so much. I owe you. I'll bake you a cake or something."

"Bake it for my mom. She's the one with no appetite."

"Done."

Candy rang off and got back to her boxes, thinking on and off about the ways people reached out to each other and did things for one another, and owed each other things and thought about them and sometimes even put them first, just because they liked each other and felt warm things for each other. Or, they said stupid things and hurt that person's feelings, and then what happened? In Candy's experience you just walked away or moved past or went to your room and turned on the TV, or whipped through the pages of a *Better Homes* magazine and let the hours pass until the hurting voice became a whisper and then a faint echo and then nothing. But in real life, how did this work?

What was the next step when it wasn't a job buddy or a family member or a business transaction? What if it was kind of like a friend? And a guy? Candy knew you were supposed to look out for friends and they were supposed to look out for you. You cared for their feelings and thought about their thoughts because they were IN your life. They occupied space in your place, like a couch or a coffee mug.

As she was finishing packing up the extra kitchen stuff, Clint texted back, confirming he could make it and telling her he would be in touch. She scrolled back through their text thread. Over a month's worth. Almost two. Lots of short little two-or-three-word dialogue boxes. Then longer ones contained contact info for tradespeople, and how to talk to them, and sometimes what to say. And then really long ones about Maeve. A thread. A real one that was growing thicker. A rope. She wondered what that meant. Their texts bounced around inside her head as she went to sleep and tried her hardest to stay that way.

No luck. She was up in the middle of the night, it seemed

like, even though her phone read 6:52. She cursed herself for being such a weakling. She ground her teeth again and decided. How bad could it be? She might watch the thing swing to its death and then she would start again and that would be that. Staying away wasn't going to prevent bad things from happening. And she also had an itch to see Clint. To check his face for hurt or anger, if she could. She scrounged up a cup of coffee and poured it into a travel mug and pulled on clothes without thinking that Clint would see her in the crappy old sweats she had chosen because they were nearest the bed.

Then, at the truck, she paused. Wait. This was An Event. Maybe the Biggest Event in her life outside of her mother leaving her and Candy hadn't really exactly been there for that. And now she was going to show up in stained sweatpants? She slowed down, about-faced, marched herself back upstairs, and changed into clothes that could present themselves to the world as clean and at least thought about. Not an outfit exactly, but not from the bottom of the hamper either. She suited up again for the outdoors and brushed her teeth, in that order, tumbled back down the stairs, got into the truck, and made it turn over in the cold, dark air of the morning. She put it into gear once the windshield cleared and made her way out Lasso Road to her lot, then pulled the truck in behind the pine trees, well out of the way of whatever was about to happen. The ground was hardened by frost. She turned off the engine and listened to it tick and kept her gaze on the rearview mirror and sipped her coffee and waited. She occasionally tried to take note of the sky, a deep winter blue, and the pines, their steady green, and the air, cold, but the details of place and time slipped under the buzz of nerves jangling through her entire being. Her hand shook and splashed coffee down the front of her coat.

Then Clint pulled in, hopped down from his truck, smiled when he saw her, but made no move to leave again, or comment, beyond a hello. Candy scanned his face. He didn't look hurt or mad. Just interested. After some "hellos" and "thank you agains" and "no worries, this could be fun" preliminaries, they came to stand silently next to each other when the doublewide noisily arrived, looking precarious and fragile on the back of a tractor trailer. Instead of it being delivered in two slices as Candy had seen on the internet, her doublewide was already assembled, and so they had hired an extra wide-bed truck and there were flags and yellow signs all over it announcing "Oversize Load" although that seemed pretty obvious since the sides of the thing were hanging dangerously over the sides of the wide bed. The doublewide itself was circled by huge blue straps wrapped all the way around it and then attached to the truck bed, holding it together against the wind or the bumps or anything else that might rip the thing apart. There were also two escort pickups, one in front and one in back, and although Candy was relieved she hadn't seen the actual transport, she was certain that the job of these escorts had been to run other drivers off the road.

It was here. She held her hands on either side of her head, waiting to duck or hide her eyes, anticipating the moment when she would not be able to stand one more creaking, swaying second of it. She wanted to grab onto Clint and instead continued to squeeze the sides of her head. She forced herself to watch for a disaster to unfold up in the air, but nothing really got lifted. The trailer with the wobbling Mystic on the back got disconnected and the house sat there on its trailer bed, swaying a bit as the truck rolled away. Then a bunch of guys tumbled out of the "CAUTION: OVERSIZE LOAD" trucks and started unloading all manner of tools and blocks and jacks and things Candy couldn't name from the trucks' beds. Then, quick as lightning, they started moving and rolling these various things under the doublewide and jacking it up and winding or maybe unwinding winchy-looking things, all the time speaking some sort of shorthand secret language to each other, most of it involving the words "yep," "ready," "hold," and "go." Then they moved more rolling things from one spot to another and repeated themselves as they made their way around the house. Then in what looked like some kind of magic trick, the trailer got re-hooked up to the truck and pulled right out from underneath the doublewide.

And now the house was lowered onto what looked like greasy planks sitting on top of what looked like toothpicks set up in triangles all around the place. To Candy it looked like a breeze could topple the whole mess. Occasionally one guy would answer a phone call or make one. Candy tried to hear what he was saying, already certain that she wouldn't know what any of it meant if she could. But no, she was just going to have to stand it, like a trip to the dentist or the first days of school.

All of these years and all of this money, and the final big jump from singlewide to doublewide, and now it felt like it was a mistake. Candy's first post-panic thought was that it was so BIG. A singlewide fit on the back of a truck. It came in one piece instead of two. Never before had Candy considered this. But here now, with the doublewide wobbling and honestly looking like it was going to bust apart at the center seam like a pair of cheap blue jeans, she could only wonder at what a mistake it had all been. Should have stayed with a single. She didn't need all this square footage. She had gotten ahead of herself, started thinking things and believing things and handling things that were way too big for her. Doublewide. She wasn't raising a family. She wasn't married. She didn't even have a dog. This was too big for even her britches.

This glum, anxious milkshake of feelings made her pace back and forth, back and forth, pine trees to the lot and back to the pine trees, knocking her knuckles on the bed of her truck at each turn for good luck.

Meanwhile, Clint had wandered over to the site and walked carefully from guy to guy, keeping out of the way and exchanging what looked like jokes. After a couple of minutes, he would move on to the next guy and repeat the procedure, always smiling, sometimes laughing, always staying out of the way. Finally, he circled back to Candy and said it all looked good. These guys were old hands at this stuff. No newbies on the job. He turned to look at Candy, asked if she was good, and she said she was, which was, at that point, only a half lie, and then turned to leave.

"I appreciate it, Clint," she said. His name in her mouth sounded awkward. She spoke the words to his back.

He paused and turned back, waved a hand toward the teetering house. "Nothing to it. I sort of enjoyed it. I've learned a bunch tagging along with you on this ..." he paused for a word, "adventure," he finished.

"More like a roller coaster ride."

"Like I said. Adventure," he chuckled.

"I'm guessing you were one of those kids who loved the field trips to the amusement park," Candy added.

"Best day of my school year. I'm guessing maybe not for you?"

"Well, there were the Slurpees and the corn dogs," Candy said, venturing a laugh at herself.

"Always," he replied, then waved another goodbye from his truck as he maneuvered it carefully around the construction site and back out onto the road.

The place looked, well, it looked terrible. Like an orphan. Like two orphans clinging to each other and at any moment Candy expected to hear a great ripping, a tearing in two of this cast-off shack that no one else had wanted. Among the many wishes that were now running through her head, she wished mostly that she hadn't come.

A young, string-bean-thin kid with a cheap cap on and huge hands dangling down from the cuffs of torn flannel sleeves ambled over to her.

"You the new owner?"

"Yeah."

"Don't worry. It always looks right terrible at first. My auntie, she's a nurse, told me that's how newborns look too. All scrunched up and deformed-like. But after a couple days they start looking fat and adorable, like they do on TV. I assure you, Ma'am, this is going to rosy up real nice. Just you wait." And he smiled at her, right at her, and then he looked back at the doublewide while he rubbed his forehead with the heel of the hand holding onto his ragged cap.

When he turned to her once again, Candy couldn't keep herself from smiling back, staring right into the kind eyes of this young beanpole of a man. What was looking back at her was a whiskered, ruddy, but generous face with a smiling mouth from which kind and generous words had come. Maybe he had seen the misery on her face and then had come over to her and said something nice. Almost as nice as Clint showing up. Maybe nicer. These two nice things crowded up against one another inside this miserable morning of her life. It was hard to take it all in.

But then, instead of her usual eyes-down mumble of a reply—which Candy could practically trademark—she kept her head up and her eyes squarely focused on his, and smiled again and then said, loudly enough for both of them to hear over the winches, "Thanks. It's all a little scary."

And the young man replied, "Won't be for long. Ima get back to it, then. More we get done, better it's gonna look." He fake-tipped his tattered cap and then turned and left.

She stayed a few more minutes and thought she should stay longer. Like a grown-up. Like a homeowner. So, for about a half hour, Candy stood her ground and watched as lots of workmen scurried around and under the doublewide. It didn't look like they were making any progress, but the longer she watched the less it looked like something a tornado had plopped down from *The Wizard of Oz*.

No place like home? She finally climbed in her truck and left. On the way home, Randy called and said it had all gone well and had she taken a turn around the building to make sure she was satisfied? And she said no, she had not, and she would do so when it was fastened down to the ground.

"Won't be long now, Miss Candy, huh?" Randy nudged her.

"I'm driving, Randy, so I got to hang up." And she did. Right in the middle of him asking when he could expect the check from the bank. She pulled into the Palace parking lot, went around front, ordered up a deluxe slice, poured herself a lemonade from the dispenser, and then sat down at one of the window counter stools, dug into her pizza and slurped her drink. Another first.

She needed to mark the occasion. Celebrate. She stared out the window at the sparsely populated Main Street, looked up and down, making the usual inventory of the post office, the shuttered ice cream store, the gift shop now open only on weekends, and the Daily Grill. Despite the pizza, she felt a kind of clean emptiness, like a now empty spool of thread or a freshly lined garbage can. A moment of liquified calm ran through her as she remembered the beanpole kid's words, and now came to see how these five years and her working and saving and planning and waiting, how it had all given her life a shape and a route. Now it was melting out of her. The feeling was almost electric, impossible to catch and explain.

The pizza surprised her with its deliciousness. She had lived on top of the Palace for two years and never enjoyed this window seat with a slice and a cold drink. She texted Clint a thank you and then Evelyn, saying everything was going according to schedule, no mishaps, and then, in a final burst of confidence, texted Randy and said she would let him know as soon as she had the check in hand, which would not be before final inspection. She added:

i'm sure you know the drill, right? security, inspection,

sign-off, banks. got to make sure all is in order before the money changes hands.

Randy did not reply, but still, Candy felt just a little like Superwoman.

Nightmares

Candy continued to live in two worlds both of her own imagining, while her body conducted the business of the real world. One was the familiar fantasy world of comfort; in it, she was already moved in and the place furnished just as she had always wanted. In this screenplay, the doublewide was stuffed, no, not stuffed, but tastefully filled with places to tumble into after a shift at work. There would be puffy, new furniture and lots of pillows and plush throw rugs all in comforting shades of navy and taupe, maybe gray and chestnut, possibly an orangey something thrown in for accent. The walls would be filled up with cool-looking art Candy would have found in made-up resale stores stocked with great art for two bucks. Here there was to be no Target "HOME is where the heart is" nonsense. Because whatever her place would look like, it would not resemble an aisle in a Target store.

Unfortunately another world had also sprung up, uninvited. This new series of dreams came in black and white, and they didn't have a mind to obey Candy's wishes. They crept up on her like nightmares. In this world, which visited her while she struggled to fall asleep, the doublewide dangled from a crane with pieces dropping off of it onto Granddah's farmhouse, crushing the old place or lighting it on fire. In other versions of this dream where Candy had seemed to have lost her job as main screenwriter, she was already moved in but the heating didn't work; she was huddled in a corner on the floor, freezing; the windows were somehow shattering in the cold. In yet another one, Randy showed up and said her check had bounced and he ordered the guys to put bizarre gargantuan belts underneath the belly of her home and hoist it away. When Candy woke, sweaty, she would try to breathe herself back into calm, fighting her own embarrassment by the transparency of the dreams.

She had become so entrenched in the many nightmares about disasters which would surely become real and rob her of the dream that it actually came as no surprise when her phone rang at work. Unknown number. Disaster coming to call. She stepped out into the hall and answered it. Her teeth were clenched in terror at what news the caller might bring.

"Is this Candace Schein?"

"Speaking."

"My name's Howard," said a man with a gravelly voice who also mumbled his last name, which sounded long with a lot of syllables. Then Candy heard the words "I'm from" and then he muttered the name of the installation company hired by Edwards to take care of seating and placing and settling the doublewide; Candy still didn't know what the word for it was, and she was so overwhelmed by anxiety while moving like a zombie through her shifts at Glencrest, that now, when she really needed to listen, all she could hear in between the words was some static, faintly like that of the lake's waves crashing in on the shore.

"I'm sorry, I'm at work and didn't hear that last thing. Could you repeat it?"

"Yes, Ma'am. I am calling to tell you that your home is now ready for final inspection. Went without a hitch. You must have someone looking over you from above. In my experience it hardly ever goes this easy."

"How's that bum corner?"

"Solid, Ma'am. Like I said, we are hooked up, aproned, stairs built front and back, although you may be wanting to think about a deck in the next year or so. People tend to want 'em."

Candy started breathing again. "Thank you. Thank you so much. I've been a little worried."

"Figured as much. Didn't see you around the jobsite. That happens. People want to spare themselves the worry until it's over. Your cousin stopped by a couple times, though. He was keeping an eye on it for you."

"My cousin?"

"Well, that's who he said he was. Maybe a boyfriend?"

"Oh no, yeah, no, he's a cousin. Cousin Clint."

"Well, he was here a couple times. Poking around, but polite-like. Stayed out of the way."

"Yeah, he's in the trades, so I asked him."

"Well, like I said, you are ready for final inspection. Inspector's name is Meyer. I'll text you the number. Homeowner's gotta call to make the appointment. And you'll need to have a rep from Edwards there. If you like, I can stand in for Randy, who I believe was your sales rep."

"That would be great," Candy bubbled.

"'Course you'll have to go back to the office and sign final papers in order to get the keys."

"The keys. Right. Right." She remembered to ask Howard for his last name and told him she would be in touch with the date and time for the inspection. Then she managed to mutter about a dozen more thank yous until she could hear Howard chuckling on the other end of the phone. She rang off, pushed herself up off the wall and went to find Janelle, who was in the break room, cursing over a broken nail.

"It's done. It's ready. I have to go through a final inspection and then it's done. It's mine."

And Janelle hopped up and gave her a hug and said reassuring "I told you so" things that Candy couldn't hear. But she asked her friend to come see it with her after work, even if they couldn't get in. Candy just had to see it and she needed Janelle to see it with her. They picked up some rosé in cans first and in a burst of rebellion, popped them open while they were still driving. When they pulled onto the lot, it was dark already and so they pulled their hoods up and turned on their phones' flashlights and walked around the place. Her place. Candy's house. The skirting was hunter green as she had asked. Folks prefer the gray or the white, Randy had said, and Candy had said no, she would take the hunter green, and when Randy said it was a premium color, Candy had shrugged into the phone and said she was taking damaged goods off him and so she figured he could eat the difference. And he had.

They climbed the stairs and tried the door. It was locked and dark inside, so they shined their phone lights through the windows and saw the laminate flooring and the kitchen appliances unwrapped and the back door. And then Janelle started complaining about the cold and they went back to the truck, fired up the heat, and shone the headlights on the doublewide. Candy just sat there, sipping her rosé and staring at the darkened place tucked right up against the pines. Finally, she shook her head, rattling herself free from the dream.

"It's real. I didn't believe it could be real. And here it is."

"It most certainly is. Just waiting for your decorator's touch and the next mortgage payment," Janelle joked. "Once you get the keys, that is."

"On it," Candy replied. And she was.

She dropped Janelle back at Glencrest to pick up her car and went back to the Palace. She entered her place, which was about to no longer be hers. It looked like a bomb had been dropped on it. No, not really, that was just an expression. It looked like a person was in mid-move and couldn't finish one thing before jumping to another. Boxes were half packed, counters were crammed with items whose fates were still to be decided. There were take-out containers in the sink, not yet tossed because the trash was full and Candy had run out of trash bags. Her bed was unmade, and the laundry in a heap, unfolded.

Clearly, she thought as she sat down on the only remaining available spot in the apartment, the arm of her couch, it was time to get a move on. She pulled out her phone, left a message for Clint, and thanked him again, apologizing again for asking so much.

Right before she fell asleep, she heard her phone ping.

that's about 23, but i've lost count.

And Candy Schein, owner of the new doublewide at 32478 Lasso Road, otherwise known as County Road 654, smiled into the darkness, her heartbeat slowed at last.

Paperwork

Way back in September, before Randy had unleashed that thunderstorm of paper in her direction, he had asked Candy to sign a contract.

"Gotta lot of interest in this one," he said, lying through his teeth. "You'll want to secure it so it doesn't get away from you."

By that time, Candy had already read enough online to know she should not do this, and that she should hire a lawyer and pay them money and they would review things and argue with the seller, and on and on. Candy didn't have a lawyer, had no money for a lawyer, and so didn't hire a lawyer. Looking back, she realized this might've been the most courageous thing she had done, even braver than watching the doublewide be rolled off of the back of a truck and settled onto supports that looked like toothpicks.

She faced the paperwork alone on her days off, laptop propped on a pillow and papers propped on a couch arm. She read paragraphs out loud. She used a highlighter. She looked up words. She consulted legal aid websites. She made herself learn things about waivers and riders. She got distracted dreaming about SUP boarders riding waves. She read about liens and imagined the doublewide leaning into a bonfire of papers. She wondered about ADHD and then did a lap around the Dump and then sat down to face it all again. She asked no one for help because every single question echoed like stupid in her head. She scolded the voice inside that told her she couldn't read right. She pored over the sentences until they changed from terrifying to mystifying to partly cloudy. And slowly, bit by bit, she finished the paperwork it took to allow the concrete to be poured and utilities to be hooked up and the doublewide to be hers.

She vividly remembered the day she had returned to Randy's office and sat opposite his desk and signed the contract. He was impatient, but she was ready for that, prepped by the invisible online lawyers who shouted out in bold type: DON'T BE RUSHED. WATCH OUT FOR HIDDEN COSTS. AVOID THIS LANGUAGE: followed by all kinds of phrases that Candy could not make sense of, but had memorized enough to avoid like the deer frozen in her headlights at night.

It took more time than Randy said he had. Candy pushed back her school-days embarrassment about being the slowest kid to finish the test and made herself read every word, whether she understood it or not, while Randy reminded her how very busy he was, although no cars pulled into the Edwards lot and the phone on his desk did not ring. She had, and this had been her own idea, put the earnest money check out on the desk in full view. She pictured his knobby fingers reaching across the desk for it. But he behaved, waited until all of Candy's questions had been answered, all of the signature lines had been filled, and until Candy, who by then was sweating from every pore and trembling, handed the papers back to him, one by one.

"That about does it now, Miss Candy," Randy said, and she slid the check across the desk and he paper-clipped it onto the contract.

"That goes in a trust, right?" Candy asked, prepped again by her online legal training. "And I get it back if this all falls through?"

"Oh, it's all gonna be fine. You'll see," said Randy. And then his voice took on an insulting coo-like sound. "It all seems a little overwhelming, what with all this paper for the lawyers, but I've walked many nervous buyers through the process, and it all comes out ok. Everyone ends up happy."

Pause. "Trust me."

Candy stifled her response, half laugh, half sneer, and an almost uncontrollable urge to spit in his face. But he held what she wanted and he was minutes, seconds even, from handing it over to her. So, instead she watched Randy sign the same set of papers, while explaining he was authorized to do so, and they had the notary, blah, blah, blah. Then he ran the whole mess through a clanking, wheezing copy machine behind his desk, slipped her copies into an official looking envelope, and handed them across to her.

"You know the next steps, Miss Candy? The down payment, the mortgage papers, the closing costs and all? Your credit union got all that under control?" He still had that tone in his voice. Talking to her like she was a child, or a moron. There was a word for that, but she couldn't grab it.

"Yep," was all she said, and she rose out of the crummy seat in the crappy office to make her escape.

"Well, if you need anything, just holler. You have my card. Call anytime."

And Candy choked out a thank you and walked back out into the autumn warmth, elated, sick, nervous, sweating.

Now it was months and mountains of paper later, and she was waiting outside the doublewide for Howard for the final inspection. It was cold and dark, but the sky promised the sun would shine soon. The plywood steps leading up to the front door were slick with frozen puddles. The down payment had been delivered to Evelyn, who promptly furnished the mortgage papers listing a bunch of extra costs that, when Candy learned about them online, had nearly taken her breath away. But she was in way too deep to back out. She told herself over and over again: it would be money spent on the dream that had kept her heart full for years, and then the money would be gone and the home would be hers, and that was that.

It was now a December Wednesday, and whatever early morning work traffic there was on Lasso Road had come and gone. While waiting, Candy took inventory of the road sounds, wondering how loud they would be inside the doublewide.

Howard pulled in, ten minutes late. Randy hopped out of the passenger side. Candy's stomach dropped.

"Big day, hey, Miss Candy?" he said, while Howard immediately started to look around. His head swiveled like an owl.

"Yep."

"No cousin today, huh?" asked Randy. Candy turned away from the smirk to see a bright red SUV with a log on the door pull in, and a well-dressed man hopped out with a backpack.

"I think I know what I am looking for," Candy replied.

Sassy. She actually sounded a little bit sassy, but it was actually impatience. She turned to greet the new guy.

"Hello. Good morning. I'm Carl Meyer, Johnson Engineering." He looked around for the owner. "Candace?"

"That's me."

"Nice to meet you. I'm here to sign off on the final inspection, but as it's a new structure, this should be quick."

"Except for the dent."

"Except for ..." he paused, running his finger over the surface of an iPad encased in some kind of gladiator cover. He found what he was looking for.

"Ah. Yes. The dent. Let's go there first."

They walked first around the outside, Carl opening some trap door cut into the forest green skirting to access the underside, cajoling Candy to kneel beside him as he shone his flashlight onto struts and pipes, pointing out the work, seals, and reinforcements. She stayed quiet besides the occasional "uh huh, I see," because what was she going to say? "Hey, that looks a bit shoddy?" or "Are those struts treated lumber?" Really, after all this time and all those hours on the internet, it came down to faith. Blind faith and a five-year warranty. She suddenly missed Clint.

Howard asked her if she wanted to take photos. She attempted to squat low enough for a view and aim her camera but couldn't manage it. Howard saw her struggle. With Randy breathing down their craned necks, Howard said quietly, "I'll snap a few." And he did. And then Candy heard her phone ping a couple of times, and she thanked him with her eyes. He asked to pull up the photos and she concentrated as hard as she could while he explained what she was looking at. Another nice guy. What was the world coming to?

They moved inside. Carl pulled out a contraption that checked all of the outlets, and then a thermometer thingy to check water temperature. Candy flushed the toilet and turned all of the faucets on and off. She lingered on the formerly damaged corner and ran her hands up and down the walls, then stared at the ceiling. It had rained and sleeted a couple of times since the move and she saw no spots. Turning to Carl again, she asked, "Can you put in there, somewhere in that report, the part about the dent?"

"I assure you it's fine, plus you have a special rider in your contract addressing any issues with it." Randy sounded aggravated.

"Doesn't hurt to document," he replied. "Looks good, though."

They went outside again, their breath making clouds in the morning air. Candy ran her bare fingers over the seams of the repair job and stared at the corner, wishing for X-ray vision, some kind of insight that would reassure her. No luck.

"Guess it looks good enough," she finally said.

"I agree," said Howard.

"Sure is," chimed in Randy. "Tight as a drum, that corner."

They went back inside and Randy pulled out yet another pile of papers, explaining that her signature on these would release Edwards Homes, LLC, of any liability for damage on the structure with the exception of, and then Candy stopped listening. The tiny words on the page blurred. She had reached the end. She grabbed the pen out of Randy's hand, signed in the three places his bitten fingernail indicated, and held out her hand for the keys. But first, she had to shake his hand. She kept her gloves on.

"Here you go. Congratulations, Miss Schein, on your new home." And Randy plopped two sets of keys, attached to one Edwards crimson key fob shaped like a house, into her hand.

Candy thanked them all, reminding Carl to send her a copy of the inspection report. They all shook hands and the men drove off. Candy carefully climbed the icy steps and locked and unlocked the door, again and again and again. With each heavy clunk of the lock turning, some kind of weight lifted off her shoulders until she felt like she would float away.

Farewell to the Dump

For the final move, she had asked Vern if he could spare a driver during a slow time to help her haul down a couple of big items. There weren't many. The dresser was the biggest deal, and you could take the drawers out and then it wasn't so bad. Candy had been surprised to discover she didn't have a suitcase. Hadn't ever owned one. Her clothes had gone in black garbage bags. She was getting a new bed and a new couch and moving the dining room table and chairs and recliner from the farmhouse.

  She had already moved what felt like hundreds of bags and boxes, hundreds, she realized, because it turned out that she was a terrible packer. She had been lugging her belongings down from the Dump, loading the truck, driving to the stop sign, taking a right on 654, and pulling into the new double-wide driveway which she had made herself by just driving in and out a thousand times. She made runs before work, after work, until she started imagining those black bags and boxes were multiplying by themselves. Then there was the unloading at the other end: trip after trip after trip. She avoided taking a good look around her new home when she dropped all of that stuff off. She just carried the bags or boxes into the room where they belonged and then turned around and left, eyes averted. She didn't know what she was afraid of seeing. Or not seeing.

On the last day, she and Max, the Pizza Palace delivery driver, managed to get the dresser and the other big items down the stairs and into the back of the truck. He had been cheerful, but seemed nosy about her belongings and Candy found herself worrying about him checking out her stuff. What, exactly, did she have of value? A TV. Ten years old. A laptop. Five years old. Her grandmother's diamond studs: hidden inside a pair of socks in her purse. A KitchenAid stand mixer. And some crappy odds-and-ends furniture. That was about it. When they were finished she thanked Max and handed him a twenty for his fifteen minutes. She had asked Janelle to help her at the other end to unload this last truckload. They timed it on a day they had a free chunk of afternoon together and the kids were in school. She pulled out of the Palace parking lot for the last time, Vern waving to her, and her waving back out the window. She was feeling both a solid good riddance, and a soft spot, sentimental now that it was over. Vern had been a good landlord: the rent cheap, her privacy respected, the water hot. The Dump had served its purpose, she thought, as she took the county road slowly, keeping an eye on her belongings tilting around in the truck bed behind her.

The new place was about ten minutes out of town, straight down County Road 654, but this afternoon she swung first by Janelle's place, which was about ten miles out of town the other way, toward Traverse. Midday traffic was light and Janelle tumbled out the front door of her split-level home as soon as Candy honked. The twins' faces were in the window, checking out the truck.

"Hey, girl," said Janelle as she hopped up and in. She pointed at her boys' faces and then waved. "They think we are on some big adventure."

Candy waved too. "Well, it sort of is."

"Glad the ground's froze," Janelle commented as they pulled out of her drive. "I don't wanna be trudging mud into your new place."

"Don't worry," Candy replied. "I got cardboard laid down to protect the floors during all this coming and going. Bed and mattress and couch have already been delivered and those guys are some dirty."

She looked down at Janelle's hands folded in her lap. "Did you bring gloves?"

"As my ex likes to say, born ready," she replied, pulling rubberized garden gloves out of her jacket pocket.

They laughed easily together and fifteen minutes later pulled into Candy's lot. She let the truck come to a rest but neither made an immediate move to get out. There was a light dusting of snow which covered the frozen ground. Candy took in the gray blue, ok, Mystic Blue, of the doublewide, and the white of the trim, and thought for the millionth time, it seemed, that it was probably the color that had done it. Mystic Damn Blue. That particular shade had screamed "this is it. THIS IS YOUR HOME." And now it was. Apparently.

The skirt around the base, which covered up all of the ugly of the foundation and supporting bits, the dark green Candy had finagled into the deal, was so deep and dark that Graham would probably have loved it. Might love it still, if he ever came to visit. The day was bright and blue and cold. Inside the cab of the truck the heater blew hot air on the women's faces as they peered out the windshield at the house.

"Well, I got ninety minutes," Janelle finally said, shaking them both out of the dream of a new home that Candy had not yet entered, not really. When the furniture had been delivered she had kept her eyes on the men as they unwrapped her new treasures. She had pored over every corner, had run her hands all along the sides and back, the top and the cushions of the new navy velour couch. She had watched as they had assembled her dark-walnut finished bed frame and made sure the plastic on the new mattress and box spring had not gotten ripped in transit. One ding was her limit. The rest had to be perfect. Which might have been why, even with all those deliveries and even throughout the final inspection, Candy hadn't really taken it in. As a home. A place where she would sleep and make toast and watch night fall. Those visions hadn't appeared since that first day she and Clint had inspected it. How long ago had that been? Months. And months. Since then it had been bedecked and bejeweled and made shimmery in her imagination and now, right here with Janelle beside her, she was, for what felt like the first time, going to open the door and walk into home.

She flashed back to that bright, warm September day when she had first pulled onto Edwards's lot, having rehearsed dialogue in her head as if she were an actress in a movie, learning her lines. How the interior of the space had shouted out its brightness in her eyes, how the windows had charted a course for her line of sight, how the space had seemed too good to be true. How the floors had glowed with yellow light. Would they still?

She unlocked the door and came back to the truck. She and Janelle each grabbed a drawer and walked in. She flicked the middle light switch just inside the door. There were three switches and she had already learned which went where: closest: outdoor, middle: entry, furthest: living room.

"Bedroom's this way," she said, and walked into the bedroom, setting the drawer on the unmade bed.

"You sleeping here tonight?"

"Yeah, I have tomorrow off to unpack. Won't take me that long," Candy replied, and headed back out the door.

"Hold on, hold on, hold ON," Janelle said, grabbing her arm. "I want to get a good look-see." She took slow steps around the room, staying on the cardboard path, turning her head back and forth, taking it in in a way Candy had not. "Ooo, the light is beautiful in here." She gestured toward the window where the winter sun was slanting through and splashing onto the wall which was still primer white. Candy was carrying paint chips from the Home Depot around in her bag. She would eventually tape them up and make a decision. Once she actually believed the place was hers, that is. She squinted into the room Janelle was looking at.

Janelle was chatting about curtains, blinds, maybe. She was standing by the sunny window, warming herself in the morning light. The unmade bed was centered on the far wall and there was a window next to her side, and another double window looking south, which she could look out of from the bed. The view was of the back, just like in the living room. She turned full around. It was big, white, full of light. She exhaled. The nightmare of disaster, of committing to a place that would betray her, of daring to make a home for herself and having that dream crumble in the real light of a real day with a real person beside her, faded. She stifled a squeal of relief.

They went back out to the living room, where Janelle complimented her on the couch, which sat in the middle of an ocean of moving chaos. They unpacked the rest of the truck, which was hard, but Janelle was strong, and then Candy drove her home and picked up a BLT and fries from the Daily Grill and then came back. Home. To the doublewide. Sometime in the last couple of weeks she had dropped the Mystic. It sounded too much like a dream. The doublewide was real. She fetched the ketchup from her new fridge and sat on the floor and ate her first meal, leaning up against the couch and looking out the windows into the dark.

It was quiet. Really quiet. When she lived in the middle of town, Candy hadn't noticed the sounds of the village, but now she heard their absence. As the night darkened around her, she turned on more lights, noting where she would need a floor or side-table lamp. She hated overhead lighting, worked under it all day and all night. Hated it.

She had no urge to turn on the TV. She felt a need to keep listening and so she did, long after the last cold fry had been dipped and eaten. Finally, she roused herself in the quiet space that was now hers, and locked the front and back doors, front leading into the living room, back out of the kitchen. The kitchen was also too white, but the new appliances were gleaming and new, their power lights and clocks blue-lit. Candy opened cabinets and put away dishes. She paused with a plate or pot in her hands, deciding what would make sense where, and how to easily unload the dishwasher. She had a dishwasher! She set the coffee maker and the KitchenAid on the counter. Emptied bags and ripped tags off of dish drainers and towel racks and area rugs and new dish towels. The kitchen was put to order in no time and somehow, that made the place look like it belonged to her. The smell of new fabrics and textiles and metals and furniture filled up the rooms. She would need a candle.

It was exhausting and her bed was unmade and suddenly Candy couldn't face doing one more thing. She dug out her comforter and pillow and made herself a cocoon on the new couch which was deep and wide. She kept the porch light on, and then hunkered down into her pillow, and waited for sleep to come.

It was so quiet. So dark. No streetlight coming in the window, no wave noise. She was now five miles from the lake. When she had lived at the Dump, she had often fallen asleep listening to waves crash or ice breaking, the occasional car passing.

Could she do it? Could she live out here alone? The porch light shone indirectly onto the living room floor. Occasionally she heard twigs cracking. After some minutes of fear she decided it was deer. Probably. She hoped it was deer. The smell of her own linens mixed in with the smell of the new couch, the new floor. She was halfway through her next to-do list when sleep finally came.

Breaking It to Granddah

It was time for the reckoning. Candy wasn't exactly sure what that word meant but it sounded big enough to hold the size of the trouble in front of her. And that was to tell Granddah. The part she dreaded the most wasn't telling him about the double-wide. It was going to be the part about why she hadn't told him sooner. She had been banking on his failing memory, but he did grab hold of things once in a while. She couldn't quite get away with the "Oh, I told you this already, you must've forgotten," lies yet, but he was no longer up to holding onto a firm timeline either. Whatever shape his memory was in, the deception or delay or whatever it was made her feel sick, sometimes turning into a full-blown bout of nausea which sent her into the bathroom to regain her composure over the toilet bowl. Afterward, she munched on a Tums and put it off another day.

And then there had been Maeve and Clint, which would have been a nice distraction if it hadn't also made her sick to her stomach. They arrived at Glencrest on a Tuesday morning in Clint's truck, and just by glancing at the truck bed, she could tell they had brought too much. Maeve had scored a rare single room but there were end tables and footstools and three suitcases and a random black garbage bag. Candy found snippets of time to check in with them as they unpacked Maeve's belongings and attempted to make the room look more homey. Clint had even brought picture hooks, which weren't allowed, but he was able to set the nails without a hammer using some kind of crazy thumb action, and hung some things on the wall. On her final swing by, she had popped in.

"How's it going? It looks lovely, Miss Maeve. That tapestry is beautiful. Did you make it?"

Maeve's eyes were set on the floor in front of her. She wasn't speaking.

"She made that, back when I was a kid," Clint replied for her, trying unsuccessfully to lighten the mood. "Mom, here's Candy, coming to see how you're doing."

She looked up. "I want to go home. This was a bad idea."

Candy's heart broke a little, her own troubles now faded into a corner of things to do later.

"I'm not going to lie to you, Miss Maeve. This is hard. Maybe as hard as anything you've had to do before. But, it ..." and the clichés rolled into her head. Candy tried to choose the least awful one.

"Here's what I know. We are going to be able to manage your pain better, and help you to feel at home. Clint here is going to be able to come anytime he wants, and he won't be worrying so much about—"

And at that Maeve began to cry.

"Aw, Mom. Please don't," Clint whispered, and stooped down and took her balled-up fist in his big paw.

"You've been lonely. I know you've been lonely and trying

not to ask me to do stuff for you, but you need help now. It's ok to ask for help. To get help. We all need help, right?"

After a minute, she touched Clint's shoulder before leaving the overcrowded room and heading back out to try to care for all the other broken old hearts.

But now Maeve was settled and it was mid-December and Candy had also finished the move into her new place. The doublewide. Home. She was sleeping there. The heating worked. The fridge was so new it didn't even hum, but it dinged when she left the door open too long. She still worried about the former dent in the corner. At least once a day, she would head over to that corner and hold her hand over the repaired section, or where she guessed the repaired section might be, and feel for coolness seeping in. She would glance up and down, side to side, trying to see the damage. The former damage. She couldn't.

Her fairy tale was not quite fully furnished. There was only a single throw rug on the floor, but the new couch was a deep navy and just as plush and deep as she remembered it in the store. Her fridge was filled with her usual combination of healthy and unhealthy foods, and the new smell was starting to fade under her almost daily cooking, made into an adventure by the new appliances. It wasn't quite a home but it was moving in that direction and there was just a bit over a week until Christmas, and she was going to bring Granddah home for Christmas if she had to carry him up the stairs herself. First she had to carry the recliner. She remembered a dolly in the barn. That would do it.

As she did with most things, Candy had decided on a calculated approach for what she had come to call "the talk." She narrowed down a couple of windows of time when Granddah tended to be the most contented, which was usually right after a meal. He loved breakfast the most, it being the one hardest to screw up coming out of an institutional kitchen. So it would be after breakfast but before reading his papers, because in his old age, Granddah had started paying attention to the nation and the world, two places he had not claimed citizenship in back in the days when they lived together and he only read the county and Traverse papers. Now he ranted about school shootings and police shootings and gang shootings. The corrupt government, the dirty governors, the socialist mayors. He railed and railed and railed at the paper. When he got on a roll people had learned to scatter, since sometimes he would turn his temper on them. So no, it would have to be before he got his hands on the morning paper. Janelle had told her it was like a flu shot; no sense thinking about it. Just walk up there with your sleeves rolled up and take it.

She found him in the TV room in his favorite chair after a pancakes and sausage morning. Candy had a fifteen-minute break; she figured it was going to take about three. She could always circle back later after he had calmed down. If he needed to calm down. When she came in he was watching the morning shows, which made him almost as miserable as the papers.

"Morning, Granddah, mind if I turn this down for a minute?" Candy asked after she had already picked up the remote and punched the mute button. Even though she had started talking to the world, she still loved a mute button. She pulled another chair close and sat down. She pulled out her phone and brought up her pictures of the empty lot and then the slab and then the doublewide on supports and then the finished, skirted home. She put the phone face down on the table next to them.

"So, Granddah."

"So, Candace."

"So, Granddah, I have some big news."

"Oh, really?" his white eyebrows rose and Candy prayed he would not burst out with a question about her upcoming engagement or marriage.

"I don't know if you remember I had to move into town, because the farmhouse, your farmhouse, our farmhouse, needed a lot of repairs and I couldn't really afford them."

"You could have asked me for the money," he said, then his eyes slid away to the carpet, telling her that he was probably just now remembering that he didn't have the money.

"Well, truth is, I been saving up. Saving up for my own place."

"Well imagine that. Must pay you pretty good to be able to save, eh?"

"Not that well. I lived pretty cheap these last couple years. And you giving me your truck, well, I would still be two years away if I had had to buy a car."

"So where you at?"

"Pardon?"

"You got it? You got the money already?"

"I got it."

"Congratulations, Miss Candace," he said, and smiled. He was with her, and with it, fully zeroed in on what was happening. Thank God.

"You buy something?"

"I did."

"Where is it?"

"Out on 654, Lasso Road."

"Near us?"

"Not near us. Same place. Your place. Our place." Candy was having a hard time with her pronouns, her mind still muddled about who owned what. Which really, she shouldn't have been. It all pretty much belonged to her. The lot, the truck, the doublewide, the mailbox, all of it.

"Well, same address, new place." And here Candy reached for her phone and showed him the picture of the finished place first. She had made sure the shot included his truck parked in front and that the pine trees were visible. Granddah squinted and stared at the picture for what felt like forever.

"Do you want a close-up look, Granddah?"

"Yeah."

And she spread her two fingers across the screen, making the photo zoom, and then navigated the image so he got a close-up: left to right, top to bottom.

"Where'd you get that, that thing?"

"It's called a manufactured home and I got it from a place called Edwards Homes, just about twelve miles east of here."

"Does it have heat?"

"Yep."

"Hot water?"

"Uh hunh," Candy nodded, and then answered yes and no to his next dozen questions about fireplace, septic system, storm windows, dead bolts, insulation, porch, driveway. And, of course, who was going to plow. Candy was beginning to feel just a tiny bit of hope, like she had aced a final exam or something, and that she just might escape without a burn. And then, he kind of shook his head and peered closely at her.

"What'd you do with the old place? My place?" he asked, suddenly leaning back hard in his chair. It hadn't taken long. He had circled back to the farmhouse. His farmhouse. Not hers. Her grandfather was not confusing his pronouns.

"Well, Granddah ..."

"You let it go, didn't you? Let it get all run down once I left, and that was your inheritance, you know. I gave that to you, didn't I? You, and you only." He was turning red in the face.

"Yes, Granddah, I know, and I am so grateful, but I had two sets of contractors out there to have a look at it and both said it was going to be forty or fifty thousand to do the roof and the windows and make it weather-tight again."

"That's because you let it go. If you had let me stay there, I could have kept it in good repair and then you wouldn't have to ... say, what did you do with it? You didn't knock it down, did you?"

"No, Granddah, I closed it up real good, to try to keep it safe until I can get the money together to fix it up nice." And then Candy began spinning the tale. She had no intention of fixing up the farmhouse and besides, she was never going to have 50K to toss into a place she would never live in. But what she did have was a vivid imagination and so she spun him a yarn, this one rehearsed, of course.

"It's a beautiful old place and it's got great bones and all. Someday we'll have the money to fix it up, right? And if we can make that work, get the old place fixed up real nice, maybe we can sell this new one." She had practiced those pronouns, memorized them. It mattered that she give his home back to him, if only in a story she had made up.

"The color's nice, isn't it? Of the new place? It's called Mystic Blue and I got the skirting in dark green like the woods out back. See?"

"I don't care what color it is, it has no bones at all that I can see," Granddah said, poking his crooked finger in the direction of her phone.

The pronoun trick hadn't worked. She knew part of this was his own frustration. It hadn't been Candy who had let the farmhouse go. It had been him. The fact was he had become unable to lift or climb or manage the tools it took to keep a hundred-year-old place in one piece, so because she had done her homework, so to speak, she was prepared for him to hate the doublewide. But. Her break would end eventually, and with it this conversation, hopefully before it turned into an attack. Then she remembered she could make her break end. Anytime. That had been part of her plan. She felt a tiny surge of control. She wasn't a kid. She wasn't a loser LPN living on top of a pizza joint and eating generic ice cream out of the carton. Well, maybe still that last one. But still, she felt a kind of power that was new to her around her grandfather. If he didn't buy the fairy tale about the farmhouse, so be it. She continued.

"It comes with a five-year warranty, which should be enough time to figure out if I got robbed."

"Five years is nothing. Good bones is a hundred. Hundred fifty."

"I know, Granddah, but I need a home now, and I wanted ..." Here she paused, pulled up the rehearsed finale from her memory. "I wanted something of my own. That I did by myself. I don't really have a great career, I am not married, don't have kids, you see, and this is my baby, my marriage, my career."

And now Candy was finished, all her best lines delivered. She waited for her grandfather's demented whiplashing. She didn't expect him to understand. Her wildest expectation had been to leave this conversation in one piece. She got up. She could see the finish line.

"My break's over, Granddah. I hope you'll come spend Christmas with me this year. I have your recliner and a TV and I'm cutting a tree this weekend."

"Huh," he said. It was all too much, she knew, but she had to get this last bit out and then make a getaway. Apparently not fast enough. To her back as she was walking out of the room, he said, "Never should have let you have it."

Christmas Shopping

However lonely and only halfway satisfying the rest of Candy's childhood Christmases had been, the breakfast part always stood out. Her grandfather taught her how to go the whole nine yards: eggs, sausage, fried potatoes, cinnamon rolls, AND English muffins with butter and marmalade and an almost always ignored side of orange slices. A giant breakfast was a family tradition, one which Granddah would say "has to tide us over till dinner." And even when it was just the two of them, the plates were heaped high with all the goodies and not much was ever left over. On more than one of those early Christmases before Candy was old enough to cook, dinner ended up being leftover cinnamon rolls, extra sausage, and a side of store-bought Christmas cookies.

As soon as she had been able, which meant as soon as she was driving, Candy had taken over the grocery shopping for the holiday and loved every minute of it. The aisles were spruced up for the holidays, all of the yummy things were on sale, and she loved buying double everything and salting items away for lonely January Saturdays. Now, as she walked the aisles of the Shop 'n Save, she was reminded that she hadn't yet cleared springing Granddah for Christmas breakfast. She'd make sure she contacted the shift person assigned to him on Christmas morning and leave directions for him to be dressed warmly, have real shoes on, and left hungry and ready to go.

The part she had missed as a kid and then learned about later from TV movies and magazines was the whole stockings thing. Then it turned out Glencrest made a big deal out of stockings, their version of Secret Santa for the residents, and so Candy signed right on to that deal. In the six years Candy had been an LPN at the place, she grew to love the art of filling a stocking well. Part of the trick to it was the budget and Candy had always been handy with a budget. Twenty dollars was the limit Glencrest admin allotted for every resident, and the shopping was done voluntarily by staff. Of course, the admin had to fill in the gaps, as there were more residents than staff and some staff didn't get as much of a charge out of the whole deal as Candy did. They had other stockings to fill and other presents to buy for home and family, so every year Candy took on at least two residents, and her stockings became a bit of a sensation. She knew how to shop, made lists and started early, stockpiled little odds and ends she saw on sale at the register, clipped coupons, went out of her way to buy things her people could use or would love. She always spent more than $20, but she didn't care. The happiness she felt as she peeled off price tags and stuffed stockings was worth all kinds of dollars.

Since Granddah had moved to Glencrest, Candy had also claimed his, so today she was shopping for three: Granddah, Mr. Frierich, who still had devoted family visiting him on the regular, and Sandy. Miss Sandy was tough. She was pretty much all gone, confined to bed and some wordless universe, but

Candy persisted, and lingered in the health and beauty section of Rite Aid. She bought tiny mints and whatever lipstick was on sale and hand lotion and kids' Band-Aids. Miss Sandy had to have injections and her skin was so thin and fragile that she would bleed and bruise, and all Band-Aids were torture. Even so Candy thought, some Princess Elsa "no ouch" Band-Aids might be nice. And those super soft scarves you could wrap around the neck and feel like a kitty was snuggling up to you. Granddah was tough too. He was such a rough cuss, but he was her rough cuss. She had started a running list for him this year in the Notes app that came with her new phone. Whenever she noticed something he could use: toothpicks, Chapstick, a college football magazine, she put it on the list. When she bought an item, she would check the box thoughtfully provided by the app. The only thing better than a list were those checked boxes.

For his present this year, Candy had done something special. She thought of it when she returned to the farmhouse to lug the recliner out to the doublewide. Tucked into the seat cushion she had found a photo, a wedding photo, old and worn. She then searched the whole farmhouse for whatever photos might be left of their family in order to make a little album for him. Just one of those soft-cover dealios that usually held twenty-four pictures. She knew she wouldn't be able to collect twenty-four photos, and so she had scoured all of the dollar stores and the Rite Aids and the Staples stores until she found one with sixteen slots. Somehow she just couldn't face leaving photo slots empty. It would remind them both that people were missing.

Even after a thorough search, Candy had found only three photos, so she had driven around to the places that Granddah had lived his life in: the Elks, the VFW hall, the county commission pole barn, the backyard, the barn with its work table and tool rack. She took careful photos and had them printed. She was trying to make it a good Christmas. She owed him. This gift would be handmade and even though Granddah was hard to please, he could still muster enough manners to not sneer at a homemade photo album. And there was a hidden agenda as well: pictures were a good memory jog. People whose minds were going could be prompted about their history and their families by looking at photos, and Granddah was fast heading to that place where his memory went in and out. Soon enough it would be more out than in. Candy had seen it before; she knew what was coming.

The recent assessment she made in her head: he remembered the farmhouse, could still recognize the doublewide for the cheap piece of construction it was, and obsess over the snow plowing as every good northern Michigander did. But Graham's name came and went and Candy's grandma, his wife, Ellie had been her name, she was fading right away. Candy found three pictures with her in them. The one tucked down into the recliner of her grandparents on their wedding day, another one of them with the grandkids at some fair or another, and one of Ellie by the stove with an apron on. In it, she was smiling, up to her elbows in pots and pans and bowls, and Candy always wondered who had taken that photo and how it had ended up in a frame on top of the sideboard. She hoped it had been Granddah.

This year, Granddah's stocking contained a new pair of wool socks, gray with red stripes around the top like he liked them. And some aftershave, even though he now needed help with shaving. A can of Stroh's. Pistachios. And then the usual travel packs of tissues, nuts and chocolate bars, Tic Tacs, and a couple of sports magazines. Even though she didn't want to admit it, Glencrest had kind of formalized Christmas in a way that made her feel like she had a place to celebrate. And give. And receive. Every year, management solicited donations from families and, in a burst of uncharacteristic generosity, matched them and doled the bonus checks out to staff. Every single one of those had gone straight into saving for the doublewide. This year it would go in the washer-dryer fund.

Back in her childhood at the farmhouse, Christmas Eve had been the hardest part of the whole holiday. As a kid, Candy developed a couple of tricks to getting through it, mostly having to do with TV. Granddah's habit was to stop off at the VFW and drink with all the other single or widowed old guys, or even some who were just escaping from too many family members or screaming grandkids. On those nights, Candy would turn on the tree and porch light and then go up to her room and find a Christmas movie to watch while waiting for him to come home. When she heard his truck roll up the driveway, she would wait in her room until he was in the house so it wouldn't look like she had been waiting for him. And then, only after he had blown in the front door, did she open hers and come down the stairs.

Granddah would have stumbled in with store-wrapped gift bags and grocery sacks, and put the first one under the tree next to Candy's carefully wrapped presents and heave the others onto the kitchen table. Breakfast. Sometimes a ham and some canned yams if he had remembered dinner too. It was Candy's job to put the food away and then they would dig into a box of Mint Milanos together in front of the TV. Granddah would fall asleep and from that first Christmas without Graham, and ever since, she had been the one to cover the old man up with a blanket and turn the volume on the TV down and then tiptoe up the stairs to finish watching her favorite Christmas movie, or really, any Christmas movie that was on. She would have already watched Charlie Brown and the Grinch earlier while waiting for Granddah, but then the more adult ones came on. Sometimes *Love Actually,* sometimes an old one with Jimmy Stewart or the one about St. Louis. She admitted she liked the old ones with the singing and the dancing. Most of the others were silly bad-guy capers or love stories. Christmas Eve was not a time for love stories, in Candy's opinion. They left you lonely, which was why as she grew older she had come to appreciate *Love Actually.* Because it was about loneliness, and even super gorgeous movie stars got lonely.

The next morning, Granddah was always up first, slurping coffee and making breakfast. After their meal, they would open presents. She remembered Granddah as kind in those times. So kind in fact, that Candy recalled how sometimes he would catch himself, then get up and go grumbling into the kitchen to pretend to figure out what they were going to do for dinner.

If he had remembered about dinner the night before, they would have ham and some sides and a pie. If he hadn't or if they had been out of hams at the store, which Candy never believed, there would be lasagna, because by the time Candy had hit junior high she had learned how to make a killer lasagna, and always asked Granddah to keep the ingredients on hand. He never complained; he loved his granddaughter's lasagna.

As for the aftermath, because the scale was small, the post-holiday letdown wasn't too bad. Really, it was the Christmas Eves that were killer. Which was why Candy always volunteered to work.

Christmas Eve

Candy loved working the second shift on Christmas Eve. Four to midnight. For one, it kept her busy. And that was when the staff presented the stockings to the residents. In the morning, after coffee and before her shift, she settled down on the floor by her tree which stood in front of the living room window of the doublewide, just like she had pictured it. She gathered her wrapping paper, her ribbon, her tape. This was a tradition that Candy had built on her own. Playing Santa to herself. From the time she first moved out of the farmhouse, she made a wish list for herself for Christmas and then went out and bought herself presents from it. And to make it feel like a holiday, and this was the most embarrassing part, the part she wouldn't ever reveal to anyone, she wrapped each of them. Carefully. With hand-tied ribbon bows. And put them under the tree, decorated with ornaments and lights and baby candy canes.

During her years at the Pizza Palace it had been a little fake tree she resurrected from the Goodwill, but this year, back on the land, she went out one sunny, cold morning and found a little sapling and cut it down herself with one of Granddah's old hand saws. She had saved her garlands and her decorations.

Her tradition had always been to decorate it on the twenty-third, which was her brother's birthday, but this year she was so tickled with her mad forestry skills that she did the trimming early. On the solstice. The tree, shorter than her, even, reminded her of Charlie Brown's Christmas tree, only not as pathetic. She propped it up in a stand that held water; the needles hadn't started falling off. Yet.

She texted Graham a few photos of the doublewide after she had moved in.

> you did what?
>> i bought a doublewide. moved it onto the land. like the blue?

A long pause. Candy imagined Graham looking at the pictures again.

> how?
>> with my savings.
> by yourself?
>> pretty much.
> what did granddah say?
>> you know, not happy.
> i bet.

And then more silence and then her phone dinged again.

> wow. I am proud of you. little candy. can I ask you why you didn't just buy a place in town?
>> because I wanted to be here. on the land. I wanted to do this on my own. and live here on my own.

He had gone on to type: **oh. i get it.** Then he added that all was well, he was spending the holiday working extra shifts and hanging with his girlfriend. And that he was taking a lot of pictures. A couple of days later he texted again to tell her he had put something in the mail for her. Graham had never put anything in the mail for her before. And a few days after that, the FedEx truck pulled into her drive and dropped off a big flat package on her front porch that could only be a picture of some sort. It was now under the tree. She hadn't taken it out of the purple and orange FedEx box in case Graham hadn't wrapped it.

Usually Candy would wake up on Christmas morning and open her presents after she made herself breakfast. But this year, Granddah was coming to her place and she couldn't open presents from her own self in front of anyone else, so she decided she would do it tonight when she got off of work.

She arrived at Glencrest early because she had presents for Janelle's kids and wanted to be sure she could make the handoff. Janelle usually booked pretty quickly after her shifts. Candy asked her every year what to get her kids and then went out and bought some little things that hopefully they would love. The girl, Christine, was easy. This year she wanted new UGGs, so Candy slipped some cash into a card. The twins were always impossible. All they wanted these days were expensive electronics so she picked up gift cards to help them buy whatever it was they were wishing on. Janelle was always so appreciative and Candy told her, as she did every year, that Christmas was for kids. She rushed from the parking lot straight into the staff room to catch her friend—her friend, she caught her mind using the word—before Janelle flew off to do her many pre-Christmas Eve errands.

She handed Candy a gift. Long, flat. Janelle wasn't big on surprises. Or wrapping.

"It's a calendar. I want you to put it on that wall next to the bathroom so you can see it all the time and write yourself little reminders. I also put my birthday in there. I want diamonds and champagne, just so you know."

They laughed and thanked each other some more. When they exchanged a hug, Candy got poked by the many ornaments Janelle had pinned on herself.

"Do you know who else is on tonight? I forgot to look when I came in."

"Marcos, Billie Jean, Cindy."

"No Miss Vicky Scrooge?"

"Lucky for you. She was on with me today. Keep it down, I think she's still around. Here," she said, handing Candy a stocking, "this is for Bernard, the grouch."

"I'll deliver it with your love."

The staff delivered the stockings on Christmas Eve for two reasons: first, it didn't get in the way of family visits if there were any, and there were almost no family visits on Christmas Eve. And secondly, and Candy knew this was true even though no one said it out loud, it was good PR. Families showed up on Christmas Day and their loved ones had new little goodies on their side tables or around their necks. Or on their feet.

The evening shift walked or followed or pushed the residents to their holiday meal. The tabletop centerpieces had been switched out from leaves and gourds to snowflakes and speckled plastic pine boughs. They used to have plastic candy canes but the residents would try to eat them and so they were tossed.

There were the usual ham and green beans and mashed potatoes and cornbread. Cornbread was a disaster of crumbs. The residents loved it but they also loved to try to butter it, and all manner of crumb hell would break loose. Then the staff walked and pushed and prodded the residents into the largest TV room and brought in extra chairs and wheeled in all of the stockings with name tags on them. Candy and Marcos distributed them one at a time because unpacking a stocking could be tricky and the residents often needed help. Many of them were tickled, and others watched passively as the staff oohed and aahed when they revealed some little gift the seniors could make no sense of.

Miss Maeve was missing because Clint had come by earlier to take her to church. Of course. The dutiful son. The poor thing had been miserable, first holidays being some sort of salt in the wound of breaking up a home. Candy had taken to looking in on her several times a shift, regardless of where she was assigned, trying her best to cheer her up, but Maeve just continued to look around her new room in distress, no doubt wondering what had happened to her house, her kitchen, her china cabinet, her life. Candy was heartsick thinking of this woman losing the home she had spent her life building. But, what had also disappeared was her arthritis pain, and so although Miss Maeve rested easier, the lines of pain on her face smoothing out, it was clear her mind had not yet let go of home, if it ever would.

Granddah, despite his grouchiness, loved his stocking. Candy had scored a series of bull's-eyes, especially with the socks and the NCAA football magazine. He chomped on his pistachios as fast as Candy could shell them.

"Are you taking me home?" he asked in between nuts.

"Tomorrow. For Christmas. We're going to have a big breakfast and some gifts and then watch the game and all."

"Where's your place again?"

"Same old place, Granddah. Your place. Only a new house. It's very warm and I got your recliner and chips and onion dip. My cable is real good too. You probably have a choice of what to watch."

Her grandfather chewed, picked nut pieces out of his teeth with a gnarled finger. Candy could practically hear the rusty gears turning. Finally, he said, "Want to see the Lions play."

"We'll make it happen, Granddah, I promise."

After the stockings were folded up and put back in the bin for next year and the residents had been tucked into bed with their gifts displayed all around them for the family to take note of, Candy made her way through the quiet halls. She ran into Marcos emptying garbage.

"That's not your job, Mister. That's what you went to school for, so you wouldn't have to empty garbage."

"My mom taught me to do what needs doing. The older I get the righter she is."

The sight made Candy angry. Marcos had worked so hard to get past dirty dishes and drippy garbage bags. He deserved better. He deserved to expect better. She leaned into him for a side hug, her arm reaching up and around his broad shoulders and she rested her head on his muscled arm. She pushed the anger down and let the sadness turn sweet.

She said, "Ok, Marcos. Merry Christmas. You're one of my favorite people to work with. Don't let the assholes get you down," and then squeezed his arm once more before breaking the hug.

Marcos looked down at her, surprised. Candy had surprised herself too. Had she never talked like this before? Been friendly to Marcos? She also realized she had never hugged him before. Now, he cocked his head at her and smiled.

"Why, thank you, Miss C," he said, "you have yourself a good holiday too. Coming back tomorrow?"

"Only to pick the old man up and bring him back to my new place."

"New place?"

"Yeah, I have a new place. A home. Moved in two weeks ago."

"Well, aren't you all grown up," he chuckled.

"Yeah, mortgage payment and utility bills. The whole nine yards."

"Your grandpa must be pretty proud of his granddaughter."

"Can't really tell," Candy said, and then paused. "But actually I'm sort of proud. I had to save for four years. And talk to all kinds of scary dudes who did septic and electric and permits and such."

Marcos laughed, "Scary dudes?"

"Ok, not scary, but I am not really out there in the building trades world that much. So it was kind of a new thing for me."

"Well, I AM proud. And you should be. It's gonna be years before I can move into my own place. I mean a place I own. If ever. The school loans are killing me." He shook his head.

"Worth it though, right?" Candy replied, remembering the day she had talked to Marcos in the kitchen back when he was a dishwasher. Told him it was doable. Told him about the salary and the benefits which were nothing great but much better than kitchen staff. And had brought him a catalog from the college. She had done that. And then, she didn't know if it was the Christmas spirit or what, but she now reminded herself with a kind of fuzzy feeling that she had friends. Plural. She had Janelle, and Clint and Marcos, and even Miss Maeve counted now. There were people who knew her, who called her by her name, who asked after her day. And who she talked back to now, more than she remembered ever having done.

Marcos was working a double. He'd be here all night until eight. He promised to dress Granddah up good and warm and make sure he didn't eat the crap Glencrest breakfast.

"I'm gonna put on the ritz for old Granddah."

"The breakfast ritz, huh?"

"Yeah, I just love a good fourteen-part breakfast." Candy laughed. She loved joking about food with other big people. Marcos was big people. They smiled at each other, exchanged another hug, a real one this time, and Candy left, crossing the cold, dark asphalt to her truck.

The best part of working second shift on a Christmas Eve, besides the stockings of course, was driving home through the cold, sleeping town, taking in the blinking holiday lights that many families didn't turn off on Christmas Eve. If they had little kids, it was to light Santa's way. If they had older ones, it was to light theirs, as they came home from celebrating with their friends. There were garlands and Santas and three or four crèches with baby Jesus finally put in his cradle.

She passed through town and the surrounding neighborhood slowly, soaking up the late holiday night, but saw no sign of any revelers on the roads. The dark night was electric with something, as it always was on this night. Candy took in the monster snow banks on the sides of the roads and the smaller ones piled beside walks and driveways. She slowed the truck in the late night to sneak a peek through lit windows; some people were still up. Candy imagined parents assembling toys for their kids, or maybe enjoying some hot drink or another with each other. From the truck there was no view of the night sky, but Candy would get that when she got home. The thought made her warm as she rolled up to the familiar stop sign, hung a left, and headed out 654. Now it was just her and the truck and its headlights on the dark road cutting through the forest, lit only occasionally by a streetlight at a crossroads. Candy flipped on her brights and forced herself to pay attention to the shoulders. Deer were everywhere.

Her doublewide was lit from within and the porch light was on. Candy's entire security system up till now was to leave the lights on and watch the house windows from the truck for about five minutes when she got home. This was silly of course, but it made her feel as if she had done something. Like it or not, Candy was coming to accept that living alone out here was different. She didn't quite feel safe enough. Granddah's farmhouse was only a black, half-hidden shadow, and there was no Palace downstairs. Surely she would hear a car pull up. And no fool would be wandering around here in twenty-degree weather looking for a big haul out of a mobile home, she told herself. Candy knew people owned guns for just this reason, but Granddah taught her early and often that guns were for hunting animals. And only then if you were going to eat them.

As soon as she was inside, the scary outdoors evaporated and Candy descended on her presents. She opened them recklessly, tearing paper and flinging ribbon about. She shook out her new sweater, pulled on the fleece-lined mittens, and admired a new cupcake tin. Even though there was no surprise, it didn't lessen the giddy excitement of opening presents. Unwrapped now, she placed each of them back under the tree as she did every year, so they could maintain their gift status for a day longer.

Then she wrestled the FedEx packaging off of Graham's gift. She had been right; it wasn't gift wrapped. It was bundled in bubble pack. Out of the many layers of plastic came a photo, of course, framed. Instead of his usual, almost always entirely black, forest landscapes, this was a picture taken at the lakeshore during the day. She had a hard time imagining Graham taking pictures in daylight. In one of the few conversations she and her brother had ever had about photography, his photography, he had said he was interested in shadows, and in the way the more you looked at something, the more things came to light. The more you really saw.

"It's your eyes getting used to the dark. But not in the real world, in the picture. My pictures make you look, really look. No one ever really looks. I want people to really see things. Hunt for them and see them."

"Hmm," Candy had replied, the little sister not wanting to offend her big brother, but thinking to herself, no one stands in front of a black picture for long enough to let their eyes adjust to see something besides the dark. But, at the same time, this had also been more words than Graham had probably said to her combined in the two years prior and so she had taken it in, the explanation, as a kind of gift.

The things in this picture were all visible. You didn't have to stand there for five minutes letting your eyes adjust to the black. It was a photograph of rocks, or pebbles, she couldn't tell which, and the stones were wet, glistening, a thousand different colors and shapes but all of them round and soft and beaten into beautifulness by the pounding of the lake over thousands of years. Graham had taken the picture from above, it looked like, but there was no sign of any human, no shadow, no footprint. Just those beautiful stones all wet and nestled into each other on top of the sand, like a wave had just washed over them.

The photo was in color. And inside a frame. A nice one. Gray to match some of the stones. Her brother had done this for her. He knew, or had remembered, how much his sister loved the lakeshore. Loved lakes and rocks and color. She cried some, sitting in front of the tree with the photo in her lap, then wiped her nose with the back of her hand.

There was no card. When she had recovered, she set the photo down in front of her tree, snapped a picture, and sent it to Graham.

it's beautiful. thank you.

No response. He was probably out there in the woods taking pictures of night shadows. But he had sent her daylight.

Home for the Holidays

Candy slept in, or tried to, but the sun, when it finally topped the pines out back, was harsh and bright and streamed into her room and woke her. She needed curtains. Although Candy loved Christmas she did not love Christmas clothes. She had never owned an ugly sweater, or a hair band with antlers or candy canes bobbing around, nor did she ever wear striped red and green pajama pants. No, in Candy's world, Christmas was about Stockings and Trees and Breakfast. And Snow. She so loved the snow on the trees. She loved snow, period. She loved winter and the couch lounging which seemed like a sin in the summer. She loved hot stews and soups and baking. She didn't even mind the dark, although last night, coming home had made her feel weird. What should she do? More lights? An alarm system? Would the alarm people laugh her out of the store once they saw what she was trying to protect?

She hurried to dress, then went to open the back door and let the cold air blast her skin. Her coffee cup sent up clouds of steam. She shook her curls and listened. Birds were cheeping and chirping and calling out to one another, squirrels clicking and cracking nuts or working over pine cones. When she had lived over the Palace she could almost always hear the lake. She would listen as it slowly froze over in the winter, first, waves as always, then, as winter set in, a weird slushing, sweeping sound, then by late January, a weird silence with occasional great cracks when the ice broke up or got moved around by winds or storms or brief thaws. She had learned of the lake's annual transformation from water to ice by listening from the top step of the Dump's back stairs, where she had gone through this same morning ritual: getting an extra shot of wake-up from the air. Listening to the world. The wake-up view at the Dump had been the parking lot: people coming and going on Main Street which she could hear but not see. The dumpster. Vern's car. The delivery truck. Here, it was trees and the sky and deer rattling the snow out of the pines, and crows and jays squawking. Candy ran her warmed hands through her tangled curls and then retreated back inside to begin the holiday. Her holiday.

Before leaving to get Granddah, she took her breakfast ingredients out of the fridge, gave a last look around the doublewide to see that all was as she wanted, planned, and dreamed, and then climbed into the truck and barreled her way to Glencrest. Empty streets again. She wanted to steal her grandfather away before the day got going and he got his mind set into the Glencrest routine, but halfway to Granddah's room she looked up and saw Clint slumped against the wall outside his mother's. He was wearing a stupid Santa cap and an ugly Christmas sweater. It had things sewn on it; ornaments, it looked like. Why did people do this to themselves? He saw her and raised up from his slump. Then he swiveled and came to a full stand right in front of her. His eyes were filled with tears. If it had been a dark alley, Candy would have thought she had been cornered. He was blocking her way.

"I don't know how to do this," he began, pathetically.

"You're doing fine." Candy was trying to be patient and kind, because Jesus, she scolded herself, on this day of all days, you should be patient and kind. But Candy wasn't feeling patient and kind; her movie was on play and he had hit the pause button. She wanted the old Clint back, the one with the tool belt and the answers. This one, the one who had become a real person, attached to an aging mother with tears in his eyes and a look on his face like he couldn't find his way home, this one she wanted to delete.

Clint was beginning to reminisce about his Christmases as a kid and how his mom made the place hum with sweet things and love. He sniffled and snorted through descriptions of how she had made all of the kids clean themselves up and go to church on Christmas Eve and then they came home and got to open one present. They had homemade cinnamon rolls and hot chocolate for breakfast. Then, suddenly, he switched gears, wiped his nose on his green sleeve, and started talking about how he didn't ever believe in God but loved the crèche his mom would set up on the mantel, and after her fingers couldn't manage the pieces anymore he would set it up every year for her on the sideboard. This year it was still in its box. He didn't know what to do with it.

"How big is it?" Candy asked, impatient. She sounded like her grandfather.

"Is what?" Clint asked, and she saw that he had been talking to himself. Maybe his eyes hadn't even seen her, being so caught up in his own fairy tales. She could relate.

"Small enough to fit on the mantle, or the buffet, like, nothing big or fancy. There's no barn or sheltering structure or anything. Just the people and the manger and the animals and the baby."

Candy thought about the words "sheltering structure." Then she told him to bring it to Glencrest. This will give him a task, an errand to run, she thought.

"Isn't it too late?" Clint had begun to compose himself, but he was still sniffling and wiping his nose on his sleeve. Candy reached around and found him a tissue. She thought about the word "caregiving." She wondered if these pauses were inside her head and whether or not the people around her could detect them, and she also wondered how long she had been wondering about whether other people detected things about her. Her mind reentered the hallway and she picked up the thread of the conversation. She tried again.

"Well, time can get weird around here, not for your mom, but for other residents. They'll ooh and aah and we'll make sure we take it down by New Year's so they're not asking for candy canes in March." She sounded now like she had found her kinder self again; no more echoes of Granddah. She attempted a smile. Clint was looking at her face and saw the smile and smiled back. He agreed to the crèche plan. It would give him something to do. Candy asked about his family.

"Coming up this afternoon. You know, they got their own kids and their own presents to open."

"You get left off the list?"

"Hell no. I'm the single uncle. I'm on everybody's guest list every year. More presents, an extra dish washer. Someone who can put together the toys. Nah, I just told 'em to come up in the afternoon. We have to figure out what to do with the house and I don't want to leave Ma alone, this being her first go around not at home, you know?"

"Oh, I know. I do know," Candy said. She did indeed remember the first year, Granddah kicking and screaming and her not able to get him over to her place because of the stairs and so they had gone out for pie and coffee at a place in Traverse out by the mall. Talk about depressing. She had handed him a present over the table and he had put it aside and left it wrapped. It had been dark and depressing that first Christmas. They went to a movie the next year. And then pie and coffee. And then they could talk about something. And she gave him a present every year, and every year he said he hadn't had a chance to get out. Candy would wrap up a hat or some magazine. It got harder every year. He didn't wear out winter clothes and he didn't go outside and he didn't fix things or have a tool shed anymore. He mostly seemed content enough to eat pie and drink endless cups of coffee without being scolded by a nurse.

Candy thought again about the word "caregiver" and the word "family." Then the word "blessing," which turned into "compassion." Then, all kinds of words were ricocheting around inside of her head, while Clint slumped again in front of her. She felt as if she were having an out-of-body experience. Then they were both brought back to the present by the sound of a toilet flushing behind Clint.

"Ima go back in and set a while," he said. He sounded one hundred years old.

Off the hook, Candy hurried to find her grandfather, fully dressed, with his winter clothes set out on the bed. He looked hungry.

"About time," he grumbled.

"Merry Christmas, Granddah. I'm going to take you back to my place and we're going to have a great big Christmas breakfast. How's that sound?"

"Just as long as I get fed. I'm hungry. Been smelling the sausages up and down the hallway for an hour now."

"I know. But I got homemade. Sausages from the Fulton Market and eggs from Lookout Farm and homemade cinnamon rolls, and I chopped the potatoes myself."

Candy and Granddah ran into Marcos in the parking lot. He looked tired but was smiling. He was headed out toward family, too.

"Actually, we do scrambled eggs with chorizo and onions and we have papas and grilled grapefruit. And my mother bakes. Oowee. Does she bake. I'm going to be in a food coma just about an hour from now. Merry Christmas, Mr. Schein."

"Yeah, Merry Christmas," Granddah replied. Then he seemed to realize that he'd been sprung from Glencrest for the day. He unfolded himself from his walker slouch and looked like he might grow wings. He waved and smiled at Marcos with more holiday cheer. "Best wishes to your family," he added. Candy's mouth practically dropped open.

Back at the doublewide, she had been careful to shovel and sand the pathway up to the front door. There were only three steps but she had made the installers reinforce the railing because she knew she wouldn't be able to handle the walker and her grandfather at the same time. Halfway from the truck to the stairs, Granddah stopped to take in the doublewide. Candy loved the way the mystic blue looked against the sky; gray or blue, it fit either way. And the green apron against the snow was just as she pictured it. The line made between dark green and white was crisp and fresh.

He said, "Looks warm enough," and then, "siding seems snug." Then he continued to the stairs.

Candy followed behind him, her arms open wide to catch him if he stumbled. She had a moment of terror. She wouldn't be able to catch him if he fell. She watched as he concentrated on pulling himself up one step at a time. They were going to need a ramp.

Inside, together, they managed his outer layers and then she tucked him into his recliner, spread a napkin over his lap, and fed him her cinnamon rolls and coffee. His chair faced the back window and the trees and the sky. Candy watched from the kitchen as her grandfather settled back into his old chair. He had a view of that familiar grove of pines. At least she hoped it was familiar. He hadn't yet asked to turn on the TV, which had to mean he liked the view. Last night's wind had blown the top layer of snow frosting off the needles, but the backyard was still white, with clean, mostly untrampled snow. On some of her first nights there, Candy had bundled up and ventured out to stare up at the slivered or quartered moon. She had wandered out past the reach of the back-porch light and turned around and looked back at her home, its windows filled with light, its true identity as a formerly dented mobile home on concrete blocks concealed by the night. In the darkness with its lit windows and layer of snow, it could have passed as a cozy cottage. A real one.

Breakfast. Nap. Presents. He didn't get her one. This time his excuse was anchored to the real world.

"I been locked up. They won't let me out."

"Granddah, you got me a present, although you may not know it."

"And what is that?"

"This place. The land that this place sits on. You may not remember but you gave that to me. Way back last year, I came and asked you to sign papers for me to become a co-owner of this land. And you did. And that is how I was able to buy my own house and bring it here and set it up and now here we are. Heat, water, a nice view, and good cable. That's because you signed a contract that says we now own this land together. Candace and Albert Schein." This was not entirely true. She was describing the power of attorney day with the lawyer, but that had been a miserable one and so she had revised it, cast him in the role of generous grandpa.

Despite this, Granddah's face looked as if he had lost the thread, and so had Candy. But she hadn't felt like herself for weeks now it seemed, what with her having woken up in a world that was now hers. One hundred percent hers. It felt like she had landed on the moon and it was impossible to explain, even to herself. And so this strange new Candy bent down, kissed her cranky grandfather on the top of his head and said thank you into his sparse white hair. She lingered there for a second waiting for the rejection or the swatted hand or the shrug. She was waiting but she was not holding her breath and it left her and warmed his head. Finally he said, "Well, I don't remember it, but I'm glad I did it. That's a hell of a nice view right out onto the pines and the sky."

"I know, right? I can see the moonrise and the Milky Way sometimes."

Then they sat there, quietly. She had checked the schedule

and knew the Lions game had already started but she wanted to sit in this place, her place, with her family and the tree lit up and the dishes soaking in the sink and the sun way low in the sky illuminating parts of the snow, for just a minute more.

And what she felt, in that exact moment, in that real place, with her hand on her grandfather's arm and both of them admiring the afternoon from inside the doublewide, was that she'd arrived after a long trip on a slow train.

She was home.

The Magi

Candy and her grandfather had both fallen asleep in the dark afternoon with the Lions losing in the background when her phone rang. She thought immediately of Graham. She had been dreaming about the pebbles in the photo. She still didn't know where to hang his picture.

It was Janelle.

"Merry Christmas, Miss Candace. Are you home and receiving visitors this afternoon?"

"Merry Christmas to you. Granddah and I are here just soaking up the afternoon rays and listening to the Lions lose."

"They haven't lost yet," Granddah snorted from his chair.

"He sounds chipper. You must've fed him up good."

"Oh yeah. We ate real good. There's even leftovers. How's your day going?"

"Crazy. But good." Janelle sounded happy as she rattled on about food and gifts and the mess that was now her living room and her ex's sudden appearance with armloads of presents and another plea for getting back together. This Janelle dismissed with a snort, not unlike Granddah's, and went back to complaining about her kids with a laugh in her voice. Janelle's idea of heaven was to go home to them and start hollering about the mess they had made. "My kids wanted to thank you for their gifts. You going to be there for a while?"

"I'm going to head out in a bit to take Granddah back. I think I want to get him down my stairs before it gets dark and all."

"Text me when you're on your way home."

"Sounds mysterious."

"Don't get too excited."

"Kids loved their presents." Janelle added, "You are too nice to remember them every year."

Neither Candy nor Janelle could ever afford the things Janelle's kids really wanted: new phones, games, expensive shoes, fancy boots. But the gift cards Candy bought them every year seemed to help. Although this was the first year she was getting an in-person thank you. She was beginning to feel like an auntie.

She knew Glencrest dinner was at five. She wanted so badly to keep Granddah here, knew how he hated the place, but she couldn't risk moving him by herself in the dark. It was too cold; ice patches were hidden everywhere. As she backed down the stairs in front of him, she couldn't decide which was worse: up or down. Again: ramp needed. And another railing. And maybe pave the driveway? Thoughts spiraled as she heaved Granddah up into the truck and lifted his weakened legs into the footwell. They were right in front of him, his legs, that is, and he was staring at them, but he couldn't lift them by himself. He had to watch his granddaughter move his body for him. Hard. Candy tuned the radio into the Lions game and they listened to the home team accept defeat on the way back to Glencrest.

The parking lot was dark and empty when they pulled in. Before she moved to get out of the truck she turned to her grandfather.

"We had a good day today, right, Granddah? A good Christmas?"

He was looking at the lit windows of Glencrest. She was not sure he knew where they were.

"Huh?"

"A good day. I am so happy we got to spend it together in my new place."

"Your place?"

"Yeah, Granddah, my doublewide. We had breakfast, remember? And you looked out the windows to the pines and we watched the sun set through them. You liked my tree, which I cut myself this year."

"Huh," he replied, then perked up, seeming to remember the day now fading behind them. "If you say it was a good day, Candace, then I believe you and I thank you."

"You're welcome, Granddah. I was glad to spend it with you."

"You did yourself, uh ..." he paused. "You did yourself justice."

She wasn't sure he meant it, thought maybe he had gotten hold of the wrong word. Still, Candy blushed in the dark of the cab, then leaned over and patted his leg.

"Let's get you back inside. Dinner's waiting."

Inside there were staff working who Candy didn't recognize. Corporate must've had to call Manpower, or Nursesource or some other temp agency. The temps were almost always older Hispanic women who spoke a quiet kind of Spanish to each other in the hallways. The permanent staff at Glencrest were mostly white, except for Janelle, and Marcos and Manny in the kitchen. Seeing the worn-out faces of the temps, Candy registered this ethnic divide with a sharper eye, although it had been here all along. Candy spent five years working shifts other staff didn't want and so she had worked alongside these women more than a few times. Why hadn't she seen them? And then this new view triggered all kinds of childish questions. Why didn't these women get permanent jobs at Glencrest? Did they not speak English well enough? Did they not perform up to standards? Were they illegal? Candy knew this was the wrong word for not having papers but she couldn't put her finger on the right one. The tired women smiled at her as she helped Granddah to his room; to them Candy was just another family member to be polite to.

It didn't always matter to the permanent staff if Glencrest offered double time on Christmas Day. The regular wage was so low that employees got frustrated and wouldn't extend themselves to do the place a favor even if they cared about the residents. Candy had spoken up once or twice, but only in her head, playing out conversations where she became a leader and a crusader. In her imagination she looked her supervisors right in the eye and said they needed more staff or they needed a raise or they needed some other sign that the Glen Life Corporation gave a shit. She once spoke these thoughts out loud to Marcos, who told her it was like pissing into the wind. But still. While Candy walked down the hall and passed the temps in their terrible uniforms with their tired faces and they smiled at her without seeing her, she felt bad. No double time for them. She thought about the families they had left behind to work. How they got to work on this cold night. Did they have cars? Maybe they were alone, families back in another country. Maybe they were always alone. Maybe they lived in places worse than the Dump. And the glow of Candy's Christmas evaporated. Just like that.

She helped Granddah into an empty seat in the dining room and someone she didn't know carefully placed a dinner plate down in front of him, then turned to Candy and asked if she was staying for dinner. She was not. She knew the word "gracias" but she said thank you instead. Dinner was all a kind of white-beige and all mashed together on the plate. Disgusting. There would be yellow cake for dessert, with some holiday icing decoration to distinguish it from all of the other endless pieces of yellow cake served at Glencrest. She felt like the worst granddaughter in the world but was also so overwhelmed by the misery of the place that she had to get out. That minute. She handed Granddah the salt and pepper shakers, kissed him on the top of his head, and said goodbye.

Now, as she turned the truck toward home, she let the false grin drop from her face and felt herself sinking down into a funk. She couldn't shake those gray faces of the tired women. They didn't even get real uniforms, just crappy turquoise T-shirts with the company logo printed on the back, so they could be identified as ... what? of no value? of the no-name-tag variety of person? the bargain BOGO human? And as distressing as these thoughts were, the worse ones that crowded into her head were those she now had about herself. She had worked at Glencrest for five years. FIVE YEARS. And this was the first night she had recognized them? Looked into their faces? Guessed at a name or age? There was something very wrong there, Candy realized, and she now knew she'd been part of it. Not because she turned down the overtime shifts, but because she got paid overtime. She had benefits, comp time. Her rare, missed shifts were covered by someone, in-house or out. Her job security had bought her a home. She saw wealth in her life for the first time, but it felt like the opposite of comfort or joy. She snapped off the radio. The darkness had fallen over the village of Cutler as she passed through it and the holiday lights didn't make the same gleeful glow they did only one night before.

She pulled into her drive and texted Janelle from the truck.

home

    over in a jiff

Not thirty minutes later, Janelle's battered old Lexus swung into the driveway, and out of the back spilled the twins.

"Christine couldn't make it. She says she just had to meet up with friends. Christmas night is the most important social date of the year, apparently," Janelle groaned, but it was a happy sound. "Teenage girls. But she asked me to say thank you for the gift card without me reminding her, so there's that. She's almost halfway to those UGGs that will get ruined two days after she buys them and forgets they are really not for the great outdoors."

Candy let the family into her home, which still smelled like breakfast. Carter and Curry slid, tackling each other down right in front of the little tree, and began to examine Candy's loot. They started to comment but Janelle hushed them. There were too many rude questions kids could ask about the weird, single lady with a tiny tree and three unwrapped and certainly unexciting gifts sitting under it.

"Do you have something for Miss Candace, boys?"

Curry paused and then raised his eyebrows. Candy thought he might raise his hand. "Oh yeah, thank you for the gift card, Miss Candace," he recited, and his twin echoed him.

"And don't you have something else?"

"Damn, we left it in the car," one of them said. Candy didn't know if it was Carter or Curry. She couldn't tell them apart without Janelle calling their names so she could attach them to a shirt or a cap.

"Don't say damn, Curry." Ok, Candy thought, Curry had the Pistons hoodie on. Carter was rocking some Mario-emblazoned shirt.

"Go on then and get it, you rascals," Janelle scolded, and they raced back out the door, leaving it open.

"What is this?" Janelle said, lifting up Graham's photo.

"From my brother. Graham. He's up in Munising. Takes photos as a hobby."

Janelle was looking at it deeply. "It's gorgeous," she said, and lifted it up and out in front of her and began to turn it and herself around like they were dance partners. She walked toward walls and propped the framed picture up into open spots, each time leaning back and tilting her head this way and that. She and the photo disappeared around the corner into the bedroom and then back and through the kitchen and dining area. The twins came bounding back in with a covered baking pan.

"Look, we even decorated them," one of them said. Carter: Mario. Curry: Pistons.

Candy lifted up the lid and saw their work: sure enough, they had made and decorated cupcakes with little pieces of peppermint and green sprinkles.

"Candy. Get it?" Curry pointed at the decorations.

"I get it, thank you. Would you like one now?"

They did that twin silent communication thing with a quick glance and then said, "Yes, please," in unison. Honestly, they were so well-mannered Candy felt like she'd landed in a Hallmark movie. She sat them down at the table and looked around to intercept their mother's objections, but Janelle had disappeared. Candy found her in the bedroom.

"It belongs here," Janelle was saying as she lifted Graham's photo up over the dresser. "You can move that." She pointed with her chin at the mirror which Candy had finally hung just yesterday.

"Why there?"

"Because that's where you'll see it every day. It's special. It's from your brother. He made it and framed it for you. His sister. That's something."

"It is." Candy agreed, taking the photo from Janelle and propping it on the dresser, saying she'd give it some thought. She was distracted.

"I have to ask you something," she began. "You know the temp service Glencrest uses when they are short?"

"Yeah, they use a couple different ones, but yeah."

"Have you ever thought ..." Candy stumbled. "Have you ever seen the women who work for them?"

Janelle gave her a strange look, a stare. There was no smile.

"Of course I have seen them, poor souls. And I mean poor." Janelle had stopped moving. This was unlike her. Janelle was always in motion. Suddenly, it got very quiet in the room and Candy listened for the boys. They, too, were quiet. She had an urge to whisper so they wouldn't hear her.

Candy waited with her confession. It was shaming her.

"Why?" Janelle was asking. And again, "I mean, why do you ask?"

"Because." Candy was halted by her embarrassment. Would Janelle stop being her friend? Would she think her stupid and cold and selfish and not worthy? Would Janelle never hug her again?

"Because what?" Janelle was laser focused now. Candy could feel her face, a burning red.

"Because I haven't." Candy blurted. "Seen them. And then I did. Tonight. And all I could think about was how could I not have seen them before, you know?"

"I'm sure you have," Janelle said. There might have been a sneer in her voice.

"No. I mean seen them. As people. As women. Like, as mothers. Or daughters. Belonging to somebody besides that temp agency."

"Do you speak to them?" Janelle asked. The sneer was gone from her voice, but she still stared intensely in Candy's direction.

"No. Do you?" And she forced herself now to look at Janelle. It was a very, very hard thing to do.

"Every single time. Every single one. I made Christine teach me some Spanish, like phrases and such so I can say more than hola or gracias."

Candy was silent. She was grateful to hear the boys arguing softly in the next room.

"And do you know why? Why I do that? Because it dignifies them. Because it means I see them. There's a way worse game of invisible than the one you've been playing, Miss Candace."

Janelle waited for a beat, and then turned and walked out of the room. Candy followed. She had nothing more to say. She had been called out by someone she called a friend and maybe had never really seen before either.

Back in the dining room, the twins, in more Hallmark TV moves, had set out plates with a cupcake each on them for Janelle and Candy, who settled down to eat. Candy made nice comments to the boys about the cupcakes and they thanked her again for the gift cards and began to talk about games and upgrades that Candy couldn't follow. They seemed happy. Soon enough they started bouncing off walls, and Janelle corralled them back into their coats and gave Candy a quick hug.

"Glad to see you were remembered at this time," she said, nodding at the gifts under the tree. "Here's one more," she slipped a small box out of her coat pocket, "from the kids."

"Stop it," Candy protested, searching Janelle's face for forgiveness.

"Miss Candace. Candy," Janelle began. She looked confused, which surprised Candy. Janelle never looked confused, or at a loss. Part of Janelle's magic was her rock solidness. Candy had come to depend on it. She waited, while Janelle seemed to make some sort of decision.

"Girl, you are a kind and generous person and I am happy to know you," she finally said, and a wave of pink relief surged up Candy's neck and onto her cheeks.

This time it was Candy who went in for the hug and they held on tight enough to each other that she no longer felt she would keel over in shame. The family tripped out the door and down the stairs, yelling out Merry Christmases and thank yous, and Candy waved and waved and then closed the door and almost fell into the navy softness of the couch, but then caught herself and moved instead to clean up the cupcake storm on the dining room table. She moved a wet cloth across the marred surface and scraped the crumbs into a cupped hand and then shook them into the sink piled full of dishes from earlier, and into this mound she now slid the cupcake plates. She looked at the mess, couldn't remember a time her sink was so full. She decided to leave them till morning.

Boxing Day

Candy woke up early, checked her phone for the weather, and saw it was Boxing Day. She had never known what this meant. This year, she was curious and so decided to Google it and discovered that, although it was just another Black Friday kind of deal, it started out as a holiday for servants. This was the day they got presents, and sometimes got the day off because they had to work their tails off for Christmas. The boxing part, according to Google, came from their gifts being cast-off stuff that their bosses handed down to them. In boxes. Which they had probably packed themselves. Sort of an old-fashioned Goodwill. Candy guessed they didn't get overtime either.

She was relieved the holiday didn't have to do with boxing of the punching and knocking-out kind. Football was bad enough. As she was doing some boxing up of her own, mostly having to do with her own wrapping paper, she heard a truck pull in her driveway.

Clint.

She answered the door. He seemed overly polite, started by saying he was sorry to bother her and sorry he hadn't texted beforehand, and Merry Christmas, and then he ran out of steam. The whole time he was talking he had been looking everywhere but at her: the yard, the trees, his boots. She now knew him well enough to recognize looking at his boots was a standard Clint move.

"Do you want to come in?"

"No, not now, though I'd love to have a look around sometime." He looked up at her briefly. "I'm running in between jobsites, actually. We got people wanting to use their houses for New Year's so they got me bouncing all over the place doing this and that." He looked back down at his boots, which were covered in a kind of mucky, snowy wetness. He stood on the bottom step. Nervous vibes floated up in her direction.

"Hey, if you wouldn't mind, could you come out to my truck for a minute? I've got something I got to ask you about."

Candy looked out at his truck, which appeared to be empty although the sun glared off the windshield so she couldn't see into the cab. "Yeah, sure. I've got to suit up though, do you mind?" she said, pointing to the door which stood open, letting the heat out.

"Sure, sure, no problem, I'll just be out here," he said, and turned back to his pickup.

Candy shut the door, bundled into her winter clothes, and headed out to his truck. Clint now beamed a great big smile which peeked through his whiskers. He opened the passenger door and out bounded, or rather, tumbled, a beautiful black dog from the front seat. The dog immediately started circling both of them and nuzzling their gloved hands and wagging its tail so hard its butt wagged along with it. Candy started laughing; she couldn't help it. The dog seemed to be laughing too.

"This is Rusty."

"Hi, Rusty," Candy said, and the dog came in for a head pet. "A new addition to your family?"

"Me? Oh no. Actually, he belongs to the Andersens, a family I've done some work for. They are moving and can't keep her."

"Why did they name a black dog Rusty?" She was still petting the dog, which seemed to have an endless need for attention.

Clint replied that it was something to do with the Andersen kids and a favorite TV show.

"So, dog sitting?" Candy kept guessing.

"Um, no. I can't keep him, I mean her; she's a her. I've got my mom's dog now, and he's one of those little yappers who can't stand big dogs. So." Clint's face now froze, halfway between looks of joy and anxiety, his mouth twisted up in confusion.

"I was wondering," he started, and then, "I was thinking," and then he stopped.

He looked like he wanted her to finish his sentence.

"You were thinking?" This came out sounding like an insult, like Clint had never had a thought before.

"Yeah. I was thinking that maybe out here on your own and all, and it being in a new place far out of town and everything, you could use ..."

Candy felt her skin beginning to prickle.

"Use?" she asked, the anger heating up like a sudden flu. It was an old feeling, but familiar.

And then he really stepped in it. "I thought maybe you were lonely or—"

Candy cut him off. "I don't need a dog."

"I just thought you maybe could want some company out here."

From his face it looked like he had more to add to his sentence but clamped his mouth shut instead, swallowed the rest of his rescue plan for the lady all by her lonesome in the country. Sad Lady. Lonely Lady. Candy turned away for a moment, back to her beautiful new home which she now lived in alone, yes, and it was a little scary to come home late at night, yes, but lonely? Not in a million years. She had worked for the chance to live alone, to be by herself, to not have to run into people or hear people or react to people. A tiny voice inside started fighting to tell her that Clint was a nice guy. He was being nice, looking out for her, as he had these past months sometimes asked and sometimes not. She could almost see this tiny voice, a new voice, trying to stand on its tippy toes and pull the screaming maniac of rage back into its cage. No luck.

"I'm fine. I don't need a dog. I don't want a dog." Candy's voice was loud, close to a yell, offended and angry, even as she knew she shouldn't be. Inside her head, this adopting a dog scenario exploded into a big deal, an insult. The tiny voice retreated, then went silent.

"I don't need a dog. I don't want a dog. What a stupid idea. What gave you that idea?"

Her words were a harsh sneer. Then her eyes cleared and she registered Clint's reaction, mouth now downturned in a grimace, eyes on the ground, and she was filled with regret, wanting to reel the crazy rant back in. But she couldn't. Words went out into the world and you couldn't take them back. They stayed out there.

She watched his neck redden and he finally stuttered, "Sorry, I made a mistake, sorry. The Andersens were in a bind and they're super nice people, but I made a mistake."

"I don't appreciate anyone telling me what I need or what I want or what I might like." The crazy voice softened, and Candy was suddenly exhausted in the morning sun, and the exhaustion was caused by the instant regret which felt like lead. Damn.

Clint said nothing and her words hung in the cold air, sharp and cutting.

"Ok then," Clint finally said.

He turned away, called for Rusty, but the dog had booked into the woods and was joyfully kicking up snow and chasing squirrels up trees, her short legs not seeming to slow her down much. The animal seemed to be a stupid bundle of happy. Candy forced herself not to retreat back into the safety of the doublewide. She stood next to Clint, trying hard to figure out how to apologize. It seemed he might have been waiting for it.

"God, Clint," she began, "I ... Oh, shit."

"I didn't mean—" he started.

"I know. I'm just," and the next word came out before she had even thought it, "damaged. Sometimes I ..."

She could hear him exhale.

"Sometimes I just don't know how to be when people ..."

"Try to tell you what you need?"

"No. Yes. Fuck." She sensed how alone they were here. Just the two of them on this clear morning when the world was exhaling too, after all the holiday buildup and then the joy and the disappointment, and suddenly Candy remembered that the world was filled with lonely people. No gifts, no trees, no jolly, no homes, even.

Clint dared to laugh at her last mumbled remark.

"No? Yes? Fuck?" he repeated back to her.

And she smiled.

Then he added, "That word. Damaged."

"Ok, not exactly damaged," she said, "but ..."

"Dented?"

And the spell broke. They laughed together, hers a stuttering giggle, his a kind of throaty rumble. Candy shared her coming-home-at-night ritual and her ideas about security systems that were stupid and too expensive anyway.

Clint pointed down at the dog and said, "That one there is free-ninety-eight a month. No contract."

Rusty had apparently sensed it was safe to return and started nuzzling again.

She grinned down at the dog. She tried out its—her—name: "Rusty," then began murmuring in some kind of new pet talk. She patted the smooth black head, rubbed the thick black flanks. Rusty nuzzled Candy some more, Clint having been forgotten. She lowered her face into the dog's fur. Rusty wagged. The butt waddled. The tail swished. The nose nuzzled. Candy petted and rubbed some more, and murmured, "Good dog, silly dog," over and over. And then she gave in.

Not twenty minutes later, Clint was gone. A dog bed and dog bowls and a bag of kibble and a leash were now in Candy's home, along with a dog. Before he left, Clint had promised to take Rusty back if there was any problem or Candy couldn't handle it. The dog could go to a pound or somewhere else, he said. Candy couldn't recall exactly how this all transpired but besides the wagging and the nuzzling there had been the hangover from the harm Candy had done. She still hated herself for it, but also felt a little tiny bit proud that she recovered enough to explain. She didn't run, she hung in there and tried to make it better. Not all the way better. She had, after all, been Vicky mean. In the middle of her attack on Mr. Nice/Shy Guy, she had felt powerful. She had lashed out and he had been silenced. Was this why Vicky did this stuff? Grabbing for any kind of power in a world where she had so little? Didn't matter, Candy thought, as she watched her new dog settling down into a carefree nap. It was just wrong. Maybe she'd make a better dog. No talking, for one. No tricky feelings to hurt or to have hurt. Being human felt heavy sometimes, all the words, the hurts, the confusions. Like she was carrying rocks on her back and they made her ache in a new way.

Candy and Rusty felt their way around each other the rest of the day. The dog seemed to understand some English: "sit," "lie down," "c'mere," and "no." She didn't jump on the furniture, although every inch of everything got a solid sniffing. Candy let her out in the back twice more before trusting that she was housebroken, even though she looked kind of old. How old was an old dog? She texted Clint with dog questions about meals, walks, work hours.

> do dogs get cold?
>> dunno, but it doesn't seem so.
>
> do they chew furniture?
>> depends on the dog.
>
> should I use the leash in the woods?
>> not as long as she knows where her food comes from.
>
> why does she run around in circles in the living room?
>> no idea. happy?
>
> why does she whimper in her sleep?
>> dreaming of squirrels?

The last text Candy sent before she headed to bed that night was two words:

i'm sorry.

She finally fell asleep trying to count up all of her apologies.

12/31/19

The last day of the year dawned late and dark and cold, but the snow, deeper out back in the woods than by the road, lit up the northern world. The pines, which were now Candy's silent companions while she drank her coffee in the morning, were still crusted over and bowed down by snow puffs which thawed in the midday sun and then refroze in place as the night drew in. The branches this morning looked painfully bent over. The next storm or big wind would blow them free. Candy's backyard—and it was truly hers now that Granddah knew, at least as much as he could know or understand about the doublewide—looked like a postcard, or a jigsaw puzzle of a winter wonderland. An occasional jay squawked in to land on a branch and shook loose pieces of snow, creating a snow necklace around the drip line of the trees. The frosted pines had begun to feel like neighbors, distant friendly ones who waved from their back doors but stayed where they were.

The coffee smelled good. Tasted good. She didn't work again until the New Year. 2020. Until then, two delicious days off. Nothing to schedule or budget or move or unbox. She hugged her mug to her chest and looked around at this new house which belonged to her. Even better, she belonged to it, this patch of sandy ground that she had lived on top of but had never, until now, really lived in, her whole life. Before she had always been on other people's terms, under other people's roofs. She looked up at her ceiling which sheltered her from winds and storms, and above that was a roof that was also hers, and tiny twinklings of wonderment traveled through her veins and made her rise from her couch cocoon, and in a gesture that felt ridiculously like some kind of daily church ritual, she again walked the length and then the width of her home. When she reached a wall she touched it, pressed and then held her hand against it, and felt the things that moved or vibrated within and without. She could tell the direction of the wind from which wall felt the coldest.

Candy moved through this exercise almost every morning. And now Rusty looked up from her bed under the front window and watched her, probably wondering if it was time for a walk. Wondering when her new owner? parent? caretaker? was going to stop pacing off the place and head over to the boot tray and suit up for a walk. Actually, Candy still didn't have the slightest idea what dogs thought. If they thought at all, in human thoughts, that is. Rusty had four gears: running around chasing something, pacing around the food bowl, following Candy around looking for love rubs, and napping. So, yeah, maybe human. This new being in her life certainly had thoughts about peeing and eating and chasing squirrels, all of which seem to be followed by naps.

She pulled up the weather on her phone. Cold. Snow: possible tonight and probable tomorrow. And so it would go for four months of the year, or used to before the winters went weird. The resorts would be happy. Snow meant money, snowmobiling and skiing, boosting an otherwise hibernating economy. Candy didn't mind. The tourists with their well-insulated clothes and four-wheel-drive vehicles pulling flashy snowmobile trailers just passed her and all the other year-rounders by without seeing them, unless of course they were serving them at a bar or checking them into a hotel. For the rest, the ones who lived here and scrabbled out a living beneath those who floated above, winter was a slow time. Candy liked a slow time. The sun didn't rise until almost nine in the morning and was gone by four. If she paid attention, and she did more so out on Lasso Road with the natural world all around her, the skies became navy blue instead of black at night, when they were clear and the stars glistened. Sparkled, even. But you had to pause and wait and pay attention to see the sparkle.

Candy was paying attention. Her eyes felt more open and this made her think that maybe she had been squinting through her days and nights before the doublewide, closing off ugly things and hazardous people. Pain. Sorrow. Sparkle. The blue of midnights. Now that she had moved off Main Street and back into the country, her eyes seemed hungry, even, and so she fed them meals of the Milky Way and had even caught sight of the northern lights once or twice after a late shift when she didn't have to work in the morning and had a late-night wander with Rusty. She had never caught them before, even though she had lived up here all of her life. Maybe it was because she had never really looked up. Or maybe it was because the farmhouse had been surrounded by trees and the doublewide stood in a clearing, the pines far enough away in her backyard so that she could stand at her window with all the house lights off and watch the sky. Some nights she pulled up a chair and wrapped a layers around her shoulders like an old lady and peered out, then up. There were no words in the universe for the blanket of contentment that had settled around her. She couldn't possibly explain why this dented, vinyl clad, mobile home—because, really, that was what it was, no matter what Randy called it—how this place had so completely cloaked her life. For so long, Candy had wished and hoped and dreamed, in a kind of scared, wishing way that held no hope of any real treasure ahead. But here it was, here she was on this dark, cold morning, living inside a treasure. That was the only way to describe it. She was golden.

There was now the open day ahead and the four walls of her house that surrounded her, and the mortgage on auto pay, which got processed two days after her paycheck on the first of the month. The roof sat over her head and the baseboard heaters ticked when they switched on and off. Despite Janelle's advice, Graham's photo hung on the wall in the dining area, where she looked at it when she ate, and she almost always ate now at her table away from the TV. She had once read something on the internet about how overeating gets worse if you eat in front of the TV. Of course the article had gone on to talk about family time and ways to engage kids in the meal, which Candy ignored. Or tried to. Instead of HGTV, she now looked out the window. She didn't know if she was eating less, but it felt right to be at the table she and Granddah shared back when they had lived as a family, there with Graham on the wall.

The table was one of only a few things that had been moved from the farmhouse into the doublewide, the one major piece of furniture Candy decided did not need replacing. It didn't carry with it any trace of poverty or dirt or pepperoni smell. It brought along with it only her own life with her brother and her grandfather and she found she loved it now, in its new home. She noticed it, ran her hands over the pine planks which were nicked and stained: an outline of a jar bottom here, scratches there, grease drops, dabs of white paint smudged into the grain of the wood. The thick legs were steady and the corners intact. It was good. Old things could be good.

Like Rusty, who now paced. She seemed to have figured out that she had to wait for the coffee ritual to finish. Candy let her out to pee first thing, but the walk, the real fun, back in the woods where she could snuffle out all the smells from under the snow and chase squirrels and dash ahead and then come crashing back to Candy, all that fun she had to wait for patiently. But pacing helped.

Candy looked down at her dog. How did this happen? How did she say yes to this beast that she now shared her double-wide with? She knew it was because Clint said full return policy, no questions asked, but she also guessed that he had known that once Rusty had been invited into her life it was going to be next to impossible to back out. And, truth be told, Rusty did rouse and growl whenever anyone stopped by, which was only the mail carrier, but it did make her feel safer. Safer from what, Candy didn't know, but she was sleeping better. These woods always felt safe, like home, they were home, and this town was home, and now there were people she could call. There were people whose phones might even have her name in them, so if she called it would say "Candy" on the screen.

And now Rusty. Safe. Clint was right. Again.

Candy dressed and then dressed once more for the outdoors. Fleece, scarf, hat, coat, mittens, boots. She usually tried not to look in the mirror when she was bundled up because a pink-faced roly-poly snow lady was surely what she looked like. But today she looked. And there was the round snow lady, grinning back at her.

"Wait until next summer, girl," she said to Rusty as she opened the back door, which the lab joyfully bounded through. "The beach, the water, the sticks, the balls. We are going to have ourselves a good old time." And she smiled at herself for talking to a dog.

She thought again about the rock-lined driveway story she told herself so many times. The rocks she had collected were still in a bin in the back of the pickup, providing winter weight for back tires to navigate the icy roads. Right now, her "driveway" was just a two-track of mud and sand carved out of the snow. She had the number of a guy who plowed but in a fit of ambitious self-reliance after the first snowfall, she went out and bought a snow shovel instead and did the first three or four rounds of driveway clearing by herself. It took a long while, but Rusty loved it and jumped after every shovelful of snow she tossed aside. And after, she went back inside and made cocoa and ate popcorn and watched a show. And felt like she earned it. This glow she felt had to do with the ownership, she knew, but it was ridiculous how many crevices and cracks of her life it had shone into. The snow shoveling, the dining table, the key holder by the door, the bathroom exhaust fan which worked, the towel rack which she hung right over a heating vent so when she stepped out of the shower she could wrap herself in warmth.

Still, the big snows were on their way. No doubt about it.

Granddah waved the *Farmer's Almanac* in her face and warned her.

"No joking, Candace, you're out there on your own and them tires on the Tacoma is old, probably no tread left on 'em, and you don't have no one out there to look out for you."

"I got a guy's number, Granddah, don't worry. I'll call."

"You call before the storm. There's no reaching them guys once it starts falling. They're all booked up and out on the road. They ain't taking no calls. I wouldn't neither."

"I know, Granddah, I remember how you did that with Willy Stevens. Always called him the night before."

"And I was right, wasn't I?"

"Yep, Granddah, you were."

This conversation was repeated almost every time she saw him as he scrutinized the weather outside the Glencrest windows. Sometimes it ended there and sometimes he persisted. Sometimes, the persistence was painful.

"Damn, I don't know why I can't go on out and live there. Why can't I live out there?" The first sentence spoken in anger, the second in a kind of childish whining.

Candy tried to inhale, holding it before plunging back into the worn tracks of this horrible exchange. "Because you can't walk by yourself and I can't risk leaving you while I go to work. Who's going to pick you up if you fall? Rusty?"

"Who?"

"Never mind. I would move you back there with me in a heartbeat if I could, but I can't."

As Candy and Rusty plunged deeper into the woods, she thought about how her safety had become an obsession for Granddah, and then she tried to remember if he had been that anxious back when she was a kid and they had lived together and the heavy snows came. It was a sign, she now realized, of how much she had had to depend on him, had no one to trust but him, that she now couldn't actually recall if he had. He just must've done it, cared for her, watched out for her, and as a child, she must've just taken it for granted. At any rate, he had done all those things, the shopping and the plowing, keeping the heat on and the truck filled with gas and the cable bill paid. And she had been safe as a result. He had been her parent. She had been loved. Or at least looked after. No, loved. She made herself settle on the harder word.

She tromped on through the snow and called for Rusty. The dog raced back from her squirrel hunting, the only sounds in the woods the jay's screech and the dog's panting. Her collar ID tag had Andersen's info etched on it and if she decided to keep her she'd have to get a new one made. Then she laughed out loud in the frigid morning air and the laugh made a cloud of steam above her, then she scratched Rusty around her neck because the dog asked for a rub with her eyes and nose, which Candy was beginning to be able to read.

Clint texted once to ask how it was going and was the dog behaving.

She replied that they (they!) were fine and she was still deciding. She tried to be nice in the text. He hadn't asked again.

Candy turned them around and headed back into the warmth of the doublewide. She considered French toast for breakfast but didn't have maple syrup. She made herself some instant oatmeal instead. Added some milk. Sat down at the table.

Her phone was on the kitchen counter, connected to its

charger. She hadn't checked it yet this morning because there was no way she was going to get called in to work. It always happened around holidays. Staff got all ambitious, or hard up to pay the holiday bills, and they rushed to sign up for the New Year's shift and then called in sick when it meant they had to actually crawl out of bed and into the cold and dark and go to work. Candy used to be one of their most reliable fill-ins. Before the move, when every cent counted and every dollar earned went to fill in the contours of her dream, she would grab any shift. But not now. Not anymore. The extras were done with. She had herself on a budget and she was good.

She reached for the phone, and sure enough there was a missed call from Glencrest. And a voicemail. She had to listen in case it was about Granddah. It wasn't.

"Hey, Candace," her nicest supervisor, Velma, cooed into her voicemail. "Sorry to bother you, but we're in a real bind for tomorrow's p.m. shift. Please call if you can help us out. Thanks. You're a doll. We so appreciate all you do for us."

Candy tapped the trash can icon. She was not a doll. And she was not so sure she felt appreciated on any regular basis. Except maybe by Miss Alice when she petted her, or even Granddah when she brought him the papers. Not today. Today and tonight were hers. A new year. Her new year. She was going to order in and eat ice cream and watch the snow fall. The Nursesource women flashed through her mind. Shit. Damn. She pushed them away, or tried to, while she put the phone down, but just as she did, it dinged with a text message.

Clint.

hi there. how's rusty?

Candy looked over at Rusty, who was snarfing her kibble noisily. This whole dream, thought out down to the last detail of the key rack and the color of the new towels and the replacement set of dishes, all this had had a cast of exactly one. One. And here was this damn dog who was, well, wonderful She sighed, scratching Rusty under her ear. It was beginning to feel like it might be love.

> **rusty's good. rusty needs a new id tag. how do I get one of those? does that mean…**
>
> > **guess so.**
>
> **that's great. really great. i'll tell the andersens.**

The Andersens had been heartbroken to give up their dog and Candy could now see why. She looked down at Rusty, who had finished her own breakfast and was now eyeing the oatmeal bowl. She put it down so the dog could lick it across the floor.

> **hey i have one more question**

Candy waited while the dots dotted inside the dialogue box.

> **what are you doing for nye?**

Candy paused, her circuits threatening overload. A dog was one thing. A guy who knew guys and had a mom and needed advice and all that. That was also one thing.

> **you mean tonight?** she finally managed.
>
> > **yeah**

New Year's Eve? With someone? That was never going to

be a thing. Never. Not in one single dream about the double-wide or her own home or her future or living inside a winter wonderland postcard, had this ever been a detail. Never. So she'd been forgiven by Clint, which was a relief. Even so, New Year's Eve? No. But then why was she circling the dining room table like she was playing musical chairs? Why was she sweating all of a sudden? Why was she dropping the phone and then picking it up again? Those were all "I am thinking about scary things" moves. A simple no, no thanks, not now, maybe some other time, got something else going on, did not result in pacing. Or sweating. Considering saying yes? That was sweating stuff. She glanced down at Rusty, who was looking up at her, worried. Could she smell Candy's fear? Her sweat? Sweat and blushing. Blushing and sweat. Private. These were things she did in private. And private was what she was.

But.

No.

But.

She kept pacing, circling the table, running a sponge over its already clean surface. She didn't need this. It would end badly with a rude comment or a sneer or he'd say something and she'd snarl again, and that would ruin everything. Or it wouldn't and that would be worse. Plus she didn't know how to do this, whatever this was; even putting words to it made her itch. Do what? she then asked herself. She didn't know what exactly "it" was that she didn't know how to do, but whatever it was, she was pretty certain she didn't know how to do it. Wouldn't be able to control it.

This new clean aloneness she lived inside of was a certain happiness, a safe joy. Of this she was also sure. She walked the length and width of the doublewide. This was hers. Alone. She made it herself. This was all she ever wanted and she had now made it. Created it and paid for it and filled it with beautiful things, at least as beautiful as she could afford, and that made her life beautiful. To her. And Rusty was enough, right? Already one more heartbeat than she had ever bargained for. Any more and she might have to armor up again and freak out about the world getting too close, coming in for a jab. Of this she was also sure.

Or was she? She remembered Clint letting her measure the dent first. Stepping in with the cousin story. Sending her names and phone numbers of contractors but then respecting a kind of radio silence. The granting of that huge favor on the doublewide's moving day. Taking care of her fear. He had taken care of her. And asked for nothing in return besides help with his mom, and for that he was desperate.

He never sneered at her.

He never talked over her.

He never crowded her.

Who was this guy? She had no idea. Ok, that was a lie or half a lie. She had a pretty good idea. She remembered her own private joke about Candy 1.0 and Candy 2.0. Candy 1.0: slow, young, murmured but didn't speak, red, fat, alone, but not lonely. And Candy 2.0? Ok, all those 1.0 things except less murmuring and more speaking, better vision, that was for sure, and just a little cocky. Quicker. Still red. Still fat. Ok, large. But still. Candy forced herself to reboot, looked down at the screen, felt her skin wet and now cooling. She started typing.

my nye plan involves pine trees and snow and moon

He responded instantly.

wow. like a ceremony?
   no. like looking out the window at the snow falling on the pine trees under the moon.
you do know if snow is falling that you're not going to see the moon. clouds.

A joke.

all right. i get it. but that's my plan. you heading out to tip some mgds? Candy typed lightly, pushed send.

nah. i'm here at home. tbh, it sucks. woke up feeling terrible about putting my mom in gc. went to visit. she is so sad I can't stand it. should of taken better care of her.
   sorry. imho you made the right decision.
yeah, so, not really feeling the party thing.

Candy paused. Waited. Waited some more. Checked in with Rusty, now asleep on her bed, which meant the ET waves of anxiety must have died down. Imagine having a dog tell you how you feel.

Her. Him. They. Him. Her. Her. Him? Candy had the strangest sensation of wading into the lake in June when it was still cold and you just had to get the first swim over with. She positioned her thumbs over the phone's keyboard. She paused. Then she typed.

maybe you could use some pine trees or some snow or possibly some moon?

She pushed send and this time did not toss her phone away like some kind of bomb.

Again, he responded lightning fast. He must've been waiting for an invitation. From her. Candy. Candace Schein. Voice number one sneered: yeah, he just needs a favor. For his mom, or maybe a stray cat. There had to be some kind of desperation.

But Clint had already clearly jumped ahead, moving the conversation along.

i'll take any two out of three. sure it's ok? can i bring anything?

Candy looked over at the clock on the stove. Plenty of time to run to the store for lasagna ingredients. Maybe make some lemon cookies. A salad. One of those Caesar salad packets.

just yourself. whatever you're drinking.
7? 8?
8
great. see you.

not if I see you first, Candy typed and blushed, all alone in her home except for Rusty, who snoozed on her bed, all right in her world.

Shop 'n Save

All the way to the Shop 'n Save, Candy had the bizarre sensation of watching herself from the outside: a person who was driving calmly to a grocery store to buy ingredients to make a dinner that was for someone else besides herself and her grandfather. She entertained no dreams about the future. She was squarely in the now of the cold, gray, final day of the year.

"This is where I turn."

"This is where I try to memorize the grocery list."

"This is where I check the passenger footwell to make sure I brought my own bags since they charge now for plastic."

"This is where I pull into the closest possible spot."

She wasn't sweating, she wasn't shaking. She was listening to herself. Change.

Until, that is, she pulled into the closest parking space, stared down at the tote bags in the footwell, and turned off the ignition. The truck did that shuddering thing for about a minute trying to turn itself off, and that was when her body picked up on the vibration and continued some trembling on its own. She pulled out her phone. If she made this call, it would commit her. She wouldn't be able to back out. Why this was so, she didn't know, but it was a certainty to her. Intuition. She pulled up her new favorites screen, populated now with two names: Janelle. GC.

She pushed the name.

It rang four times and Candy almost hung up after each ring. If Janelle didn't answer, then she couldn't ask for advice and if she didn't ask for advice she could just send a text, back out and say ... change of plans, had to go see Granddah. Blah, blah, blah.

"Hello?"

"Janelle?"

"Miss Candy, how's it? Happy New Year. Almost."

"Hey. How's the family? You got any time off?"

"Working tomorrow. What's up? You need an extra shift? Want me to call in?"

"Not exactly." Candy paused. "I actually need to talk about something. Do you have a minute?"

"I got several. Shoot."

So Candy began. Clint. Clint tonight. She had already told Janelle about the bust at the peninsula site and the referrals and even him showing up at the pouring. But she rebuffed all of Janelle's joshing. Not like that, are you kidding, not for me, you know I fly solo, happy as I am. And Janelle, being the kind of friend that Candy had always treasured for not being nosy, had always eased off after a friendly nudge or two along the lines of:

"What can it hurt?"

"He could be interested."

"Oh well, your life. Suit yourself."

And like that. Around and around two or three times and

then Janelle would let it drop. Now, Candy could almost hear the intensity with which Janelle listened on the other end of the phone. She stumbled to a halt.

Then she heard Janelle close a door and then there was only quiet on the other end of the phone.

"So. Tonight." Janelle said more than asked.

"Guess so. I'm in the parking lot of the grocery store. I was thinking about lasagna, maybe a salad."

"Huh."

"You know. It's a holiday. And he sounded terrible on the phone. I mean over text. That's how we talk. Over text. Said he's still bummed about moving his mother. How sad she is at Glencrest."

"Huh."

"So."

"Huh."

"So?"

And she waited. Janelle was not the silent type, was never at a loss for words. Now she was silent. After a minute, Candy couldn't stand it.

"Are you there?"

"Yup. I'm here. Did you have a question? Like is lasagna a good choice?" Janelle's voice contained a smile.

"Not exactly."

"Ok, then what to do when he snuggles up next to you on the couch and moves in for a wet one?"

"Janelle, puhleeze."

"Candy girl, I'm not sure what you're asking for then. Permission?"

Candy was stumped. Did she have to keep crawling out on limbs like this with people? Swaying in the cold breeze of the world? The two of them on her new navy velour couch?

"Are you kidding?"

"Then what are you asking for?"

"I'm not asking anything, I guess."

And then Janelle's voice warmed over the phone, right into Candy's cold ear.

"Yes you are, sweetheart." Pause. "It's ok."

"I feel like an idiot. I want to change my mind. I have no idea why I let him."

"Let him what?"

"Let him get to me. Make me feel sorry for him."

"So call him back."

Silence.

"Ok, then have him over."

"What if he says something ... mean, like about my weight or my stupid hair or my bad clothes or ..."

"Like an insult? But, with everything you've told me, which isn't much by the way, he doesn't sound mean."

"But."

"But then, if he is, you boot him. Tell him to shove it and lock the door behind him. He's not a monster. I think we can be pretty sure about that, right? You take care of his mom, for crying out loud."

This reminder felt reassuring to Candy. There was a tie there. Candy worked at the home where Clint's mom now lived. Candy took care of Miss Maeve. And Clint had sort of taken care of her. Clint had cried seeing his mom hurt and sad. In front of her, wiping tears on his sleeves like a little kid. Candy let the list of things she knew about Clint scroll through her mind.

"You know, Candy," Janelle was saying, "there is a possibility that this guy likes you. Is choosing you, not just using you. And that he's a nice man. There are still a couple out there."

Candy wiped the fog from the side window with her sleeve, and watched as people passed by the truck. She could think of nothing to say. The Clint inventory list kept scrolling: he gave her phone numbers, arranged discounts for her, made jokes over the phone without emojis. Candy heard Janelle's voice again coming from her phone.

"This is the way it's gonna go, Candy," she was saying, her voice slow and low as if Candy were supposed to be taking notes. "You'll go home and cook. I love your lasagna. I've tasted your leftovers, remember? And then you'll shower and decide what to wear. Go comfortable but not sloppy, because this is gonna be hard enough for you. You're a beginner. Novice level, my twins would say."

"Yeah. Ok."

"Then you'll get dressed and then you'll be nervous, and you'll open a window to cool down."

"Yeah."

"And then he'll arrive and then you'll talk and then you'll feed him and maybe you'll both ease up enough to tell some jokes and have some laughs, and then you can tell him to leave."

"Yeah."

"If you want him to."

"Christ, Janelle, I hardly know the guy."

"Well," Janelle chuckled, "in the real world this second part is called hooking up and you might be surprised at how little people know each other before, you know ..."

"I don't want to hook up," she whined. "I feel SORRY for the guy."

"Are you sure about that?" Janelle's voice was quiet, almost a whisper.

"Of course I am. He sounded pathetic on the other end of the phone. His mom and all."

"I don't doubt you feel sorry for him, but feeling sorry and connecting are two different things. You've done a lot of one in your life and not much of the other."

Candy let that sit in the Tacoma's cab alongside her. As she felt the air around her cool, she watched people wheeling carts filled with groceries and cases of beer out to their cars. The parking lot was landscaped with pickups and mountains of cleared away snow, now turning sandy brown in the filth of the holiday traffic.

"You still there?"

"Yeah. Freezing and sweating."

"Sounds about right."

"Really?"

There was another long silence as they listened to each other breathing. Then suddenly Candy heard Janelle inhale sharply and then let out a long sigh.

"Candy, let me give you a news flash, ok? You set yourself apart, wear your extra weight like a damn suit of armor, even though I know you could probably work on that if you wanted to. You managed that new house, didn't you? All alone and on an LPN salary? You can do anything you want to, but I believe you stay large because it keeps you small. Hidden. You smile and shut up and wipe butts and clean off chins and wheel around old folks for a living. You do so with love and caring worth a whole lot more than what they pay you, or me, for that matter. And then you run back into your little life in your little house where you control everything and you lock the doors to the outside world, and you call that living."

"It is living. I like it that way."

"Doesn't sound like it, the way you beat up on yourself. What's wrong with your clothes? Nothing. What's wrong with your hair? Nothing. At least nothing I couldn't fix in one afternoon. And your size? Girl, the only problem I see with your weight is in your own head."

"Wow. Glad I called," Candy joked weakly.

"Yeah, the new year's coming up and I am on a roll. You like your life alone, lonely, whatever word you wanna put there? Fine. Keep it that way. You hate being large? Lose it, or learn to love it. You invited this Clint man over for some reason and I don't believe it's pity. Or only pity. But if it is, just feed the dude and send him home and then shoot him a text once a month."

"Are you done?" Candy asked.

"Yeah, I'm done. Aren't you glad you called?"

And then they laughed a little. A settling, finishing laugh.

"Ok?" Janelle asked.

"Ok," Candy answered.

"Thanks, Janelle. You ... I ... I mean, you ... you're ..."

"I know I am."

"Thank you. I'm headed into the store."

"Happy New Year, girl. I'll be thinking good thoughts for you."

Candy clicked off, pocketed her phone, grabbed her bags, and headed into the store, adding to the grocery list in her head with every step. Because there should be cookies.

Snow, Moon, Sky

That evening, Candy found herself thinking that if this were a movie there would be a long scene with the two of them at the table, eating dinner and drinking dark red wine from long-stemmed glasses. He would flirt and she would flirt and by the miracles of Hollywood CGI, she would shed thirty pounds and he would have shaved and put on a shirt with a collar, etc., etc.

But it wasn't a movie. He had arrived a little after eight, looking as sad as he was, and Rusty greeted him like family. He clutched a paper grocery bag of bottles to his chest, beer for him and cider for her. He popped one open and offered one to her, which she declined. She took his coat and hung it by the door and turned back to him. His shirt actually had a collar. It was one of those lined flannel ones, and the plaid was lake blue and beige sand. She stared at it long enough for him to notice and look down, then smoothed it over his chest. "Nice color, that plaid," she said, and then she showed him around, Rusty following them in and out of rooms, staying close. He complimented the place and then paused in front of Graham's photo.

"Where'd you get that?"

"Christmas present. From my brother, Graham. He takes

pictures, mostly black and white. But I guess he broke his own rule for this one." Candy paused, then added, "He knows I love color."

"It's beautiful." Clint leaned closer into the photo, accidentally knocking over another picture in a plastic frame on the sideboard countertop.

"Oops, sorry," he said, examining it as he put it back in place.

"That's him. And me. At the fair."

"How old are you there?"

"I think eight or nine."

"Ooo wee, look at that hair." In the photo, Candy's crazy red ringlets were caught up in a topknot ponytail falling around her face like a lion's mane. Graham was in a Metallica T-shirt and black jeans, already a teenager. Little Candy was in pink all over, leggings, striped top, hair tie. She heard the armor start to clank around inside her head.

"Yeah, well the personal grooming was on me from an early age," she replied, an edge to her voice that even Rusty seemed to register. So did Clint, it seemed.

"Did the best you could, huh?"

Candy waited for more. For the snicker or jab.

Instead, she heard Clint say softly, "So, no mom ..." Not a question.

"No mom."

He didn't apologize, just smiled down at the picture, and gently fingered its black plastic edges to make sure it was secure. Then they headed back into the dining room. He found his beer and guzzled deeply.

They were both so nervous she decided to serve dinner

right away. He drank his beer from the bottle after pouring her some cider into a jelly jar. His cheeks flushed red and Candy noticed that he had tried to comb down his hair. It was as hopeless as hers. There was a funny moment as he yanked the cork from the Martinelli bottle and they smiled, almost laughed, together. The cider fizz made her nose itch, but it tasted good. Sweet and sour together at the same time on her tongue.

They gobbled down two servings each of Candy's lasagna with barely a dozen words in between them, mostly Clint saying, "wow, delicious," and "seriously, this is delicious," and "man, so delicious." Candy thought about telling him the story of her and lasagna but stayed silent, except for the chewing, of course.

Afterward, they leaned away from their plates and managed some small talk about his mom and her grandfather and brother and their years in school (he had been three years ahead of her). They talked, sometimes joking, about the summer people and his work up on the peninsula, and it didn't feel so nervous. Candy had followed Janelle's advice and worn comfortable clothes. They were clean and brown hued and she found herself not sweating. Then, after the conversation wound down into a kind of silence that didn't feel too awkward to Candy, they both leaned further back in their chairs and looked over each other's shoulders, Candy into the whites of her kitchen and Clint out the black windows behind her.

And then Candy turned around to see what he was seeing. Or trying to see. Boldly, she got up and turned off the overhead lights. Clint murmured approval. The snow had stopped and the moon appeared. The snowy landscape beyond the doublewide had turned a faint aqua that darkened to navy in the trees' shadows. Candy tried to memorize that shady aqua. She thought she might have found the color for her bedroom walls. As they both looked out, their view into the backwoods seemed to ease them away from all the expectations and nervousness of this not quite a date, date. At least that was what Candy was thinking. Because they both were watching the night move outside. It was, after all, what she had offered.

"Wanna head out?"

"Hell, yeah."

By the time they bundled up, half tripping over Rusty as she ran circles around them, the moon had slipped away again. Clint opened the back door and Candy stepped through it. They tumbled down the temporary steps, Rusty leading the way and disappearing quickly into the shadows, Clint closing the door behind them. Candy had the strange sensation that he was watching her descend the icy stairs but she didn't turn around. The night dark closed in again, so they stood for a minute, letting their eyes adjust. Snow started falling, a hard, icy snow, so Candy could hear it fall in tiny clicks, and she was grateful for Clint's silence.

As the night world became visible to them, they found and followed Rusty's tracks in the new snow. Clint asked questions about the land, her land. They passed by the old farmhouse and without asking, Clint said he'd return in the new year to board up the windows.

"Won't be beautiful, but it'll keep the house safe until you decide what to do with it."

"I couldn't take Granddah out here, his old home locked up and empty, when I brought him to my new place. He still thinks he has left me something of value, and I'm going to keep it that way."

"But then again he has, right?" Clint said, spreading his arms out and up into the night. The moon must have been close because she could see his face as he said, "This. All this." He was smiling. Not at her, but into the trees and the sky.

Candy smiled too. "I feel like I'm not even in my own life anymore."

"I know what you mean," Clint replied, gazing at the moon's ghost light, and then at the animated pine tree shadows. The swishing noise of Rusty making her way through the night was the sole background music.

He didn't. Know what she meant, that is. She didn't mean the pines, or the snow, or the night with its weird moon glow or the sound of Rusty rooting around for treasures in the ground.

For just a moment she thought about keeping this thought to herself, and then decided against it.

"No, I don't mean this," she said. "I mean me."

"Huh," he murmured, and then, without taking his eyes away from the night, put an arm lightly around her shoulders.

She leaned in.

Afterword

This novel was inspired by the caregivers who held my failing mother in their arms and hearts during her long decline. In every corner of this world there are people taking care of those who cannot care for themselves. The word "caregiver" came into common parlance during the pandemic, when even those whose families did not (yet) need the strength and talent of these amazing professionals, were forced to see them and their invaluable role in our world. There were banners outside hospitals and yard signs in front of homes, ads on TV and memes all over Twitter.

And yet, when are we going to give caregivers their true due? A middle class wage, benefits, workplace safety, a retirement plan? When are we, to use that tired phrase, going to truly see them?

Candy inhabits places all over the world. She works doubles, wipes asses, comforts family members. During any given shift she is called to act as doctor, nurse, parent, child, nanny, server. She doesn't ask for a lot: a home, money to pay the bills, respect for her own family, a workplace where she is respected and valued. It's time we gave that to her.

If you employ a caregiver, pay them more than they ask.

If they need time off for their own family, pay them still. If you have a loved one in an assisted living facility, ask the corporate heads to disclose the wages and benefits of those who keep their facilities running. And demand more for them.

If you are a caregiver, know that you deserve more. Reach out to us who value you and get our help. Organize, educate, demand the professional treatment you have a right to. Our families and yours depend on it.

And thank you.

Acknowledgments

Thank You:

To all my first readers, thank you for letting Candy into your hearts. And for saying things like, "this is good, I mean really good," and "I want more Candy!" And offering astute suggestions for revisions. Your encouragement fueled my desire to see The Doublewide in print.

To Mission Point Press, from my first, hours-long phone call with Jen Wahi, through serious editing work with the brilliant Tanya Muzumdar and then to hammering out sales copy with Heather Shaw, that is after she taught me what sales copy was. Throughout the whole "bring the DW to life" process, Heather has been steady and smart, agile in all phases of editing, formatting, covers, and not a few hand-holding sessions. Jeff Bane and I spoke for less than 30 minutes and a week later he had created the perfect cover. In the initial stages, Chris Johns answered all my 20th century questions about how to sell a book in the 21st with patience and clarity and Leslie and Julie took it from there, helping me to navigate the marketing world. Also, Darlene: proofreaders help us authors face the world without goobers on our faces. Thank you.

Every time I turned to MPP I was welcomed, heard, and read and responded to with professionalism and care. Any writer couldn't ask for more, but for this new author, it was more than I dreamed was possible in the publishing world.

Anna Murphy has helped me navigate the "social" universe since my first forays into website building and has stayed by my side. Her patience, creativity, humor, and brilliant ideas have helped me immeasurably. If you see anything on my socials that impresses, it's because of Anna. If it's lame, that would be me.

To my soul sister Beth Callaghan. Girl. Walking this path with you has been one of the great gifts of my life. To Gail Siegel, one of my earliest readers who first spoke the word "publishable" out loud in a way that I believed.

To my children, Johnny and Sophie, for being shining lights in my life and in this world. You both inspire me to be a better writer and a better human.

And to Richard. I'm rarely at a loss for words, so here's a couple from Bonnie: "Your love was like a diamond right away on a sea that calmed my mind." You took my breath away and then gave it back, helping me to fly. Always and forever, my love.

COMING IN 2026

Sheltering in Place

the romantic sequel to

The Doublewide

Follow author Ann Goethals on FaceBook
and get updates and insights at

anngoethals.com

Sometime in early July:
MICHIGAN:
confirmed COVID cases 64,132.
COVID deaths: 5,951.

Back before the pandemic hit, Candy and Clint had fallen into a routine: Friday nights and Sunday afternoons together if Candy didn't have a shift. Dinner or coffee and pastries. Movies and popcorn. They had progressed to the making out stage, which had prompted Candy, more than once, to take her clothes off in front of the bathroom mirror and take good long looks at herself. This is what he would see, she told herself. Would he be turned off? Disgusted even? On the plus side, mysteriously, her eczema had almost disappeared over the winter, as long as she remembered to wear her gloves while doing dishes. So her skin was clear. White and pink and smooth. Her boobs were big no doubt but they didn't droop that bad and her hips were round. Ok, really round, but that meant she, or he, could or would? actually see her waist.

That was in February. Then March 15 arrived right in the middle of their heat up, Clint reaching under her sweatshirt and stroking her back and kissing her neck which made her nuts down there, and then suddenly, all touch was gone and not just between them. The whole world had pulled away from itself. Retreated in the face of this insane sickness that could not be tamed and was killing people. Candy's own fear had restricted them to phone screens or six feet apart. Neither of them liked FaceTime, so they really didn't even see each other much less touch each other just when Candy was beginning to get the hang of it. Then came that fateful cafe meetup, which was supposed to be about figuring out how to be together and ended up with Candy stomping off with her coffee unlidded and spilling all over her scrubs. In her rage, she had vowed to not pick up his calls. Then the weeks got swallowed up in work and fear and more work and more fear. Making contact, making up, explaining and listening and "working it out," as Clint said. Just too much energy. Too much time.

But here was a pan of lasagna he had clearly made himself and the new firepit he had bought. Bought and brought here and placed in the right spot and gathered kindling from the woods and, and, and. Jesus. She can't ignore all this kindness, let it pass unthanked for. That would be an asshole move, all caps. So, after dinner with the Aguilleras, she goes back into the doublewide, plops down into her beautiful empty couch, and pulls out her phone.

thank you

There is no reply.

for the lasagna and the firepit

Nothing.

and the wood and the kindling

...

and everything

...

we are having a fire tonight if you want to stop by

Finally a bubble appears and the dots are in motion.

we?

long story. Marcos has family that needed a place to crash.

are they safe?

Candy doesn't know what this means. Are they safe here? Are they safe to be around? Is she safe?

i think so. we just ate dinner together. apart. outside.

i might swing by.

The "might" stings, but Candy might deserve it.

Rusty nuzzles her. She has been whining about being left inside while there was outdoor fun and food she was missing. When the sun disappears below the tops of the pines, Candy opens the door and the two of them come back out. The chairs are empty. Rusty wanders off to pee and then returns to sniff at the table. The plastic forks have disappeared, and a fire has been laid with the dinner paper plates folded neatly under the kindling. The Aguilleras soon emerge from behind the barn again and Julio produces a lighter.

"A good time for this?" he asks.

"Yes. A good time."

As the fire catches, the wind becomes visible and they laugh quietly while they rearrange chairs upwind. It becomes quiet in that way that fires always seem to quiet humans. Candy is grateful for it. Rusty has nuzzled her hellos and seems to understand "perro" and "buen perro" and "muy negro y grande," then settles herself as close to the fire as she can stand.

Some minutes later, they all hear a truck engine, then the sound of tires on dirt and a door closing and the sound of boots walking and then from around the corner of the doublewide, Clint appears. Candy can feel both her stomach and the Aguilleras clench, stiffen.

And then, oddly, Julio gets up and smiles and says, "Hey, Clint," then turns to his parents and says something about an amigo and they loosen and smile, but Candy can only wave from her seat because she is shaking too much to stand and she has also apparently lost her voice.

There is no chair for Clint at the firepit, but Julio quickly offers his and then Candy goes back into the doublewide and lugs one of her dining room chairs back out. As Julio rushes to take it from her, she remembers Clint has sat in that same chair back in the before times when people shared inside spaces. Julio explains in both Spanish and English that a couple of the day gigs he has picked up from the Home Depot parking lot were at the same site where Clint has been working, and that he loaned him a hammer and some gloves.

Clint smiles, takes the beer Julio offers, snaps it open, and takes a long pull. He doesn't say anything. Finally, Candy finds something approximating a voice, croaking but audible at least.

"Clint helped me with this house. He hooked me up—" this may not translate? "He helped me find people to get this place—my new home—to here," she says, and gestures to the doublewide with her hand without turning back to the house. Julio translates for his parents who nod and smile at Clint.

"It helps to know people in the trades," he says.

While Julio is quietly speaking to his parents, his mother continues to nod and smile but she is looking first at Candy and then at Clint in a way that seems to say, "I know what's up here."

It is now fully dark and the moon has risen. Only faces and torsos are visible in the firelight and all seems settled, but only "seems" because Candy is still vibrating. With shame. Shame about what exactly she is not sure, but there is a long list: the blocking calls, the walking away, the fear of being touched with and without the pandemic, and most of all a new kind of embarrassing hunger she has for this guy, this man, who, it turns out, she has missed and is just this minute realizing how much.

In the weeks they've been separate, if Candy's being honest, she has felt like the wind's been knocked out of her. She's been more tired than she should be, even with all the extra shifts and the rising anxiety and extra protocols. She's been kind of bummed out tired, hitting the snooze button two or three times before rolling out of bed and into whatever clean scrubs are still in the dryer. She has also taken to doubling up on meals: one dinner at 4 another at 8, all the guardrails dropped, and until the Aguilleras arrived, Candy had done little else besides go to Glencrest, try to protect the residents—especially Miss Maeve and Granddah—the best she could, and then return to the doublewide and crash.

As summer rolled in she noticed that on the roadsides the wildflowers had begun to bloom. She had cried silently in the truck at first. How wrong all this insane beauty seemed. Flowers going crazy with color in a dying world. Every otherwise forgettable roadside had suddenly burst into pink or magenta or burgundy or violet. One day after work, in an effort to delay her usual doomscrolling, Candy had downloaded an app and learned the names of them: wild sweet pea, lobelia, chicory, something that grows everywhere called knapweed. Then she lost interest and went back to her usual jumping between graphs and data showing the world coming to an end and large size lingerie websites.

Her favorite is one called Dare me Bare, because it's the one with the most honestly fat models. Candy had started using the word "large" or "plus size" in an effort to fix her self-esteem, but now self-esteem is the last thing on her mind and fat sounds right. Three letters that land hard, just there. No floating around in the atmosphere threatening to kill you in a vaporized drop of spit. Candy wants all things hard. Factual. Known. None of this weird "what if," "does he or doesn't he," "will we and when?" The unknown takes too much energy now, and her crush seems like a bizarre luxury she can no longer afford.

This luxury, this big, hulky man across from her, in the flesh, is right now looking through the firelight at her. Unashamed. Unembarrassed. Perfectly comfortable with his new best friends.

It is so hot tonight that Candy wears only a tank top with her bra straps peeking out—lavender tank, taupe straps. She listens but the people around the fire are quiet, and Candy starts to feel that, at least for now, this is a place of peace, of safety. They are outside, the chairs are spread apart, the breeze is blowing, the harsh light of the day and the virus have faded into the night. It is so calm Candy imagines catching it, the peace, like a virus. She feels the shame fade, senses herself slowing and tiring. She slumps in her chair and stretches her legs out in front of her, careful not to melt her flip-flops.

After a while the Aguilleras murmur goodnights. Candy is guessing they too are doing day labor, wherever they can and as they rise, Candy asks Julio to ask them if they have enough masks for where they work. It turns out they are running low, and Candy uses her phone light to go out front to the Tacoma and grab the box from her front seat. They start to take one mask each from the box, but she pushes the whole box at them. Glencrest finally has enough masks, they are actually drowning in masks, which is a surprise considering how many times a day residents will pull theirs off and let them drop to the floor. New litter.

After several *buenos noches,* they are gone. Clint has gotten up to stir the embers.

"Probably time for this to die down right?" he asks.

"Yeah. It was real nice though, Clint, a really nice thing for you to do."

"How'd you know it was me?"

Candy laughs. Because of course it was him. Clint is that guy and what's better than the firepit or the beautiful embers pulsing in the ashes is the fact that that guy, that type of guy is standing, right now, in her future, ok her present backyard. And he is waiting.

"So I went to Traverse. And I tested. And I'm negative."

"Oh Jesus, do we really have to?"

"Ok fine," he says but not angry. As a matter of fact he sounds as tired as she feels.

"That 'Oh Jesus' is meant for the world, not you. I appreciate it, the testing and you telling me and caring and all."

"I'm doing it for me, and my mom. And you."

After another minute, he drops the stick into the pit and comes over to her chair, straddles her flip-flops with his boots, and pulls her up to standing. The force of his lift sends her right into his arms, and he wraps himself around her. The last time they were like this it was winter and they each had a couple layers of clothes on. Now it is skin on skin. She feels his hair and his rough hands and the muscles through his T-shirt.

She pulls away or tries to, bracing her hands against his leaning in chest.

"I haven't tested Clint. I haven't had time, but they're promising we'll have on-site testing as soon as Munson does and that should be soon. And then—"

"Yeah, no. Now." And he kisses her. Just like that, deep, long, open. He tastes like beer with maybe some mint gum behind it. She kisses him back, and then she grabs his face just like in the movies and says, "I want this. I want you to know I want this." And kisses him again.

But then not like any movie she's ever seen she adds, "But I'm scared. Of all of it, you, the virus, my body, your body, all of it."

"Ok. Well, this is what I think. That kiss? We just crossed a line. And we can't cross back. At least not tonight. So I am going to ask myself inside and I'll wait for your permission but I'm going to be super pissed if you say no."

He looks down at her, but she has no answer. The discarded stirring stick cracks in the firepit behind them. Rusty hasn't budged, but her ears are up, alert.

"And then when we get inside, I'm going to ask to use your shower because I worked late and you called just when I was going to hop in and then I couldn't wait and came straight here."

He pauses but doesn't loosen his hold.

"Then I'm going to put on enough clothes not to embarrass myself or you, and then I'm going to ask if it's ok if I come into your bed."

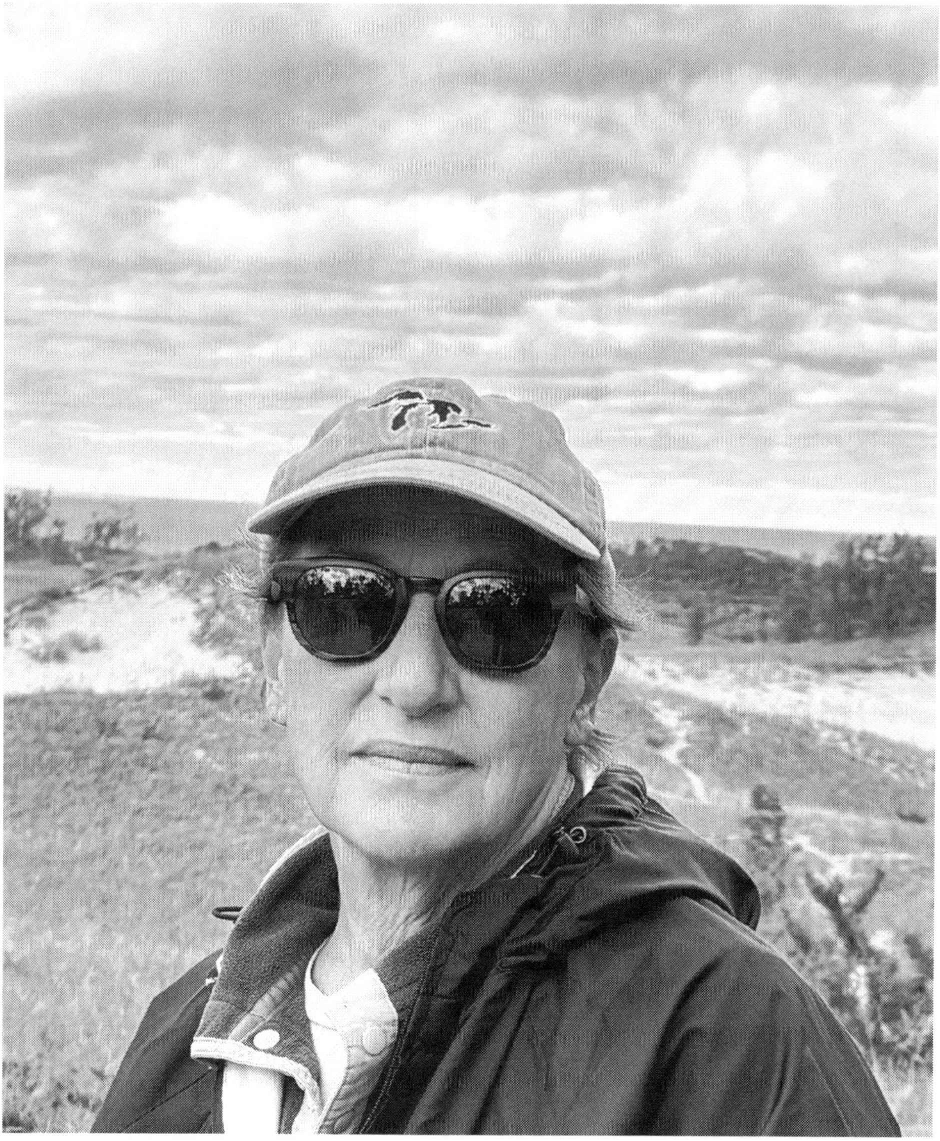

About the Author

Ann Goethals is a retired high school English teacher who set aside her own writing aspirations for three decades to nourish those of her students. During that time, she also developed new teacher training programs, created a student writing center, and worked in union leadership. She retired "into COVID" (a not unhappy coincidence) and has since focused her energies on her own writing. Goethals works in all genres and has had several pieces published in online journals. *The Doublewide* is her first novel and she is busy working on a sequel.

Goethals divides her time between Northern Michigan and Chicago, accompanied by her partner Richard and their dog Dude. She is never far from the lake.

Made in United States
Troutdale, OR
10/13/2025